BY THE
LIGHT
OF THE
MOON

JODI VAUGHN

Lin,

So great meeting you in
Atlanta! Enjoy my
werewolves!

Jodi Vaughn

ACKNOWLEDGEMENTS

There have been so many people that have helped me along this journey to get my Arkansas Werewolves to the readers and out into the world. Tracey Steele, without your undying love of my characters, unending encouragement, and brilliant ideas for my career, this book wouldn't be possible. Thank you Amanda Sumner, my critique partner and sister of my heart, for your professional eye, your attention to detail and for having coffee with me (via FaceBook) every morning. Jaye Garland, thank you for your wonderful critique, your loving words of wisdom and your excitement for this series. Thank you to the LaLas and your unwavering support and being a shoulder to cry on when I needed it the most. I want to thank my Chick Tale ladies, (KC Klein, RL Syme, Krystal Shannon and Lavender Daye), who've talked me off the ledge, picked me up when I was discouraged and have truly been a family to me. Last, but certainly not least, I want to thank the amazing and talented, Jennifer Ashley. Jennifer, your words of wisdom and encouragement for my werewolves, and your generosity have meant the world to me. I hope one day I can repay the favor.

ALSO BY JODI VAUGHN

PARANORMAL ROMANCE

RISE OF THE ARKANSAS WEREWOLVES Series

BY THE LIGHT OF THE MOON
BENEATH A BLOOD LUST MOON
DESIRES OF A FULL MOON
DARKSIDE OF THE MOON
SHADOWS OF A WOLF MOON-coming 2016

VEILED SECRETS-coming 2016
VEILED ENCHANTMENT- coming 2017
UNVEILED- coming 2018

CONTEMPORARY ROMANCE

SOMEWHERE, TEXAS series

SADDLE UP
TROUBLE IN TEXAS
BAD MEDICINE

The CLOVERTON series

LOST WITHOUT YOU
LOST ALL CONTROL-coming 2016
LOST AND FOUND LOVE-coming 2017

CHAPTER ONE

Damon Trahan shoved a hand in his jeans pocket and leaned against his black Harley-Davidson Breakout. For three long hours, he'd been standing watch outside the dilapidated bar constructed of cinder block walls, rusted tin roof, and grim desperation. The seedy bar was a well-known hangout for rogue wolves that had no respect for Wolf Law, making it the perfect place for his suspect to hide.

He grimaced as the scent of stale urine and fresh vomit wafted over him, making his stomach clench in a violent spasm. He regretted parking in the dark alley away from the blinding security light, but tonight's mission required stealth, so he'd sacrificed fresh air and comfort. His saving grace from the repugnant odor was the occasional breeze carried on the October wind.

He narrowed his gaze on the door, as if willing Raymond Wilson to exit so he could apprehend him. Why any werewolf would risk outing their species to the world for easy drug money was beyond his comprehension. Risky behavior, whether criminal or not, wasn't tolerated by the Pack. The U.S. Government knew about the existence of werewolves. In fact, some of the military's best soldiers were werewolves. On the other hand, the civilian human population had no clue their species even existed. If humans discovered them, it would be an all-out war. Werewolves would be hunted down, one by one, until they were eliminated.

No one deserved to live their life in fear. No one.

His cell phone hummed against his thigh. Gritting his teeth, Damon fished it out of his pocket. "I'm a little busy right now, Barrett."

"Damon, we need to talk."

Damon bristled at the sharp command of his Pack Master. Since he'd moved to the Natural State, Barrett Middleton regulated his schedule, day and night, twenty-four seven. That's what happened when a wolf joined the elite ranks of the Guardians. You gave up your life to protect the Pack and watch over civilian werewolves.

Damon wasn't complaining. Being a Guardian had given him a purpose, a reason to keep going. He was ready to lay down his life for the better of the Pack.

Their small community of werewolves, located just outside of Little Rock, Arkansas, functioned like a military compound to the human world. In reality, it was a training base for elite werewolf soldiers, also known as Guardians. Barrett was Pack Master over Arkansas, but he still answered to the General and the Council. The power was too great for any one wolf to rule alone.

A white male shoved the exit door of the bar with such force, it bounced against the wall with a bang and the resounding boom ricocheted in Damon's ears. Country music from the jukebox bled out into the night on the wisps of cigarette smoke.

Damon clenched his hands, his gaze never wavering from the suspect. "Can this conversation wait? Your culprit is leaving."

The suspect, in his late thirties with muddy brown hair, hurried out of the bar. Dressed in a red flannel shirt and ripped jeans, the man made a beeline for a beat-up blue and white truck. He cast a few nervous glances toward the shadows where Damon crouched.

Damon tilted his head back and sniffed the brittle air. His nostrils flared as the familiar scent of wolf hit him. The drug dealer might look human, but there was no denying his scent was all wolf.

"I need to go." He straddled his Harley.

"Goddamn, Damon. Forget about him."

"Why?" He shifted in his seat while his gaze darted from his suspect back to the bar. Something was wrong.

Barrett never left an assignment unfinished. His Pack Master was relentless when it came to keeping order and protecting the werewolves in Arkansas. Calling off the investigation when they were so close to catching a suspect was completely out of character.

Unless...

Unless Damon was being pulled off the case and being reassigned to another Pack.

Damon rolled his neck side to side in an attempt to loosen the tension that had suddenly blossomed. Not again. His last Pack in Louisiana had thrown him out without warning, leaving him on his own to find another state, another pack, another home. He thought he'd found a home in Arkansas. For once, he almost let himself believe he'd been accepted.

He'd been a fucking fool to entertain such a thought.

"Which Pack are you reassigning me to? Alaska? Antarctica?" The comment smacked of sarcasm and he winced at the lingering bitterness his words left behind.

"I don't think you understand," Barrett's tone lowered, the same way a mother might do when she was about to discipline an unruly child. "An emergency assignment has come up. I'm putting you on it. Alone." The grimness in Barrett's voice had unease snaking up Damon's spine like a night crawler.

He'd never been on assignment alone. Barrett had always put him with at least four other Pack members. In fact, the other three Guardians, Zane, Lucien and Jaxon, were probably tailing the suspect and bitching about Damon's absence.

"One of our females has been abducted." Barrett's voice came out low and laced with deadly intent.

"Who was it?" Damon's lips curled a feral snarl as his pulse raced. Some things were punishable by death, and taking a female ranked number one.

"Ava Renfroe."

The blood drained from his face and pooled in his stomach in a nauseating rush. The rest of the conversation turned to white buzzing noise between his ears.

Ava Renfroe was the General's daughter.

She lived near Jonesboro and he had only seen her once, from a distance, when she visited the General over the holidays. With silky black hair, eyes the color of emeralds, and a body made for sin, Ava was a female any male would fight over.

"What are the demands?" Damon tightened his grip on the cell phone. The plastic squeaked, threatening to break under his sweaty palm.

"The kidnappers have made no demands. No demands for money, prisoner exchanges, or territory."

The only thing a wolf Pack needed more than food and territory was a female. A female to ensure their population and increase their numbers. He knew exactly what kind of hell that would be for a female as beautiful as Ava Renfroe.

"Why did you call me, Barrett? Why not call one of the other Guardians?"

"The other Guardians are too far away."

Didn't that just warm the fucking heart? He was Barrett's last choice. Or maybe he was Barrett's only choice.

"You have the skills and the ability to infiltrate the compound where we believe she's being held."

"You mean they won't be able to smell the scent of your Pack on me." Fully belonging to a Pack always seemed beyond his reach. What was the use in trying anymore?

"This is your Pack, too, Damon. Once your trial period is over, you'll be initiated into the Arkansas Pack."

"Yeah, right. You keep believing the shit that's coming out of your mouth, Barrett," he snarled.

"Watch your tone when you address me," Barrett growled.

Barrett always called him on his shit. For that, Damon respected his leader.

"Right now, my main concern is getting this female back before they can do God knows what to her." Damon clenched his muscles, fighting the anger racing through every cell of his body. This wasn't the time to shift into a wolf.

"It's an isolated wooded area. I'll text you the coordinates to the compound. According to the Intel from our surveillance planes, that place is locked up tighter than Fort fucking Knox."

"I'll be ready to go within the hour." He slipped his phone into his leather jacket and glanced at the yellow glow of his Luminox watch. He needed to run home and grab a few items. Thankfully, he was already packing most of his weapons. Two Sig Sauer 45s holstered to his chest, a ten-inch blade in his right boot, and some thin strips of C4 in his pocket.

All he needed were a few detonator caps, a remote control, and he was in business.

Lethargy seeped into the recesses of Ava Renfroe's foggy mind and threatened to pull her back into the blackness she was so desperately trying to escape. She'd never felt this tired, so drained of energy, and she wondered if she might have a bad case of the flu. It was too much to fight and she was sucked back into unconscious oblivion.

An eternity later, she pried open her heavy eyelids.

She blinked, letting her eyes get adjusted and glanced around. Cold, musty air stung her nose and each breath made her lungs ache. A cold sweat popped up across her skin as she gaped at her bleak surroundings.

Pushing herself up to a sitting position, she hissed as a deep pain shot through her back from lying on the concrete floor. Where the hell was she? She clamped a hand over her mouth to keep from being sick and focused on taking slow, even breaths.

The last time she felt this bad was a few years ago, after a night of shooting tequila. After that, she'd sworn never to touch the stuff again.

Wincing from the glare above, she cradled her throbbing head between her hands. An ancient, incandescent light bulb hung overhead, illuminating rusted tin walls that soared upward to a metal beamed roof. She was in some sort of warehouse.

How the hell did she end up in a warehouse?

"What the hell is going on?" She flinched as her voice reverberated throughout the cavernous space. She closed her eyes and tried to calm her racing heart. *Think, Ava, think.*

She remembered getting up at dawn, drinking coffee, and reading the newspaper on the back deck of her tiny country house. Nothing special happened on her noon shift at the Golden Lair Restaurant and bar. After that, she had gone home.

She remembered her doorbell ringing. A shiver raced down to her toes as the next memory came into focus. She'd opened the door to a figure standing on the other side, dressed completely in black. Then she remembered . . . nothing.

Her eyes popped open. Icy, wet fear trickled through her veins like a winter stream.

Why the hell couldn't she remember what happened next?

A door creaked open somewhere in the shadows. She jerked her head up and immediately wished she hadn't. Her stomach churned at the sudden motion.

"Glad to see you're awake, female." The man's deep voice slithered across the room, making the hair on her arms stand up.

"Who are you? Where am I?" Her voice cracked. "How did I get here?"

"We brought you here. You're our special guest." His accent was more redneck than southern. Raised in the South, she could tell the slight difference.

"I think it's time I left." A chill skipped across her heart, hard and quick, like a pebble on a frozen pond. What had happened in the last few hours that she had ended up here, alone?

"It doesn't matter what you want."

"My family knows I'm gone. They'll be looking for me." Anger and terror paraded up her spine, racking her body with tremors.

Evil laughter, echoing against the metal walls, hung over her like a vile promise of what was to come. Booted footsteps tapped against the concrete floor as her captor circled her in the safety of the shadows, his identity concealed.

"Your family has no idea you're missing. And when they do, they may try to come for you, but it'll be too late. We'll be long gone."

Rage pumped through her body. This asshole had another thing coming if he thought he could keep her here like a prisoner.

"You're the key to our survival, Ava."

"What the hell are you talking about? Survival of what? I'm just a bartender." She squinted, trying to make out the dimensions of the room and find a way out.

"We need to increase our numbers, Ava. We need children. We need you to provide those children for us."

She froze. Her breath whooshed out of her lungs like a deflating balloon.

She shook her head. This wasn't happening. She must be trapped in some kind of nightmare.

Nausea engulfed her. She dropped to her hands and knees and emptied the contents of her stomach.

"That's it. Get that nasty drug out of your system."

Sitting back, she dragged the back of her hand across her mouth, and glared into the shadows. "You drugged me?" It would explain the drowsiness she felt earlier.

"It was the only way to get you here without a fight." The shadow chuckled. "I hope you're ready. It's almost time."

She squinted, trying to make out his features. "Time for what?"

"It's time to present you to your lovers, of course. All forty-five of them."

Damon tore down the dirt road on his Harley, kicking up a wave of dust in his wake. According to the surveillance coordinates, he should be quickly approaching the destination where Ava was being held.

He white-knuckled the handlebars. *Ava.* He hadn't wanted to bring his Harley to make the rescue. He wasn't sure what condition Ava might be in when he found her. Though the bike had a slender second seat, his Harley-Davidson Breakout was more suited for one person than two. But showing up in his Hummer would have definitely blown his cover as a Rogue wolf. Rogues didn't make the kind of money Guardians did and he didn't need to stand out. He needed to blend in.

Rounding the curve, he slowed his bike and headed off the road into a field and drove toward the tree line. He killed the engine and eased off the motorcycle. He stilled, listening for any sign that he had been followed.

The cadence of an occasional barn owl and the rustle of dead leaves filled the night and assured him he was alone.

Within ten minutes of hanging up with Barrett, a messenger had met Damon with a package containing a pair of Ava's pajamas. He needed something with her scent in the event he couldn't locate her visually. He reached into the leather saddlebag and pulled out her pink pajama bottoms. The soft material slid through his fingers like silk as he lifted it to his nose. Her sweet feminine scent hit him right in the gut, sending his body careening and making his cock harden.

He shook his head, shaking off the daze she'd put him in by scent alone, and forced his mind onto the objective of his mission.

He lifted his face to the sky and sniffed. The scent of decaying leaves and crisp October air mingled in his nose.

A jolt shot through his body as he caught another scent settling upon the wind.

Ava.

Her scent, like honeysuckle baked in the hot July sun, was unique and like nothing he'd ever experienced. His He squeezed his eyes shut and forced his body under control. He was on a mission. Now was not the time to fantasize.

From the aerial map he'd gotten from Intel, the compound where they suspected she was being held was located another two miles deeper into the forest. If he could smell her from that distance, she must be putting off some major fear pheromones.

His pulse sped up as he bared his sharp teeth. Every vile image of what they might be doing to her invaded his mind. He curled his fingers into fists, clenched his muscles, and forced his wolf side under control. *First things first. Must find Ava.* Her safety was his priority.

He walked his Harley underneath a nearby oak tree and flipped the kickstand with his boot. Reaching inside the saddlebag, he pulled out a bottle of camouflage scent. He covered his entire body with the masking spray, concealing any odors he might have picked up from being near his pack.

The plan was simple. Get in, find Ava, and get the hell out before they both ended up dead.

He hit his red and black bandana with a couple sprays before retying it to his head and then slipped on his Oakleys. Despite the darkness, wolves had excellent eyesight and the sunglasses didn't impede his vision in any way.

Damon snapped off branches and laid them around the chrome of his Harley. The last thing he needed was some redneck asshole out in the middle of a bean field trying to get laid and running upon his motorcycle.

The camouflage scent would only last about an hour before it wore off. He needed to get in, find Ava and get out before that happened. He set the timer on his Luminox watch, patted himself down in a last minute weapons check, then launched into a dead run.

Ava's scent guided him like a ghostly finger, leading him deeper into the thick woods. His feet slammed into the cold, dead ground as he sprinted, dodging low-lying branches. The forest was quiet except for a startled raccoon that snarled and jumped out of his path as he raced through the trees.

He approached an illuminated break in the trees and slowed. Keeping his body hidden within the forest, he surveyed the open grounds.

Several werewolves in human form congregated around five small campfires. Old school Kid Rock blared from an old truck's radio, breaking the solitude of the night.

He squinted at the wolves as he caught a whiff of their scent.

What the fuck? They were not just any wolves. They were red wolves.

How was that possible? Red wolves had been extinct in Arkansas for years. They had become so savage that they'd managed to kill each other off in their bloody rages. Gray wolves, were the only wolves left in Arkansas.

A shout echoed through the camp. Damon dropped to a crouch and palmed the cool steel of his .45. He steadied his breath and waited for the attack. When no one rushed him, he stole a glance at the camp.

Two red werewolves shoved each other as they argued over the choice of music. Apparently, not all of them were Kid Rock fans. The rest of the group drew closer, shit talking and urging on the fight. One wolf shoved the other and then fists were flying.

"Fucking bunch of idiots."

With everyone's attention on the fight, no one was watching the perimeter.

He eased away from the tree line and stepped into the camp, attempting to blend into the group. His stomach clenched as their overwhelming scent grew stronger.

He hated having people touch him. What he hated and what he needed to do were two different things. He knew their repulsive odor would mask his own. Passing the wolves, he rubbed his shoulder against members of the motley group.

Blood lust vibrated in his veins. Visions of his past rose up behind his eyes, almost blinding him with rage. It was all he could do not to rip their throats out for being so close.

He stepped away from the group and made his way to a pull-behind camper. Kneeling, he pretended to tighten the laces on his riding boots while he slipped an explosive to the underside of the camper.

Damon stood and grabbed a beer from the nearest cooler. He leaned against a rusted white truck and took a long drink from the icy bottle. Watching the fighting, he tucked his fingers under the hood and secured the second explosive.

He tossed the beer and looked around. He needed to find Ava and get out.

Making his way further into the camp, he spotted a large warehouse. Two werewolves stood on either side of the rusted door, shooting glares at anyone who ventured too close.

He raised his Oakleys, made eye contact with one of the large guards, nodded and then turned his back.

"Hey, you," the large guard yelled.

Damon smirked. He tensed and waited for the guard to make a move. One thing a wolf didn't tolerate was the disrespect of another wolf turning his backs to him.

"Hey, asshole, I know you heard me!"

Anger boiled low in his stomach. He wanted nothing better than to jump the guard right there. *Get Ava out first.* He swallowed his rage and held his ground.

"Hey, you fucker!"

Okay, the fucker part got him.

Damon turned.

The guard deserted his post and now stood several feet in front of him. His greasy brown mullet hung over his thick shoulders, reminding Damon of the movie, *Joe Dirt.* Dressed in jeans and a dirty white wife beater, the guard snarled.

Damon slipped his sunglasses up on his head, looked the guy in the eye, and gave him the finger.

The second guard roared with laughter. "I don't think he likes you too much, Bubba."

Anger flashed through Bubba's eyes. He bowed up and threw a punch. Damon dodged the blow and grabbed Bubba's arm and twisted. The guard cried out in pain. He planted his boot on Bubba's back and pushed. Bubba landed with a thick plop in a mud puddle.

"What the hell's going on?" A white male in his late forties came trotting out of the warehouse hoisting a shotgun over his shoulder. His gray hair was styled in a high-and-tight military cut and his weathered face had more mileage on it than an eighteen-wheeler. He stopped short when he spotted his guard lying on the ground. "Bubba, what the fuck you doing in the mud?"

"He's in the mud because that's where I put him." Damon cocked his head and met the old man's stare.

The second guard broke into another howl of belly-splitting laugher.

The older man drew his disgusted gaze from Bubba up to Damon. He leveled his shotgun at Damon's forehead. "Who the hell are you?"

"Demon." Damon knew better to give his actual name. He was also smart enough to keep it close to his real name in case someone called out to him.

"What the hell kind of name is Demon?"

"What the hell kind of name is Bubba?" Damon held the older wolf's gaze, refusing to look away.

The guy's eyes widened for a second before he barked out a laugh.

"What the hell you laughing at, Carl?" Bubba scrambled to his feet. He wiped his face with the back of his hand, smearing the mud and making an even bigger mess. "He don't belong here." He pointed a thick finger at Damon.

"Shut up, Bubba. You're not running things here. I am." Carl continued to glare at Damon. "What Pack are you in?"

"I don't belong to a Pack."

Carl lifted a bushy gray eyebrow. "No Pack? That means you're lying or you've gone rogue."

"The last wolf that called me a liar is wearing his dick for a tie," Damon growled. "Like I said, I don't have a Pack."

"Then what the hell are you doing here?"

"I was passing through and caught the scent of blood. I didn't realize you were having a private party." He nodded toward the fight in the middle of the camp, but didn't break his gaze.

Carl's thin lips twitched like a rodent's. He lowered his gun. "It's not every day a wolf admits to looking for a fight. These days Packs are trying to be more tolerant, more politically correct." Carl spit a thick stream of tobacco juice on the ground. A slimy drop trailed down his chin. "Bunch of pussies, if you ask me."

"Fuck that. Wolves are animals," Damon snarled.

Carl's weathered face relaxed, as his lips broke into a smile. "Seems like we're of the same thinking, boy."

"Don't call me 'boy.'"

Carl laughed. "All right, all right. I can respect that. It seems like you got more balls than some of these dickheads I'm rolling with." He cut his eyes at Bubba who lowered his gaze.

"Are you looking to join up to a Pack?" Carl lifted his chin. "We could use someone like you."

"I don't play well with others."

"I like that. But I bet I could change your mind." Carl smirked and rested the shotgun against his shoulder.

"I doubt that." Damon crossed his arms over his chest. No need to appear too eager.

"Once you see what we got in this here warehouse, you'll be begging to join our Pack." Carl snorted.

"Carl, you said I could have her." Bubba pressed his muddy lips together like an impudent child.

"She ain't ready yet, dumbass. Keep up your whining and I'll castrate you. Then you won't be getting any at all!"

Bubba went wide-eyed and then bent his head in a submissive gesture.

Damon snorted. What do you know? Bubba might actually have some brains after all.

His gaze drifted casually to the warehouse. Ava's scent was overwhelming. She was there. His stomach tightened to the point of pain.

"You got a female, so what? It's only October. Females don't go into heat until spring."

Carl leaned in close. A smirk lurked at the corner of his thin lips. "Well, we got us a special formula that will force her into heat."

He uncrossed his arms. "That's impossible."

Females were only in heat for a few weeks in February and March. This was only October.

Carl grinned. "Our formula will shorten the pregnancy and allow her to stay in heat so she can have multiple pregnancies within a year."

Damon swallowed back the nausea rising in the back of his throat. Females were only fertile every two years. Even having twins was rare. What Carl was suggesting was beyond evil.

"I guess her mate is going to keep her busy. Is this lucky couple going to start their own pack with all those offspring?" He clenched every muscle in his body to keep from beating Carl's ass right there.

Carl narrowed his gaze. "She's not mated and she's not going to be. She's what you'd call community property."

Ava would be enslaved and raped. Judging from the wolves Damon had seen, not one of them would think twice about violating her. She wouldn't last two days before they killed her in their lust.

"I don't like sloppy seconds."

"I'm sure you'll change your mind once you see her. She's one hot little piece of tail." Carl whistled through his tobacco-stained teeth.

Damon nodded, not trusting his voice. Rage edged through every corner of his body.

"Round everyone up," Carl barked at Bubba. "It's time for the unveiling."

The only thing that separated him from Ava was a wall of rusted tin. With one hit he could tear through the tin walls of the warehouse and reach her.

He sucked in a deep breath. It wasn't that easy. He was outnumbered and couldn't risk her safety.

Damon followed Carl into the warehouse and scanned the darkened room. The rest of the Pack hurried in behind them, cursing and shoving their way inside as their stench filled the room. He focused his gaze on a covered object in the middle of the room.

Ava.

Someone flipped a switch, bathing the room in blinding floodlights. Everyone let out a string of profanities and covered their eyes.

"Bubba, you dumb fuck, turn that shit off," Carl bellowed.

Damon slipped his glasses on and blinked, allowing his eyes to adjust. Bubba staggered to the wall and attempted to flip the switch with one hand while shielding his eyes with the other.

"Sorry, boss. I thought you wanted her lit up real pretty, you know like one of them game shows where they show off the prizes." Bubba patted his hand along the wall, feeling for the switch like a blind man.

"That's what wrong with you, Bubba. You think too damn much." Carl made his way over to the wall, slapped Bubba across the head, and cut the lights.

Under the blanket of darkness, Damon's hand brushed the cool metal of his gun. His fingertips itched to clasp it and put a bullet in every wolf's head. The urge to tear these wolves apart by hand coursed through his heated veins, but he knew he was racing against the clock. He had to grab Ava and get the fuck out of there, even if that meant using his Sig Sauer.

"All right boys, I know you've all been dying to meet our new female." Carl stopped beside the covered object as someone passed him a lantern.

"Boys, meet our newest bitch." Carl grabbed a handful of canvas and pulled.

Damon stepped forward as his stomach lurched.

Ava, clothed in only her black bra and panties, was gagged and tied down to a doctor's exam table. Her black hair clung to her dirt-streaked face, and her green-eyed gaze flashed around the room in fear. But that's not what made him sick.

Her feet were up in stirrups, her legs restrained with ropes, spread open for every male's viewing pleasure.

The group of werewolves edged closer and the hum of panting drifted through the room. Their nostrils flared as they caught her feminine scent. Growls erupted around the room and one by one they shifted into wolf, their urge to mate too great to control.

"That's it, boys; get a good look. In a few more days this one will be all hot and ready for you." Carl's lips curved into a sadistic grin as he held up a syringe. "Once she gets this, she'll be begging for it."

The scent of testosterone surged to a lethal level within the tin walls. There was no way in hell these assholes were going to wait a week to have Ava. They wanted her now.

He fingered the remote device inside his jacket. It was time for a distraction.

The wolves edged closer, crowding Damon. He stuck his foot out and the guy closest to him tripped, tumbling into the next wolf, setting off a domino effect. Two wolves growled and snapped their elongated teeth. They bowed up and circled each other as they shifted back into their naked human form. The rest of the wolves shifted into human form, eager to watch the fight. A punch was thrown, and an unruly brawl ensued.

This was his chance.

Damon pressed the button.

A deafening explosion rattled the walls of the warehouse and shattered the window. Shards of glass rained down as the rabble members fell to their knees.

Damon strode to Ava's side as the Pack scrambled like ants out of the warehouse.

He reached for his knife. Ava's eyes widened as she tried to scoot away from him.

"I'm not going to hurt you, Ava." He shoved his sunglasses up on his head and made eye contact. Her gaze landed on the scar on his left cheek. His disfigurement certainly didn't make him look less intimidating. He knew that for a fact.

"I'm going to cut you lose and get you out of here, okay?" He held his hands up and waited for her permission.

She nodded once.

He untied the gag from her mouth and made quick work of the thick ropes. Freed, she scrambled off the table.

"Who the hell are you?" She snatched a shard of broken glass from the ground and held the weapon out in front of her.

"I'm Damon. I'm here to get you out."

"How do I know you're not one of them?" She jerked her head toward the empty doorway, but her gaze remained on him.

"Trust me, I'm nothing like them." He slipped the knife back in his boot and stood. "Ava, we can't stay here. I need to get you out before they come back." He held out his hand, hoping she'd take it.

If not, he wouldn't give her a choice.

He'd just throw her over his shoulder and haul ass.

CHAPTER TWO

Ava's heart beat against her chest like hummingbird wings. She couldn't take her eyes off the large man dressed in black. His dark hair trailed out from a black and red skull bandana and brushed his broad shoulders. His eyes, the color of a tumultuous ocean, were hard and unflinching. An angry scar ran from his cheek to his jaw line, the only blemish on his good looks, making him look even more sinister.

Damon looked more like the devil than her rescuer.

Unlike the others, he hadn't made a move to touch her.

And unlike the others, he hadn't done the whole freaky, change-into-a-wolf thing. That was a definite plus.

A shaky laugh erupted from the back of her tight throat. Surely that really hadn't happened. People did not change into animals. Not in the real world. She must be hallucinating from whatever drug they'd given her.

One thing was certain. If she stayed here, they'd rape her and then kill her when they were done.

"It seems I'm low on options." Ava placed her small hand in the heat of his palm.

His gaze drifted down to her panties. Her body heated with humiliation. She snatched her hand away and attempted to cover herself with her hands.

"Put this on." He scowled and shrugged out of his leather jacket as he averted his gaze. He shoved the jacket into her hands.

"Who are you?" She stuck her arms into the warm jacket and wrapped it around her body. It smelled like sandalwood and leather. He didn't stink like the other men.

She cringed. Between being sick to her stomach, and sweating in fear as she was tied up like an animal, she probably didn't smell any better than her kidnappers. Damon might not want his jacket back if she ruined it with her not-so-fresh scent.

"I'm Damon Trahan. I've been sent to bring you back home."

"Thank, God." The police in Arkansas were really on the ball. She was definitely sending in a donation to their charity this year instead of hanging up on them when they called.

He lowered his gaze to her bare feet. "Where are your shoes?"

"That asshole took them when he strapped me down." Ava glared and pulled the jacket tighter around her.

A muscle twitched in Damon's cheek, yet he said nothing. He headed for the door and peered out. "Fuck."

"What?" She winced as she hurried to his side, trying to ignore the tiny shard of glass that found its way into the bottom of her foot. She grabbed his arm for balance and dug out the sliver.

He stepped away and snarled. "We've got to go. They're making their way back."

"Then, let's go."

"They're blocking the road. Our only way out is through the woods. And you don't have any shoes."

"I don't care. I'd rather have bloody feet than stay here and let them touch me." She lifted her chin. She would not stay here. No way. No how.

"Just keep up," he growled and grabbed her hand. They ran out of the building, past the frantic men who scrambled to put out the raging blaze with coolers of ice. Damon ran, pulling her along as he hurried toward the forest. She stumbled as she fought to keep up with his long stride. Chaos ruled the camp, but luckily no one paid attention to them. When they reached the protective cover of the tree line, Damon stopped and cast a glance at the camp.

Ava jerked her hand free from his hard grasp. She sure as hell wasn't going to wait around and give those freaks another chance to capture her.

She pushed past him and ran deeper into the forest. Briars and underbrush tore at her feet and legs like a thousand needles. She clenched her teeth and pushed down the pain. Escape was all that mattered. Bloody feet would heal. She would not, if she didn't escape.

Swamped in darkness, she held her hands out to keep from slamming, face-first, into a tree. Damon's curses echoed behind her, and then suddenly he was running beside her.

"How much farther?" She slammed hard into the bark of a tree, stumbling backward. He caught her before she landed on her ass.

"Watch where you're going." He steadied her and then shoved her forward.

She made it three steps and smacked into another tree. This time, her ass hit the ground hard.

"Can't you pay attention?" Grabbing her under her arms, he pulled her up to her feet. Despite the dark, she could imagine the impatient scowl stretching across his face.

"I can't see in the dark, you asshole." Flushed with anger, she curled her hands into fists.

"What do you mean you can't see in the dark? Of course you can see." He gave her another shove forward.

She spun around. "Shove me again and I'm going to punch you in the balls. I told you, I can't see in the dark. What the hell do you think I am? A bat?"

"No, a wolf."

The words died on Damon's lips as he stared at Ava through the thick darkness. How could she not know she was a wolf?

How could that be? Hell, he could smell her five miles away. Ava's heady scent was all wolf.

Frenzied howls of the wolf Pack erupted, raising the alarm that Ava had escaped. They needed to go before they ran out of time.

He swung her up in his arms.

"What the hell are you doing? Get your hands off me." She struggled against him, but he didn't loosen his grip.

"If you want to live, hold on."

She froze at his sharp command and then wrapped her arms around his neck. He stiffened under her touch for a brief second before getting his mind back on the mission.

Damon sprinted through the forest, dodging trees and low-hanging branches as he headed toward safety, putting distance between them and the howls of the rogue wolves.

A little while later, he broke out of the forest and into the clearing of the field. He set her down roughly.

"Jerk." She tightened the jacket around her and mumbled under her breath.

Ignoring the temperamental female, he began stripping the tree branches away from his Harley.

"A motorcycle?"

"Not just a motorcycle. It's a Harley. Ever been on one?" He seriously doubted it. It might mess up her hair.

"No."

"Well, tonight's your lucky night." He unhooked the helmet from the seat strap and placed it on her head, tugging the straps down.

"I can do it." She batted his hands away and fiddled with the strap under her chin.

"Make sure it's tight." He scowled and pulled out her pajamas from his saddlebag.

"My PJs?" She eyed him suspiciously.

"Put them on. It won't keep you warm, but it'll keep you covered."

She turned her back to him, slipping on the thin pajamas as he started the engine. The Harley roared to life, humming under his fingertips like a heartbeat. Placing her hands on his shoulders, she eased on behind him. He held his breath, waiting for her to wrap her arms around him. While his Harley Breakout could carry two people it had no backrest. She'd have to stay glued to him for the entire ride.

"You're going to have to hold on tight if you don't want to fall off."

He relaxed slightly as she tucked her arms around his chest and tightened her hold.

He reached inside his pocket and pulled out the remote for the second C4 charge he'd set inside the camp. He pressed the button. A loud explosion billowed out into the inky night followed by a bright orange fireball that lit up the woods.

"Hold on tight."

He tore down the dirt road and waited for the suffocating feeling to kick in whenever he was physically close to someone. Her fingers dug into his shirt and his heart rate quickened. But, strangely enough, this time the panic didn't come.

When he reached the paved road, he accelerated, pushing the speed until they were flying. He needed to put as much distance between themselves and the kidnappers as possible.

At the speed they were traveling, he would have Ava safe at home in less than three hours.

Thirty minutes into the ride, he felt her fingers trembling against his chest.

He'd been so busy trying to get her out that he hadn't thought about making sure she was warm. She was going to freeze to death before he got her home.

"I'm going to pull in at the next truck stop and get you some clothes."

"No, don't stop." She dug her nails into his chest.

"I have to get you something warm to wear."

"No. Keep going."

"Damn it, Ava, you're going to freeze to death." He didn't intend to rescue her from one dangerous situation only to have her die from pneumonia.

"If they catch us they'll take me back. I'd rather freeze to death than go back."

The terror in her voice made his stomach ache.

"Damon, please." Her plea pricked his heart, a place he'd never thought anyone could touch. He tightened his grip on the handlebars. He was going to make it his mission to kill every one of those red wolves for ever daring to kidnap her.

"We'll be home in three hours, but I'll stop in an hour to make a call. I'll get you something to wear then. Can you make it that long?" He frowned as the words spilled out. It was going against his better judgment not to stop now.

"Yes." Her body relaxed slightly against him.

He wished he felt the same relief.

His instinct, on the other hand, kept telling him this wasn't over. Not by a long shot.

True to his word, an hour later Damon pulled into a well-lit truck stop. Thank God. Ava couldn't go much further. Her body ached, her legs were numb, and she couldn't stop shivering.

Damon parked around the back of the gas station in the shadows and away from the lights. He cut the engine and tried to stand, but her arms were locked tightly around his waist.

"S-s-sorry." She'd held on for dear life as they raced down the highway, scared if she loosened her grip for a second she'd fall off. She forced her stiff muscles to unclench long enough to let him go.

He dismounted the Harley with the grace of a lethal animal. Bracing her hands on the seat, she tried to stand.

Her achy muscles protested in pain. Too proud to cry, she clenched her jaw.

His large hands clamped down around her waist and she jerked her gaze up to his. He picked her up as if she weighed nothing and lifted her off the bike. Her hands rested on his massive shoulders as she slid down his muscled body. Suddenly, she couldn't breathe.

"Thanks." She held his gaze, unable to look away.

He was at least six-five with shoulders like a linebacker. Judging from her brief contact with his body, he was made of finely honed steel. The more she looked at his scar on his face, the more she thought it made him look sexy.

She frowned. After what she'd just been through, drooling over a hot guy was the last thing she should be doing. Maybe the effects of the drugs hadn't worn off yet, or she was still in shock.

"I'll run in and get you some clothes. They should have some sweatpants, jeans if we're lucky."

She grabbed his arm. His narrowed gaze landed on her hand and she released her hold. "I'm not staying out here alone." She folded her arms over her chest

He raked a glare across her body.

She winced. "I'll walk in first so you won't have to walk in with me." She dropped her arms and pulled the jacket down her thighs. She knew she looked like hell. At least she was wearing pajama bottoms and not completely nude. Besides, it was late and she seriously doubted anyone would be looking that closely at what she was wearing anyway.

He said nothing, staring at her with an intensity that would scare most women. The thing was, she wasn't most women.

"Look, I know I look awful. I'd be embarrassed to walk in with me too. But, I'm not staying out here by myself." She ran her fingers through her tangled hair, trying to make it lay flat.

"Stop." He pulled her hands away. "You're just making it worse." He pulled off his bandana and retied it on her head. It, along with his jacket, wrapped her in his scent, in his warmth. In some small way, it made her feel safe.

"Don't speak to anyone," he growled.

"I wasn't planning on it."

Without a word, he grabbed her hand. She tightened her grip as they headed for the front of the brightly lit building. He stopped long enough to scan the area before escorting her through the front door.

She nodded toward the bathroom and he released his hold. She kept her head down and made her way across the store toward the restroom sign.

From under her lashes she stole a few quick glances around the store. It was fairly busy for this time of night. A middle-aged male cashier was busy ringing up a truck driver while another man waited in line to pay for some beer. Over at the restaurant, a few people were eating while a waitress walked between the tables refilling coffee mugs. At the drink cooler, a couple of teen boys with body piercings were arguing which energy drinks were the best.

Thankfully, no one was watching her.

She pushed opened the bathroom door and cringed as she stepped barefoot onto the tile.

She crouched and looked under the stalls. When she didn't see any feet sticking out, she snatched two paper towels from the receptacles. She placed them on the floor and skated toward the nearest bathroom stall.

Minutes later she stood at the bathroom sink, scrubbing her dirty face with paper towels the color of school lunch bags. She didn't even mind the sandpaper texture against her skin. She just wanted to feel clean again.

"Ava?"

Startled, she hurried to the door and yanked it open. "What's wrong?"

He held out a plastic bag. "It's clothes. Get changed. I'll stay by the door so nobody walks in."

She pulled off Damon's leather jacket and carefully hung it over the stall door. She cringed as she realized she was standing barefoot on the bathroom floor. She slipped on the long-sleeve gray T-shirt with the words "Budweiser" sprawled across the front. She ditched her underwear and pulled on a pair of black sweatpants and thick white tube socks. She smiled a little at how ridiculous she must look as she tugged on the black CAT boots.

She picked up the bag to toss it in the garbage can when she felt something heavy in the bottom. She peeked inside.

A brush.

Either Damon was very thoughtful or he thought she looked really bad. She glanced at her reflection.

She was betting on the latter.

Damon stood in front of the ladies' room door, scowling at anyone headed in his direction. Turned out, people didn't have to go so bad after all.

He glanced at his watch. One more minute and he was going in after Ava. They needed to get back on the road if they wanted to stay ahead of the rogue wolves.

The bathroom door squeaked opened and Ava stepped out. He sucked in a deep breath as his body heated with desire. Dressed in her truck stop attire, Ava looked nothing less than beautiful.

"Thanks, for letting me borrow it." She held out his jacket.

"Keep it." He clenched his jaw, reminding himself of his duty to his pack and to her. This was a job. Nothing more, nothing less.

"Won't you get cold?"

"No, I won't." He narrowed his eyes. Being a wolf, his body temp was higher than a human's. He only wore the jacket because he liked it.

He glanced at his watch. "We need to get going."

When they reached his bike, he pulled out his cell phone.

"Shit." He gritted his teeth at the numerous missed calls from Barrett. His Pack Master was not going to be happy.

He hit speed dial.

"I have Ava. We should be in Jonesboro in about two hours."

"Damon, where the hell have you been? I've been trying to reach you," Barrett thundered.

"I've been driving like a bat out of hell. Sorry I didn't stop every ten minutes to check my messages or Tweet about my whereabouts." He sneered. "Like I said, I'll have Ava home soon."

"No. Don't come to Jonesboro," Barrett commanded.

Uneasiness snaked up Damon's spine. "Why? What's wrong?"

"There's been an explosion at Ava's house." Barrett's tight voice had Damon bracing for what was next. "We've also had a breach in security. A bomb just took out the Council Hall in Little Rock."

"Fuck." He pinched the bridge of his nose and closed his eyes. "This means those red wolves knew I was a Guardian." Guardian werewolves were all spread out over the state of Arkansas, yet it was common knowledge that the Pack Master and the Council ruled from Little Rock. It functioned much like the capital of the states did for humans.

"It also means you're going to have to keep Ava with you and away from here."

His eyes shot open. "What the hell am I supposed to do with her?" He walked a few feet from Ava as she shot him a glare. Keeping Ava with him was a bad idea.

"That's up to you. She's under your protection until I call with a safe house location."

"Hold on..." It was too late. Barrett hung up.

"Perfect." He ran his hand across his face.

"What's wrong?" Ava touched his shoulder. He flinched.

"We need to go." He climbed on the bike and started the engine, his mind plotting out his next move.

She climbed on behind and wrapped her arms around him.

"Are you going to tell me what's going on?"

"Nope." He punched in new directions on his cell phone and pulled out onto the highway. He just prayed they were far enough ahead of the red wolves to get to their new destination.

It was after 2:00 a.m. when they drove into a small town just across the Louisiana state line. They'd been riding for what seemed like an eternity and Ava knew she wasn't going to last much longer. Her ass hurt from riding, cold soaked down to her bones, and she desperately needed a hot shower. She had never been so miserable in her life.

Damon finally pulled into a parking place at a low-budget motel. He climbed off the bike like he hadn't been riding hours in the seat. She tried to follow, but her heavy legs threatened to give way under her weight.

Damon shook his head. "Don't get off yet. I'm not even sure it's safe to stay here for the night."

"Look, as much as I appreciate everything you've done for me, I'm going to have to disagree with you. We're staying here tonight." She sighed. "I can't go any longer. I need a shower. Not to mention my ass is numb." She winced as she crawled off the bike.

"It's my job to make sure your ass is delivered back home in one piece. If it's not safe, we're not staying." He stepped into her space.

"Whatever." Pushing past him, she stumbled to the sidewalk and sat. She eased onto her side and curled up into a ball.

"What the hell are you doing? Get up."

"I'm sleeping."

"Ava, get your ass up now."

Her eyelids drifted shut. If she hadn't been so exhausted she would have told him to go to hell. The last thing she heard as her eyes drifted shut were angry boots stomping away.

Damon turned and glanced back at Ava. Despite his irritation, he couldn't help but feel sorry for her. For someone who'd never been on a bike before, she'd hung in there like a champ. Her ass was going to be killing her in the morning that was for sure.

After making sure the dump of a hotel was secure, he opened the office door, making sure he could still see Ava from inside. The young, skinny male with a mop of brown hair and acne-scarred face sat behind the front desk. He was too busy playing an online computer game to look up at his customer.

"I need a room for the night." Damon angled his body away so the clerk couldn't get a good look at his face. The guy was human and posed no physical danger to him. But humans were greedy and willing to do anything to make a quick buck. If those rogue wolves came here, he wanted to make sure the clerk couldn't identify him.

"Yeah, just sign in. It's sixty-five for one night or hundred and ten for two nights." His fingers danced across the keyboard while his eyes remained focused on the computer game involving dwarfs, elves and a dragon.

Damon signed in under an alias and placed the money on the desk. The guy grabbed it with one hand while typing with the other. Sticking the money in a drawer, he slid the key across to him.

He stepped out into the frosty night and stopped, unable to tear his gaze away from the female with hair the color of midnight curled up like a kitten on the cold, hard sidewalk. The sight made his heart ache.

He bent down and picked her up. This time she melded into his arms, which surprised him. She sighed and wrapped her arms around his neck.

"Please don't make me leave." Her warm breath brushed the side of his neck. His heart pounded in his chest.

"We're not leaving. We're spending the night."

"Thank you." Her arms tightened around his neck and she snuggled closer.

His muscles clenched, unable to take another step. Sweat popped out across his flesh and he struggled to breathe. "Don't do that." His mouth had gone dry. "Don't touch my neck."

Her sleepy eyes opened and she slid her arms down to hold onto his shoulders. "I'm sorry. Here, put me down. I can walk."

He let her slide out of his arms as he set her gently on her feet. He hated that his past horrors still held power over him. Embarrassed, he turned away and pulled a gym bag out from one of his saddlebags.

He unlocked their motel door and flipped on the lights. Relief washed over him when no cockroaches scurried across the floor. It may be old and out of date, but at least everything appeared clean.

"Shit." His gaze landed on the bed.

"What?"

"There's only one bed. I've got to get the room changed."

She blinked at him and headed toward the bathroom.

"Where are you going?"

"I'm going to take a shower."

"Wait until I get a different room."

She shook her head wearily. "I can't. I'm filthy and I'm not going to stay this way another second."

She walked into the bathroom and locked the door.

He raked his hand through his hair. "Great."

He checked his watch as the muffled sound of the shower drifted out into the room. Pacing the room, he rolled his shoulders as he waited. He couldn't leave her alone to go get the rooms changed. He'd wait until she was out of the shower. He eased onto the edge of the springy bed, his body weary from the past two hours, yet his mind alert for the danger. Mental clarity was part of the job and he was nothing, if not all about the job. Being a Guardian filled a void on the baser levels and gave him purpose. Some wolves had families; he had his position.

The shower turned off and he stood as the bathroom door opened.

His heart nearly stopped beating in his chest. Ava stepped out wearing nothing but a towel.

She looked up at him and smiled. Her wet hair hung like black silk ribbons across her slender shoulders and grazed the tops of her firm breasts. Her long legs peeked out from the bottom of the threadbare towel.

She was fucking gorgeous.

He forced his gaze up to her face.

She brushed her hair away from her green eyes. Unlike most women, she didn't seem afraid of him. In fact, he couldn't even smell fear anywhere on her body.

He cleared his throat and picked up his bag, pretending to rifle through it to hide his throbbing erection. "Stay here and lock the door behind me. Make sure it's me before you open the door." Not waiting for an answer, he slammed the door behind him and hurried toward the office.

A few minutes later he was back, knocking at the door.

Ava opened the door and locked it behind him.

"There aren't any rooms with two beds. We can try further down the road." He kept his gaze on the ceiling. She still had that fucking towel on and he was still sporting an erection. Another few miles on the Harley would give his body time to cool off.

"I'm exhausted. We'll just stay here. It's no big deal."

He grimaced. Despite being a wolf, sleeping on the floor did not appeal to him.

He pulled out an extra toothbrush and a tube of toothpaste out of his bag and tossed them on the bed.

"I could just kiss you for that," she moaned.

He met her emerald gaze. Heat flared in his belly and his body hardened. All that lay between them was that skimpy rag. With just one pull, that poor excuse of a bath towel would be on the floor.

Before his body could react, Ava turned on her heel and headed toward the bathroom with toothbrush in hand.

Ava walked out of the bathroom feeling wonderfully clean. All she needed now was something to sleep in. In her haste to change at the truck stop, she'd thrown away her pajamas. She didn't think she'd need them.

Damon held out an oversized, long-sleeved, T-shirt he'd retrieved from his bag. "You can sleep in this."

"Thanks," she muttered as he headed toward the bathroom. She held up a handful of the soft material to her face and inhaled. It smelled like him.

She shook her head and climbed into his shirt. What the hell was wrong with her? She barely knew this guy, yet here she was sniffing his clothes. She needed to get a grip.

Pulling back the covers, she slid between the cool sheets and closed her eyes. She had never been so happy to see a pillow in her life. Thanks to Damon, for tonight she was safe.

She wasn't sure how much time had passed when she opened her eyes and glanced across the bed. It was empty. She sat up and squinted against the darkness.

Damon lay sprawled on the floor, his muscled arm thrown across his eyes.

"What are you doing?"

"Getting some sleep. You need to do the same. We're going to have a long day tomorrow."

"You can't sleep on the floor." After all he'd done, it wasn't right for him to be spending the night on the floor.

"Ava, go to sleep."

"Damon, get in the bed."

He moved his arm and looked at her like she'd grown a second head. "What?"

"You can't sleep on the floor. You can sleep in the bed with me. It's fine."

"No. It's not."

"I promise to stay on my side. I'm too tired to make a move on you anyway." She snorted.

He gave her a horrified look. She flinched at the insult.

"If you won't sleep in the bed, then I'm going to sleep on the floor with you." As much as she didn't want to, she stood and grabbed a pillow. He scrambled to his feet.

"Damn it. Get back in the bed."

"Are you coming?"

"Yes." He made a growling noise.

She watched him make his way to the other side of the bed and pull back the cover. Satisfied, she slid back under the sheets and closed her eyes.

Damon woke up, his cock rock hard and aching. Ava's arm was wrapped around him like a vine. Her soft body pressed against his side while her arm was slung low across his stomach, inches from his throbbing dick.

He gritted his teeth as he tried to ease toward the edge of the bed, hoping to quickly slide out before she woke.

She moaned softly, her breath scorching his shoulder while her hand snuck even lower past the waistband of his boxers.

Sweat broke out across his body at the warmth of her touch. God, he wanted nothing more than to bury himself between her thighs until they were both sated.

Her breasts pressed against his arm, the outline of her hard nipples burning his skin through the thin shirt. He bet those tight buds tasted as sweet as she smelled.

She sighed and shifted, rolling to her back as she pulled his arm across her flat stomach. She tugged his hand down to her thigh, his fingers very close to the heated treasure that lay between her legs. Gritting his teeth, he used all his self-control to move his hand away. She moaned and covered his hand.

He couldn't breathe.

He should stop her. He. Really. Should.

He'd been with a lot of women, but they were usually one-night stands. A woman with Ava's beauty had never given him a second look, let alone touched him like she was doing.

But then again, she was asleep. She was probably having some dream about a Calvin Klein underwear model.

She moved and her shirt rode up dangerously high on her thigh.

Fuck. Was she not wearing any panties?

His body clenched so tight he thought his bones might shatter.

"Damon."

He jerked his gaze up to her face, expecting to see her looking back at him. How was he going to explain his hand on her thigh? She'd never believe the truth.

Her eyes were closed, her face lost in concentration as she dreamed.

She wasn't awake. She just said his name in her sleep.

The thought shot through him as his erection grew painfully hard.

He needed to get out of bed before he climbed between her legs and gave her something to moan about.

Gritting his teeth, he pulled his hand away and rolled off the bed in one fluid movement. He pulled the sheet up to her waist.

She stretched her arms over her head and blinked. Her gaze settled on him and she sat up. Her oversized T-shirt gaped open, giving him an amazing view of a firm breast.

She followed his stare to her chest. Blushing, she tugged the shirt back into place.

"What time is it?" She ran her hand through her tousled hair.

"Almost eight." He kept his back to her as he slid on his jeans and repositioned himself. Once his equipment was under control, he turned and faced her.

She narrowed those pretty green eyes at him. "I'm assuming from your phone call last night that we are not going to Jonesboro."

"Not right now."

She shook her head. "As much as I appreciate what you did for me, I think we need to have a talk before I agree to go anywhere else with you."

"There's no need for a conversation. It's simple. You were kidnapped. I rescued you. I'll keep you safe until I can get you to your father."

She gave him an astonished look. "My father?" She narrowed her green eyes in suspicion. "Did my father call you?"

"Not me personally, but he contacted my Commander."

"Commander? You mean from the military base that is stationed in Little Rock?"

He stared at her for a minute. Though no one spoke about what they were, everyone living in the compound was a werewolf. They tried to blend into the human population, even going so far as to set up a military base where the Guardians could train. The U.S. Government had known about the existence of werewolves for decades. The government made a pact with the werewolves to protect their secret in exchange for service in special operations in various branches of the military.

"Our wolf Pack, Ava. He contacted our wolf Pack."

She gave a little laugh and smiled. "Wolf Pack. Is that the code name for your team?"

He took a step toward her. "Why are you acting like this?"

"Like what?"

"Like you don't know you're a wolf."

"Is that slang for female?" She gave a brittle laugh as her smile faded.

"Look at me."

She looked him in the eye. Females rarely looked him in the eye. They were too afraid.

He stared into her green gaze, looking for the lie.

He sucked in a harsh breath. She wasn't lying.

"Ava, how can you not know what you are?"

"Know what?"

"That you are a wolf."

"Right. I guess that means you're a wolf too." She smirked.

"Yes."

"You're like those freaks that kidnapped me?" Her smile faded and her face paled. She scooted toward the edge of the bed and stood, slowly easing toward the door.

"Make no mistake. I'm nothing like those wolves." He had a code of duty and honor he lived by. Rogue wolves lived by their desires, killing and stealing without remorse.

She held her hands palms out as she continued to back toward the door. "You know what, I think I can get home on my own. I'll just go ask the desk clerk to call me a taxi." She reached for the doorknob.

The second she opened the door, he sprang. Grabbing her around the waist, he slammed the door shut and pressed her back against it.

"Just let me go and I swear I won't tell anyone that I ever met you." Her voice was a whisper caressing his cheek as he leaned into her. His cock twitched.

"I can't let you go."

CHAPTER THREE

"My father can pick me up and take me home."

"It's not safe, Ava. You can't go home."

She stilled and her green eyes widened. "What do you mean?"

"They bombed your house in Jonesboro and our Council Hall in Little Rock."

"Oh, God. Did anyone get hurt?" She covered her mouth with quivering fingertips.

"I don't know. Barrett didn't have time to give me the details. He said not to bring you back there and to keep you out of sight until he could find a safe house."

She shook her head. "I don't understand. Are you saying they bombed the Council Hall because of me? Because you saved me?"

"Yes." He took a breath. She seemed more concerned about the Council Hall than her own home.

She shuddered. "This is my fault."

"That's not true. None of this is your fault. If you want to blame someone, blame those fuckers who took you." He tilted her chin with his fingertips, forcing her to look at him. "Do you understand what they were going to do to you?"

She blinked back the tears swimming in her eyes, trying to be brave.

He hated to see a woman cry, but he wanted her to be safe. He needed to hear her say the words. Her naivety could get them killed if she weren't careful. "Tell me. Do you have any idea how much danger you were in or what they were capable of doing?"

She swallowed with visible effort, raw emotion scraped past her taut lips. "They were going to rape me."

He cupped her face in his hand. "They were going to rape you repeatedly. No one ever has the right to take someone by force, to be chained up while abused, over and over again. No one has that right, do you hear me?" His tone hardened. He couldn't stop envisioning what those rogue wolves had planned for Ava. It made him want to rip them apart.

Their gazes locked, and he couldn't stop the barrage of words spilling off his tongue.

"Don't ever think any of this fucked-up shit is your fault. If anyone is to blame, it's that Pack of red wolves."

She grimaced. "Just when I thought you were back to being normal you go and make another doggie comment."

He growled in frustration.

Her warm fingers brushed his scarred cheek. He froze. No one ever touched his scar.

"I'm sorry. I just find all this impossible to believe. I'm not even sure if what I witnessed back in that warehouse actually happened. The drug they gave me was probably still in my system and caused me to hallucinate." She gave him a worried look. "I'm really not trying to be difficult. Don't be mad."

"I'm not mad, Ava." Her tenderness rocked him to the core and the warmth of her touch made his head spin. Unable to stop, he leaned closer to her warmth.

Alarms went off in his head. He couldn't do this. He wouldn't sacrifice his future as a Guardian. He'd lost too much already. His life was his job. He dropped his hands to his sides, and stepped back. Immediately, he missed her warmth. He wanted his hands all over her.

"Prove it."

"Prove what?" He rested his hands on his hips as he studied the floor. He better get a grip on his urges before he messed things up for his career.

"If you're a wolf, show me." She lifted her brow. "Or do you have to wait for a full moon?"

He jerked his head up. He didn't know if he was more irritated or amused. In his lifetime, he hadn't come across another female like her.

He snorted. "I don't need a full moon to shift. It doesn't work like that."

"Good."

He narrowed his eyes. "Fine. But you have to promise not to scream."

"Okay."

"I don't intend on shredding the only clothes I have." He eased his tight T-shirt over his head and tossed it on the floor. He didn't miss the way her eyes widened as he shoved his jeans down over his hips and kick them off. Her gaze landed on black tribal tattoos that circled his biceps. Maybe she was one of those chicks that didn't like tattoos? Wait until she saw the massive tattoo that spanned the width of his shoulders, marking him as a Guardian.

He closed his eyes. The beast roared to life as he released his self-control, giving free rein to the creature that lived inside. His power surged, knocking him to his knees and heightening his senses. Pain licked through his joints and muscles as they stretched and shifted, accommodating his wolf body. Hair grew and spread over his entire body until his flesh was concealed in a furry pelt.

He opened his wolf eyes.

Ava stood by the door, her mouth hanging open, her eyes wide with fear.

She screamed.

Well, fuck.

He tried to shift back, but it was too soon. He needed a few minutes. What the hell had he been thinking? This had been a mistake. With his head down, he headed for the corner, made a complete circle and curled up in the shadows, waiting for the cops to bust in with animal control.

Ava tightened her trembling grip on the doorknob as she gaped at the massive gray wolf, in the corner.

Damon had turned into a wolf. Just like her kidnappers.

She kept her gaze on the wolf as her heart beat in her ears. After he walked to the corner of the room, he lay down and curled his body into a tight ball.

She could open the door and make her escape before he made it across the room. She could be free of this man who both excited and frightened her.

She wasn't so sure she wanted to escape. He may look like her kidnappers, but he had proven by his actions that he was nothing like them.

Her stomach fluttered as the wolf's blue gaze locked on her from across the room. If he were going to hurt her, he would have done so by now.

Her hand fell away from the doorknob as she took a hesitant step toward the wolf. When he didn't move, she stepped closer until she was a foot away.

Crouching down, she looked at the beast staring her through Damon's blue eyes.

"Damon?" She winced. Could he even understand English? "Can you understand what I'm saying?"

He lifted his head off his paws and let out a whimper.

She grinned. Maybe he did understand her after all.

She held out her hand. His large tongue lapped across her knuckles and she laughed. Gingerly, she ran her fingertips through his lush gray fur.

She sat on the floor with her legs crossed, staring at the massive animal in front of her. How was this possible? How could a wolf exist within a man's body? And why did he insist that she was a wolf as well?

She stroked his soft head until he belly crawled closer. She held her breath as he put his head in her lap.

"Hey, watch the snout, buddy." She shot him a glare when his nose came a little too close to her crotch.

He lifted his head and gave her a toothy grin.

Wolves didn't grin, right?

He stood and walked back to the corner.

The wolf began to change, his limbs lengthened and his pelt receded until Damon lay naked in the corner.

Her lips parted as she continued to stare, unable to drag her gaze away from his nakedness.

Damon was perfection, his body constructed of hard muscles, tanned flesh, and a face that would even tempt angels to sin.

He eased up to a sitting position, obviously comfortable with his nakedness. Trying to have a conversation while he was completely nude was impossible. She grabbed the comforter off the bed and handed it to him.

"Thanks." His gravelly voice had her stomach tingling in a very naughty way.

She stroked her arm as her gaze traveled over his body. A large, winged tattoo with eyes peeking out covered the entire span of his back. Black tribal tattoos circled his biceps. His muscled chest had a sprinkling of dark hairs, while his six-pack abs was bare. Right above the comforter, the dark hair started again in a downward vee toward his...

"What does the tattoo on your back signify?" Ava cleared her throat and squeezed her eyes shut. She needed to get a grip and stop fantasizing about how big a package the man was sporting.

"It's the symbol of Pack Guardian." He shifted his intense gaze at her. "You screamed."

Her eyes popped open. "Yeah, sorry about that."

"You said you wouldn't scream."

"What did you expect? You turned into a freaking wolf. Not just a regular wolf but a really big wolf. A freakishly big wolf." She propped her hands on her hips.

He ran his large hand across his face. His biceps rippled under the action. She wondered how his muscles moved when he was having sex. Really hot, sweaty, all-night-long sex.

"Now do you believe me?"

"What?" She dragged her gaze and her dirty mind from his massive arms up to his eyes. Her face heated. He had asked her a question. "I was wrong. You're a wolf."

"You're a wolf too, Ava."

"That's not possible. I have never done what you just did, my friend." She moved toward the door. She needed to get some air to clear her head or she was going to jump his body right where he stood.

He grabbed her hand, spun her around, and let the comforter fall to the floor.

God help her, she couldn't resist looking. Her gaze dipped down. Her breath caught in the back of her throat. He was big everywhere.

"You *are* a wolf, Ava."

She closed her eyes and tried to ignore the heat that was building between her legs. "No, I'm not. If I had been bitten by one of you, I would have known. Judging by those teeth you were sporting, the pain would definitely be memorable."

He snarled. "You don't have to be bitten by a wolf in order to shift."

"Yeah?" Her eyes popped open. "Then how does one become a werewolf?" Her gaze dipped toward his huge erection then back at the ceiling. Her face heated. She couldn't continue to hold a conversation if he refused to cover up.

"You have to be born with the gene."

"So my parents were werewolves?" She frowned as she forced herself to look him in the eye.

"No, just one of them. You father, most likely."

"You're saying there are more werewolves in Little Rock?"

He grinned. "Our whole base is werewolves."

She shook her head. "I thought it was a military town. I mean, you guys always wear camouflage and carry guns.

I've even seen all those Hummers locked inside the fence behind the Council Hall."

"We operate to the human world like military to cover our true identities. If the world knew we existed, it would be a total witch-hunt until we were all eradicated. Having the access to a few rocket launchers comes in handy when it comes to guarding our Pack."

"Guarding the Pack from whom?"

"Other wolf packs that want what we have." He seared her with his gaze.

She shifted under his stare. "If I'm a wolf, why haven't I transformed?"

"Shifted. Transform is what robots do in the movies."

He really needed to put some jeans on. Trying to have a conversation while averting her eyes from his crotch was hard work. "Fine, then why haven't I shifted?"

"How old are you?" His eyes drifted down her body like he was analyzing her every curve. She wished it were his hands analyzing her body and not his gaze.

"How old do you think I am?" She propped one hand on her hip and thrust out her breasts. It was her signature pose that men couldn't resist. That's how she gotten through college without having to pay for beer.

The corners of his mouth curved up in a sexy grin as he leaned in closer. "I don't ever guess a woman's age. It might get me in trouble."

His scent hit her, curled around her, as she inhaled deep. She gritted her teeth, irritated that he was even having this effect on her in the first place. It did nothing for her ego that he wasn't even a little attracted to her. He'd done nothing but glare and argue with her since he rescued her.

She leaned closer, her lips only an inch from his, and inhaled. "Damon, somehow I find it hard to believe you stay out of trouble."

Damon curled his fingers into fists to keep from pulling Ava into his arms and stripping her naked.

Females usually kept their distance. But no, not Ava. Instead of heeding the danger and staying away, she leaned in and sniffed him.

His gaze dropped to her parted lips. All he could think about was sinking his teeth into her flesh as he drove himself, balls deep, inside her body until she cried out his name.

"I'm nothing but trouble." It came out as a growl, as he leaned closer.

She blushed as she met his gaze, yet still didn't move away.

His gaze drifted down to her breasts. Her hard nipples pressing against the thin material of the T-shirt made his dick swell and ache. Lust fueled his brain until all he could see and smell was her.

His mind went blank, leaving only animal instinct. If she insisted on playing with fire, then he was going to light the match.

He wrapped his hand around her waist and tugged her against his chest. His mouth covered hers, dominating and hard, claiming her full attention.

He thrust his tongue inside her hot, sweet, mouth, kissing her hard and deep. His mind became dizzy with how sexy she tasted. If he kissed her for an eternity, he still wouldn't quench his thirst.

He braced himself, expecting any minute for her hands to shove against his chest and push him away. How the hell was he going to let her go when all he wanted to do was keep her close?

Her hands slid up his shoulders. He tensed, waiting for her to stop him.

Instead, she did the unexpected.

She dug her fingers into his shoulders, clinging and pulling him closer.

Stunned, he opened his eyes. Her green gaze was glued on his as she kissed him back, their tongues mating in an intimate dance. His body ached as she ground her pelvis against his rock-hard erection, nothing but the thin T-shirt stopping him from actually pressing between her thighs.

Her tongue stroked in and out of his mouth as she laced her fingers behind his neck, tightening her hold.

The wind left his lungs as he stiffened, memories flooding over the gates of his closely locked past. Struggling to breathe, he pulled away.

"What's wrong?" she breathed.

"Don't touch my neck."

"I'm sorry." She reached for him. "I didn't know."

"This was a mistake." He grabbed her hand, keeping her at arm's length. He shouldn't have touched her, let alone kissed her. This whole damn thing was a bad idea.

"I thought you liked kissing me."

"Kissing is not all I want to do to you, Ava. I think you know that."

"Maybe it's not all I want to do, either." She ran her free hand up his chest and flicked his nipple with her fingernail.

He hissed. Her touch was fire racing across his flesh. He needed space. He needed to clear his head and get focused on his duty. The careless words tumbled out anyway. "Baby, your fantasy and mine are completely different."

"I doubt that."

Why did she have to be so fucking beautiful? And completely out of his reach?

He shook his head. "It's different. You want romance and gentleness. I'm neither of those things."

"How do you know what I want?" Her hand lingered on his chest.

"Trust me. I am not what you want." It would never work. Their destinies were set by their blood and sealed by fate.

"Really?"

"Because of your status in the Pack, you will be mated to a male who is your equal. And that's not me."

Her eyes flashed and she jerked out of his grip. "Well, thank you, Einstein, for telling me what I want. It's amazing you and your ego can fit in the same fucking room." Heat sparked off her green eyes, and he could have sworn the temperature in the room increased ten degrees.

She stuck her finger in his face. "Let me tell you something. I have no plans on getting married or mated or anything else that will tie me to some asshole who thinks he is going to control me or my life. Who I let into my bed is nobody's business but mine." She turned on her heel and stormed into the bathroom, slamming the door behind her.

He glanced down. Her tirade had only made him harder.

What the hell was wrong with him? If he didn't get his mind back on his job, this whole thing could go to shit. The job always came first. No matter what.

Shaking his head, he finished getting dressed and grabbed his cell phone. He needed to give Barrett an update.

After showering and throwing her clothes on, Ava stepped out of the hotel room. She held up her hand, shielding her eyes from the bright sunlight. Damon stood by his bike, giving her a quick glance before continuing his conversation on his cell phone.

Asshole. He couldn't even spare her a second thought.

Men were all the same. Wanting to jump your ass one minute and, the second things didn't go their way, they'd kick you to the old motel curb in the next.

She shrugged out of the leather jacket under the warm winter sun. Weather in the South was so fickle. Yesterday had been cool, and now it was hot all over again. Maybe she should move to Colorado. She'd bet the weather and the men were more agreeable than what she had here.

With Damon still ignoring her, she slung the jacket across the seat of his motorcycle and headed toward the motel office.

"Ava, where are you going?" Damon yelled.

She ignored him, figuring two could play at his game.

She opened the door to the office and walked up to the young clerk and smiled.

His eyes widened. Whatever he'd been doing on the computer was quickly forgotten. He shot to his feet and gave her his complete attention.

Damon could learn a lesson from this guy.

"Hi." She rested her elbows on the counter and leaned in a little. "I'm Ava."

"I'm Michael." Michael's gaze dropped to her breasts. She resisted the urge to roll her eyes. Men were all the same, whether they were forty or four, they couldn't stop staring at a pair of boobs.

"I was wondering if you could help me."

"Sure. I can help you with whatever you need." Michael's acne-scarred face broke into a wide grin.

"Well, aren't you the sweetest thing?"

Michael blushed and puffed out his thin chest. Yeah, she still had it. Even if Damon was immune to her charms.

Damon hurried after Ava as she strode into the motel office. She clearly had no idea that keeping a low profile was of the utmost importance. Yet here she was strutting around like the Queen of Sheba without a care in the world.

The nerdy desk clerk had obviously found Ava more appealing than that damn computer game he'd been playing last night. Not that he could really blame the guy.

"I was wondering if you can recommend a place for breakfast," Ava purred.

The clerk flashed a grin. "I know just the place. It's a few miles down the road and it has the best pancakes. It's called the Apple Dumpling."

"Hmm, pancakes sound good. I was kind of thinking something healthier. I don't know if I need the extra calories." Ava poked her lips into a sexy pout.

What the hell was Ava doing, flirting with that kid?

"I don't think you have to worry about counting calories. You look amazing." The desk clerk pushed his glasses up on his nose with one finger.

"I bet you say that to all the girls." She grinned. Damon didn't know if he wanted to beat the shit out of the guy, or throw Ava across his shoulder, take her back to the room, and finish what they'd started.

"I wouldn't know. The girls around here don't talk to me." The clerk glanced away as his shoulders slumped.

Damon certainly could empathize with the guy. He remembered feeling scrawny and awkward around females before puberty hit. Still, he didn't like the way the twerp was looking at Ava.

"The girls around here probably don't measure up to Ava." Damon wrapped his hand around her waist and pulled her close. She glared and elbowed him in the side, but he didn't let her go.

"Are you kidding? No one around here looks like Ava." Michael swallowed.

"I bet in another year, you'll have all the girls after you." Ava smiled.

Damon's chest tightened. He had lived most of his life as an outcast. Ava probably never would know what that feeling was like. Yet, here she was her kind words an encouragement to a stranger who would always remember them.

"Really?" Michael gave her a doubtful look before looking over at Damon for confirmation.

He shrugged. "Yeah, but you're going to have to get off the damn computer and get your underage ass to a bar. This is Louisiana. Surely you can score a fake ID."

"Damon," she hissed.

"What? The first time I got some was in the back room of a bar."

"Why am I not surprised?" She gave him a droll look. "Although I'm surprised you waited to have sex until you were old enough to drive."

"I wasn't old enough to drive. I rode my bicycle."

"Who was the lucky girl?" Ava arched her eyebrow.

"I don't know. Some chick that just got a divorce. She was looking to celebrate, and I didn't mind being the cake."

"I don't think that's even legal." She gave him a horrified look.

Damon shrugged and looked at his watch. He had more important things to do than help this kid get laid.

He faced Michael. "The point is, you can either keep playing with your dick or you can get a girl to do it for you. Trust me, its better when a girl is playing with it." He grabbed Ava's hand and led her outside.

She dug in her heels and snatched out of his grip.

"What?" He sighed.

"You can't tell him that kind of thing. Are you crazy?"

"I was just trying to help." He shrugged.

"Yeah, well you didn't tell him anything about waiting for the right girl, or being in love, or how to be responsible when it comes to sex."

"Fine." He threw his hands up and walked back inside. Wasn't like he was on a mission or anything. "Hey, kid. Don't be a fool, always wrap your tool." He pulled a silver package out of his pocket and tossed it toward the teen. Michael caught the condom in midair.

"Thanks! Thanks a lot, man." The clerk grinned and shoved the condom in his wallet like a prized possession.

"There. He's been educated." He glanced at Ava as he headed toward his bike.

"Where are we headed?" Ava straddled the bike behind him and slipped on her helmet.

"To eat breakfast, then to meet up with a friend of mine. I'm hoping he's willing to help us find someplace safe to stay."

"Won't we be putting him in danger?"

"Trust me, he thrives on danger."

After stuffing themselves with pancakes and bacon, they made the short drive to the Lady Diamond Casino in Shreveport.

"What does your friend do exactly?" Ava asked.

"He's security for the casino." Damon scanned the nearly filled parking lot for any signs of the rogue wolves before making his way toward the entrance of the casino. The sun hung bright in the pale sky and glinted off the water like diamonds. A few people milled around the front door, smoking cigarettes and talking. There was little activity this time of the morning and he sensed no danger.

Lady Gaga blared through the speaker system. He grimaced.

"I take it you're not a Gaga fan?" She smirked.

"Not really."

"I had you pegged as more of a Slipknot kind of guy."

The corners of his lips toyed with a reluctant smile. She knew him better than most.

"I was right, wasn't I?" Her smirk turned into a full on smile.

"Actually, he's more of a Katy Perry kind of guy."

Damon growled and turned. "Jayden. I knew I smelled something rotten."

"The rotten smell is our lunch special. I, on the other hand, always smell irresistible." Jayden gave Ava a charming smile. "Especially to the beautiful ladies."

As long as he'd known him, Jayden had never lacked for female company. With his blond hair and blue eyes, he looked more like he belonged in Hollywood than Louisiana.

"I'm Ava." She stuck her hand out.

Jayden's eyes sparkled and his nostrils flared. He brought her wrist to his nose as inhaled.

Something inside him snapped. Damon lunged, catching Jayden around his throat and pinning him to the wall. "Don't fucking touch her."

"Damon, let him go." Ava pulled at his arm.

"Yeah, Damon. Let him go." Jayden wheezed in spite of the hand clamped around his throat.

Two security guards appeared out of nowhere, one on either side of Damon, attempting to pull him off.

Damon caught unmistakable fear in Ava's emerald green eyes and his head cleared. The last thing he wanted was for Ava to be afraid of him.

He released his grip.

"Still a hothead, I see." Jayden winced and rubbed his neck.

"Come on, buddy, you're out of here." One security guard grabbed Damon's arm.

Damon growled.

"No, it's fine. It's just a misunderstanding. He's a friend." Jayden waved away the guards. With watchful eyes they backed away into the shadows of the casino.

"I meant no disrespect to your female, man." Jayden held up his hands.

"She's not my female," Damon snapped.

"I'm not his female," Ava answered in unison.

Jayden snorted.

"She's in my care until I can get her safely back home."

"And since the bombing you can't exactly go home, can you?" Jayden frowned as he adjusted his collar and smoothed his shirt.

"How did you know?" Even though Jayden didn't belong to a Pack, the word would have still passed to him through other wolves. News traveled like the Internet in the lupine world.

"I got an email from Barrett after midnight. The whole compound has been moved to the safe house in the northwest part of Arkansas."

"Then, that's where we should head," Ava said.

He shook his head. "We can't. Although that area is considered neutral territory, the wolves that bombed the compound wouldn't think twice about bombing that as well, especially if I showed up with you. Lives don't matter to them."

Jayden inclined his head toward Ava. "So, the rogue wolves want the female."

"The name is Ava," she corrected.

"They kidnapped her. I went in and rescued her."

Jayden's smile quickly faded. "Are you fucking with me? Kidnapping a female hasn't been heard of since the Council set the death penalty for such an act."

"Yeah, well those red wolf bastards are willing to risk it."

"Red wolves? I thought they were extinct in this area?" Jayden's frown deepened.

"Apparently, they are making a reappearance," Damon growled, "with plans to start procreating."

Understanding reached Ava's eyes as the puzzle pieces clicked together in her mind.

"Oh, hell no. Just because you and Scooby Doo here can grow some fur, doesn't mean I can. Even if I did, I'm not dropping a litter for anybody."

Jayden's gaze darted down the hallway. "Keep your voice down."

"We need a place to stay." Damon looked at Jayden.

"You can stay here." Jayden shrugged. "That way there'll be two of us watching over her."

Damon snorted. "Since when are you a team player?"

"Says the pot to the kettle. Just because you run in a Pack doesn't mean you are part of a team." Jayden smirked.

That hit a little too close to home. Damon gritted his teeth, held up his hand and gave Jayden the bird.

Jayden chuckled. "No, thanks. You're not my type."

"If you two are finished, can we please get a room? After we check in, I need to find some different clothes."

Ava held her shirt off her chest and grimaced. "Being a walking advertisement for beer is not my idea of fashion."

"Don't worry. We've got a boutique in the casino," Jayden offered.

"That sounds kind of expensive and I'm short on funds." Ava looked over at Damon. "If I could borrow some money, I can pay you back as soon as we get home."

"My treat, Ava." Jayden reached for his wallet, but Damon moved faster.

"I got it." Pulling out three hundred-dollar bills, he handed them to her. She gave him a brilliant smile. His chest tightened.

For the first time in his life, Damon felt like he was the one in danger.

⚜ ⚜ ⚜

The sales woman dressed in a black-and-white wrap dress and sparkling black heels shot Ava a dirty look as she walked through the door of the boutique. Apparently she wasn't a fan of Ava's truck-stop attire either.

Luckily, Jayden was there, armed with a few charming words and a devastating smile. He assured the sales clerk that Ava was practically family. After Jayden left, the woman was saccharine-sweet helpful, showing her everything from diamond jewelry to designer handbags. Neither of which Ava needed, nor could afford.

Much to her relief, an older lady dressed to the nines walked in and the clerk left Ava to attend to the new customer.

Ava ran her fingertips over an angora sweater and picked it up. After glancing at the price, she put it back on the shelf.

"Not everyone who comes to the casino leaves with money. You'd think they'd know that," Ava muttered to herself. Her eyes glazed over at the array of designer jeans and trend-setting shirts that were way out of her price range.

Her heart sank. "I can't afford any of this." As she walked toward the back of the store before making her way out, a small sale rack caught her eye. She rifled through the clothing and smiled. Now this she could afford.

Ava ignored the haughty looks the sales clerk gave her as she paid for her purchases. All in all, she'd done pretty well.

She'd grabbed her bag off the counter when her pulse picked up. She knew without turning around that Damon had just walked in.

The scent of warmed leather and hot danger heated her blood. Every time he came near, she had to fight the urge to push him to the floor and straddle him.

After that very hot kiss in the motel room, she thought he was attracted to her. But by the way he pushed her away, she knew better. He probably had a girlfriend. Hell, she'd bet he had a female in every city across the Southeast.

Taking a deep breath to steady herself, she turned. Her stomach turned to jelly when she met his intense eyes.

"Did you find something?" Damon looked down at her with those aqua eyes that seemed to see into her soul.

At five foot ten inches, it was hard to find a man who actually had to look down at her. But Damon did. He made her feel petite and dainty and delicate.

"I did. But I didn't have much money left over." She handed him a little more than seventeen dollars in change.

He frowned.

"Sorry, the clothes are really expensive. I did manage to buy everything on clearance, but it still added up." Maybe she should return a few things. She could wear the same thing a couple of days in a row, right?

He shrugged. "Doesn't matter."

She narrowed her eyes. Did the man ever show any kind of emotion other than anger and irritation? She seriously needed to have her head examined for her attraction to him.

She stepped around him and out into the lavish lobby where Jayden was waiting for her with a brilliant smile.

Jayden. Now there was a guy about whom she should be having fantasies. Not only was Jayden gorgeous, he was incredibly attentive. Despite his movie star good looks and charm, when she looked at Jayden, she didn't feel anything. No bolt of excitement straight through her body, or the need to lean into his neck and inhale his scent, or even the urge to rip his clothes off with her teeth. Only Damon made her feel that way.

She was so screwed.

"Did we get a room?" She needed a hot shower and a wardrobe change to feel like herself again.

Jayden bowed elegantly and dangled a room card in front of her. "What my lady wants, my lady gets."

That wasn't true. Ava knew, this time, she wasn't getting what she wanted. Not by a long shot.

CHAPTER FOUR

It took all Damon's restraint not to knock that goofy looking grin off Jayden's ridiculous face.

He shoulder checked Jayden as he followed Ava into the elevator.

"Is your room on the same floor?" She punched the number for her floor without looking at him.

"Yes, it is."

The elevator ride was tense and quiet. She was still angry and he didn't think that wasn't about to change anytime soon. He should never have touched her. He was playing a dangerous game that would only end up hurting his career as a Guardian. If he had ended up sleeping with her and Barrett found out, Damon would be punished, stripped of his title, and never allowed back into a Pack. He'd have to go Nomad, always on the run, always alone, always without a home.

The elevator doors opened with a soft chime and they stepped out.

He waited behind her as she inserted the key into the lock.

She entered the room and turned to close the door. He pushed past her, ignoring the glare she shot him. Pulling off his jacket, he tossed it on one of the double beds.

"You don't have to stay here while I change." She crossed her arms over her chest. "I think I'll be safe enough."

"Actually I do. This is my room too." He went to the window, looked out for evidence that they'd been followed, before closing the curtains.

"You don't need to stay in the same room with me. There are security cameras everywhere. I doubt anyone is going to risk taking me here." She licked her lips.

He stared at her mouth. *Mind on the job. She was a job. Nothing more.* "We're short on funds due to your shopping spree." Her face fell and his stomach tugged with guilt. "I can't use my credit card because it's traceable."

"They have the connections to track us by a credit card?"

"Believe me, baby, the bad guys have connections. They already admitted to having their hands on the ultimate fantasy elixir."

"What do you mean?"

"It's an intravenous medication that forces a female wolf into heat so she can reproduce. They were planning on using it on you."

She dropped her arms to her side as her face paled a couple of shades. "So, they were going to force . . ."

"They were going to force you into heat."

"Like a dog?" Her voice was only a whisper.

He shook his head. "When a female werewolf goes into heat there are personality changes, loss of appetite, and an increased need for sex."

"After they forced me into heat, they were all going to take turns raping me." Her hollow voice cracked as she fully comprehended the horror at what those wolves had planned.

"I wouldn't have let them touch you." He stepped closer and cupped her face in his hands, forcing her to look at him. "Those red wolves won't be brave enough to jump state lines. They'll know by now that all the Southern states are on alert after the kidnapping. You're safe."

"For how long?" Her face tightened with doubt.

"As long as I'm alive." No question in his mind, he would stand between her and a million of those red wolves to keep her safe.

"Then I guess we need to keep you alive."

He snorted. "Yeah, I guess we do." He nodded at the bag she dropped on the floor. "Why don't you go get a shower and change clothes?"

She nodded, picked up the bag and headed for the bathroom.

He grabbed his phone and punched some numbers. Jayden picked up on the second ring.

No matter what happened to him, he needed to do whatever it took to keep Ava safe.

No matter what.

After a long, hot shower and changing into her new clothes, Ava stood in front of the steamy bathroom mirror staring at her reflection. Retail therapy had always cheered her whenever she was feeling low, but right now, new clothes did nothing to lighten her mood.

She needed to call her father, the General. She needed to let him know she was okay. Her stomach knotted with guilt. She should have called him right after Damon had rescued her. She'd been too caught up in the excitement and danger to even think about letting him know she was okay. Being with Damon had made her forget her family obligations. She was a horrible person.

Stepping out the bathroom, she cringed as the Arkansas Razorback football game blared from the TV. Damon dragged his attention from the game to her.

He scowled.

She glanced at her jeans and white cable knit sweater. "Is this okay? I have another top that's not as casual that I can put on."

"You look fine," he grumbled before turning his attention back to the game.

She clenched her jaw at his less than stellar compliment. She'd never been one to fish for compliments, but she wasn't used to men dismissing her either.

"I need to use your cell phone and let my father know I'm okay." She sat on the edge of the bed and tugged on the boots she'd gotten at the boutique. They were knee-length, black leather heels with buckles on the sides and were way better looking than those CAT boots Damon had gotten her at the truck stop.

"He already knows."

A knock at the door had her jumping to her feet. Maybe he ordered room service.

She stood to answer it, but Damon beat her to it.

"Really? I don't think a kidnapper is actually going to take the time to knock before he breaks in."

"Did the kidnappers knock at your house?" He arched a brow.

"Yeah. They did." She narrowed her eyes. Smartass.

He gave her a hard stare before reaching behind his back and pulling out a really big gun.

"Jesus! Have you had that on you the whole time we were riding? You could have shot me." She slugged him in the arm. She didn't remember feeling any weapons on him while being pressed against him on the back of the Harley.

"I had it in my saddlebag."

"How did you manage to sneak it thorough the metal detector in the casino?"

"Jayden showed me the other way in." He peered through the peephole. "Speak of the devil." Damon opened the door and tucked his gun in the back of his jeans.

"What the hell took so long? I was beginning to wonder if you two were making yourselves decent before opening the door." Jayden waggled his eyebrows.

"I was making sure who it was before I opened the door. As security, even you should know that." Damon bristled.

"If I were staying in a room with a beautiful woman, working would be the last thing on my mind." Jayden winked at her.

She sighed. Why couldn't she lust after Jayden? He was built like an expensive male stripper and charming as hell.

"I have a job to do." Damon grunted.

"He is simply tolerating my presence. Maybe he needs to get hazard pay for having to put up with me." She spat out the acrid words.

"The Damon I used to know liked the ladies, especially the beautiful ones." Jayden scratched his jaw. "You haven't turned gay on me, have you?"

"What?" Damon's eyes grew wide.

Jayden shrugged and held up his hands. "Not that there's anything wrong with that."

A laugh bubbled out of her. She slapped her hand across her mouth as he shot her a glare.

"I'm not gay," Damon growled.

Giving her complete attention to Jayden, she smiled prettily. "I'm sure he still likes the ladies. It's just me he doesn't like."

"Was there something you wanted?" Damon stepped between her and Jayden.

"I'm heading over to Granny's. I thought maybe you guys wanted to come along."

"I don't think so." Damon shook his head.

Ava clenched her fists. He had no right to tell her what to do. He wasn't her boss.

"I'll go, if you don't mind the company." She smiled.

"I'd love it." Jayden grinned. "If I bring home a hottie, it might give Granny the idea that I've finally settled down."

"Fine. We'll all go." Damon growled as he slipped on his leather jacket.

"You don't have to go. I'm sure Jayden can be my bodyguard," Ava snapped.

"Hell, yeah. I'm all over guarding your body." Jayden took a step closer to her.

"I said, we'll all go." Damon shoved Jayden out the door before he could get any closer.

※∞.※∞.※∞

Damon had never met a female who could piss him off faster than Ava Renfroe. She had a smart mouth, didn't obey, and undermined his authority at every turn. Females tended to stay away from him. But not Ava. She was fucking fearless.

When she walked out of the bathroom wearing those skin-tight pants, he almost came in his jeans. Her sweater dipped low enough to hint at her small, but firm, breasts that strained under the snug material. Then there were her high-heel boots that screamed "Fuck me up against the wall." She had a body made to be worshiped.

She walked ahead of him, her hips swaying with each step. What would that ass feel like in his hands as he pressed her palms against the wall, ripped off her clothes, and took her from behind?

Jayden cleared his throat. Judging by the looks Jayden was giving him, he knew where Damon's mind had been.

"Penny for your thoughts." Jayden grinned like the idiot he was.

"Fuck off." Damon growled and quickened his steps.

He could have Ava in his thoughts; he just needed to make sure they didn't turn into actions.

※∞.※∞.※∞

Damon shook his head as Jayden sped down the highway in his Mustang. After several complaints from Ava in the back seat, telling him he was driving like a maniac, Jayden finally relented and slowed his speed.

While they were on the Harley, Ava didn't complain once about his driving and he'd been doing way over the speed limit. That thought alone amused him.

Thirty minutes later they were pulling into Granny's gravel driveway. As Ava climbed out of the Mustang, Damon took the opportunity to scan the familiar area. Granny's ranch-style white house looked exactly the same as when he was here so many years ago. Faded yard gnomes were hidden in the flower beds while ceramic woodland creatures dotted the lawn. It looked like Walmart's lawn and garden section had thrown up on the front yard. Granny had always been a bit of a hoarder. Oddly enough, the clutter had always made him feel at home.

Jayden bounded up the front steps, taking them two at a time. He rapped a couple of times before opening the screen door. "Granny?"

Ava stopped half way across the yard and turned, meeting his gaze.

When he didn't move, she walked toward him.

"You're not going to make me go in there by myself, are you?" She propped her hands on her hips and nodded toward the house.

"No." His heart warmed. She might be pissed but she still wanted his presence. With his hand on the small of her back, he escorted her inside the house he'd once called home.

"Damon!" Granny's gaze widened, smoothing the deep wrinkles around her eyes. Her gray hair was in desperate need of a perm and several errant strands stuck out in all different directions. Her signature outfit, an oversized Muumuu in bright pink and orange, swallowed her petite frame.

"Hi, Granny." Damon ducked his head, unable to hold her gaze. Guilt tugged at his heart. He should have visited her sooner. He'd been so intent on forgetting the bad parts of his life that he'd forgotten the good along with it.

"You know Granny?" Ava asked.

"Of course, he knows me." Granny pulled Damon into a tight hug. She held onto him, squeezing hard as if making sure he was real. When he finally pulled away, he turned toward Ava.

"Granny, this is Ava Renfroe."

"Nice to meet you." Ava stuck out her hand and smiled.

"Well, bless my heart, you've actually done it." Granny's mouth dropped open.

"Done what?" Ava looked from Granny back to him.

"Damon found his mate." The old woman's face broke into a wide smile. She pulled Ava into a hug.

Ava shook her head. "I'm not his mate." He didn't miss the sidelong glance she shot him while she pulled out of Granny's hug.

Damon shoved his hands in his pockets as everyone's eyes landed on him. Granny was the biggest gossip in Louisiana. The second they left, she'd be on the phone with all her old biddies to try to set Ava up with every single werewolf in town. That could not happen.

"We're not mated, yet. Just dating," he lied.

"Dating?" Granny raised an eyebrow. Jayden snickered.

Damon shot Jayden a warning look to keep his big mouth closed. Wolves didn't date. Once they smelled out their mates they both instantly knew they belonged together. They usually had sex within hours of meeting.

Ava stiffened as he wrapped his arm around her waist and pulled her close.

"Yes, dating." He cleared his dry throat.

"Why?" Granny leveled her gaze at him, as suspicion flared in her scrunched brows.

"Yes, honey bear, why don't you explain why we are dating." Ava looked up at him with a beautiful smile and a flash of anger in her emerald eyes.

Honey bear? Couldn't she at least come up with a manlier nickname? Like anaconda?

Granny pursed her lips. "I don't believe it. You mean to tell me you two aren't mated?"

"We've not had sex."

"Yes, I can confirm there has been no sex going on." Ava stepped back from him and cut him with a glance.

Jayden snorted.

Granny narrowed her shrewd eyes. "How odd. I could have sworn you two were a match." She shook her head and shrugged. "Young people these days. They think they know it all." She shook her head again. "Come along and I'll fix you all some lunch."

Damon stepped into the dated 1950's kitchen decorated in black-and-white tile and smiled. Exactly as he remembered, just a few more dust catchers to take up room on the kitchen counter. There was even the creepy, black-and-white cat clock hanging on the wall that he hated so much. The tail swished back and forth in time as its eyes lolled side to side. He hated cats.

"Y'all have a seat." Granny pointed toward the vintage gray Formica kitchen table.

"We aren't going to sit in the dining room? There's more room." Jayden eased his big frame onto a small kitchen chair.

"Not today. I've got a little party tonight and my stuff is already set up in there." Granny opened the refrigerator and pulled out plastic containers of deli meat.

"Are you having another Tupperware party?" Jayden popped the top on his soda that he'd snagged from the refrigerator and took a long drink.

"Not exactly. But there are a lot of products made of rubber."

Jayden choked on his soda. "Oh, hell, Granny. You're not having one of *those* parties, are you?"

"I sure am." Granny straightened her proud shoulders.

"What kind of party is it?" Ava looked at Granny.

"The kind you need to stay for. Especially if you and Damon are only dating." Granny winked.

What did that mean? Curiosity got the better of him and he sauntered to the dining room. He opened the door and froze as a fresh horror washed over him.

Dildos and vibrators in every shape, size and color littered the lace-covered table. It looked like an obscene adult store.

Jayden's eyes widened. "Granny, how many times have I told you that you can't have sex parties like this? Word gets around and they'll kick you out of the church."

"Who do you think is buying this stuff?" Granny huffed as she waved a dismissive hand in the air.

Damon cringed. He did not want that image locked in the recesses of his brain.

"I'm seventy years old and I can do whatever I want. Besides, there's a lot of money to be made at these parties." Granny stuck out her chin. "Why, last month I cleared five thousand dollars and that was just to my Bible study friends."

"Five thousand dollars?" Jayden's eyes narrowed.

"Yep. Tonight, friends from my book club are coming. They're not as uptight as the church group, so I expect to make a killing."

"What, exactly, is a sex party?" Ava ventured further into the room as her smirk grew across her face.

"It's a party with products guaranteed to enhance intimacy between couples. Or, if you're single, enhance your own pleasure without going through the hassle of having a man." Granny smiled.

"Please tell me that's not the company's official tag line." Damon rubbed his eyes while wishing he'd never opened the door.

"It sure is hon. In fact..."

The phone trilled in the other room, saving him from whatever else Granny was about to say. He loved that woman, but having to hear her talk about sex toys was beyond crossing the line.

"Let me grab that. Might be a customer." Granny hurried to answer it. Jayden was right on her heels ticking off reasons why her career choice was going make him the laughingstock of Shreveport.

"What is this?" Ava picked up a purple dildo with an extra head.

His cock twitched as she ran her finger along the length of the sex toy. He wished she were holding him instead of that piece of plastic.

"It's a dildo."

She gave him a droll look. "I know it's a dildo. What the hell is this extra horn? Where exactly does it go?"

His nostrils flared. His grabbed the obscene sex toy and tossed it on the table where it landed with a thud. He leaned in, crowding her, as every muscle in his body tensed. "I'd rather show you where it goes."

"I think that would be very hard for you to do, seeing how repulsive I am to you. Or would you see it as part of your job?" Anger flashed behind her eyes as she jabbed her finger in his chest.

Lust raged through his body and his mind clouded with her scent. *Move away from her.* Wrapping his hands around her waist, he pulled her against him, forcing her to meet his gaze. "Fucking is never part of the job. Let's get that straight right now." Her lips parted as her warm breath glided against his mouth. He should let her go. He shouldn't even be touching her. She was part of his job and nothing else.

In the end, animal instinct won out.

His mouth slammed down on hers, hard, hot and possessive. First they were arguing about sex toys, and in the next breath they were kissing and clawing at each other's clothes.

He clasped the back of her head, holding her still as his tongue licked inside her mouth, her taste tattooing its way into his soul.

Her scent of arousal wrapped around him until he couldn't let her go as his fingers threaded through her silken hair. He was fighting a battle he feared he could not win.

She was going to be the end of him

Ava wrapped her arms around Damon's waist and melted, boneless, against his body, sinking into his warmth.

Her hands moved around his broad back, muscles rippling under her touch. The man's body was like honed steel, hard and unyielding, no weakness anywhere.

His lips trailed kisses from her mouth to her neck and she panted as desire swept through her body and pooled between her legs. She wanted him with a desperation that shook her.

"Fuck," he whispered. "We shouldn't be doing this."

For a second she thought he was going to push her away, like he always did. Instead, he pulled her tighter as he covered her mouth, stealing her breath with his kiss.

She sighed. His scent was driving her insane as she contemplated shoving him down on the table, pulling his pants down and riding him until they were both coming.

She'd never wanted a man as much as she wanted Damon.

"See what I mean?" Granny's voice startled them. They jerked away from each other.

"One minute alone with my toys is enough to stir the flames of passion." Granny nodded proudly.

Ava's face heated.

"Jesus, do you have to keep saying that kind of shit? Flames of passion?" Jayden grimaced.

Granny slapped him on the back of the head. "Don't use the Lord's name in the same sentence with profanity."

"Why?" Jayden asked as he rubbed his head. "Was it grammatically incorrect?"

"Jayden Alistair Parker!" Granny scowled.

"Alistair? Your name is Alistair?" Damon didn't bother hiding his smirk.

"Shut up, asshole."

"Granny, why don't I help you in the kitchen?" Ava figured distraction was the best plan right now. If she stayed in the same room with Damon and all those dildos, she wouldn't care who was watching. She was going to jump him.

"You have such nice manners, Ava." Granny wrapped her arm around her and the two of them headed toward the kitchen, leaving the men behind. When they were out of earshot, Granny patted her hand and whispered, "Don't worry, honey. He may be saying he's not interested in you, but I see the truth."

"What truth?" She held her breath as she looked at the old woman.

Granny chuckled. "Damon is just afraid of getting hurt again."

"Again?" Ava frowned.

"Yes. His last relationship ended badly."

"What ended badly?" Damon sauntered into the kitchen with Jayden at his side. He arched a brow and looked from her to Granny.

Granny didn't miss a beat. "That movie I was watching on Lifetime ended badly. Do you want to hear about it?" Granny gave him a hopeful smile.

"No." Damon and Jayden answered in unison.

The drive back to the casino had been tense to say the least. Ava had wanted to ride around and see the city, but Damon shot that idea down immediately. He knew the less visible they were the better. This was not a vacation but a mission. He'd rather have her mad and safe, than happy and in danger.

Damon dropped Jayden off in the lobby before heading upstairs with Ava. As the elevator doors closed, he glanced over at her and tried his best not to notice how pretty she was when she was mad.

"Are you going to pout all day?"

"I don't pout." She kept her gaze straight ahead, arms folded.

"Ava, I told you why we couldn't stay out any longer. It's just not safe."

"I know. But riding around in a car is not as visible as riding around on the back of a motorcycle."

Touché.

The doors opened and Ava stepped off the elevator and headed for their room, not stopping until she got there.

He sniffed and then relaxed when he didn't scent any wolf odors. He unlocked the door and ushered her in.

"Everything smell okay?" Her tone smacked of sarcasm as she passed him.

"I was making sure no one had entered the room after we left." He locked the door behind them.

"What does danger smell like?"

"I can see you're not taking this seriously." Ignoring her question, he headed to the window. She grabbed his arm.

"No, wait. I'm being serious." Between the puppy eyes she was flashing him and her hand touching his arm, he was in no condition to refuse her.

"Damon, please. I really want to know. Especially if I'm going to have to turn into..." She bit her lip and cringed.

"It's not that bad, being a wolf." He laughed softly at her pained expression.

"It's different for you. You're a guy. It doesn't matter if you get all hairy."

He laughed.

"Stop laughing. Do you know how much money and pain I go through every month to get a Brazilian wax, and now it's just going to get all hairy down there."

He stopped laughing. Her words knocked the breath out of him. "You get waxed?"

"Yes." She narrowed her eyes. "Let me guess. Wolves don't like their females waxed."

Why the fuck was she asking him this? Now, he couldn't get the image of Ava's silky sex out of his oversexed mind.

"I don't know." How the hell was he supposed to answer that? He swallowed. His throat felt like sandpaper. Avoiding her eyes, he stomped over to the thermostat, making sure the heat wasn't set at a hundred degrees. Nope, set at a cool sixty-eight.

"So, there's no protocol that says I can't get waxed?" she asked hopefully.

"God, Ava. You're killing me." He palmed his eyes and rubbed.

"What? Look, I need to know these things. How am I supposed to know what's acceptable and what's not?" She arched her brow and gave him a perfectly serious look.

For someone who had just discovered that she was a werewolf, Ava was holding up pretty well. It must have something to do with that stubborn streak running through her.

Trying to swallow but finding his mouth had turned into a desert, he walked over to the mini bar and pulled out complimentary water. After downing half the bottle, he eased onto the edge of the bed. He felt like he was about to give a talk on the birds and the bees.

"You're right." He rubbed the back of his neck.

"So you'll answer my questions?"

He flinched. He had never considered that she would have questions about being a werewolf. He'd been too busy doing his job to consider her feelings. He was such an asshole.

"You'll be getting a man's point of view." He was pretty sure she needed to talk to another female, not him.

She sat down on the opposite bed and crossed her legs. "Can I ask you anything?"

"Of course."

She frowned. "Does it hurt when you shift into a wolf?"

He chose his words carefully so as not to frighten her. "The first time it happened, it hurt. But after that it only feels sore, like the day after you've worked out really hard at the gym."

"When did you know you were a werewolf?"

"I've always known I was different, even when I was young." He shifted his weight on the bed. He'd never shared his first shifting experience, with anyone, not even Jayden. "I guess the first time I shifted I was ten. It scared me at first, but then I realized that's why I always felt so different from everyone else."

"Didn't your parents tell you?" She frowned.

"My parents died when I was a baby. I was raised in an orphanage."

"I'm sorry." She uncrossed her legs and reached for his hand. The gesture made his chest ache a little.

He shrugged. "I had no other relatives so I was placed in an orphanage run by nuns."

"Were they nice?"

"The nuns?" He chuckled. "As nice as a nun can be, I suppose. They didn't beat me if that's what you're asking."

"That's good." She relaxed her shoulders. "Granny asked if I was your mate. What's the difference between a mate and a girlfriend?"

"A mate is your life partner. Once a male and female are mated, it's like being married except there's no divorce."

"By having sex with someone does that mean you're mated?" She wrinkled her brow, awaiting his answer.

"No, it doesn't."

She blew out a breath. "Good, because I thought I mated myself to my ex-boyfriend."

His chest clenched at the thought of some other male touching her. He tightened his grip on her hand. "How long were you together?"

"Only a few months." She snorted. "I broke up with him. I knew things were never really serious between us. I think I was lonely more than anything. After seeing what Granny had laying out on the table, I'm more inclined to start handling things myself. I mean, did you see the size of the one called the Bad Beaver?"

Clenching his jaw, he closed his eyes, trying to get the image of Ava masturbating out of his head.

"I hate when you do that."

His eyes popped open. "Do what?"

"Roll your eyes like everything I say is stupid. You're probably not used to women having an opinion." She snatched her hand away and stood, glaring at him.

Fuck, she was pretty when she was mad.

"I never said you were stupid."

"You don't have to. I can see in the way you grit your teeth or fist your hands, like you want to strangle me." She stomped toward the bathroom.

She made it one step.

He pounced, shoving her up against the wall. He pinned her with his chest while his hands rested on her slim hips, holding her captive. His heart pounded in his chest, threatening to leap out of its cage. Curling his hands around her small waist, he shoved his face into the crook of her neck and inhaled, deeply. He'd longed to do that ever since he laid eyes on her. Her scent washed over him, fueling his lust.

"You couldn't be farther from the truth," he growled against her neck.

"Really?" She breathed out the word. He could feel her heart racing against his chest, knowing she was feeling the pull of desire as well.

"I fist my hands to keep from touching you. Do you know how hard it is, to be so close to you, to have your scent on my flesh, to want you like my last breath and not be allowed to touch you?"

Desire flashed through her eyes. "What if I wanted you to touch me? Would you touch me if I asked you to?" She reached up and pulled his head closer into her neck, rubbing against him like she wanted him to claim her.

He growled as her lush body rubbed erotically against him, teasing him to the point of pain. She felt too damn good.

He squeezed his eyes, trying to rein in his desire. He could not do this. It would cost him everything. "This is a bad idea. If I touch you, Ava, I'm not going to stop."

"I'm counting on it." She pulled his palm to her breast, molding his hand to those delicious curves he'd dreamt about.

Ava looked into Damon's heated gaze. His blue eyes burned with need so strong, it was almost animalistic.

She sucked in a ragged breath, suddenly deprived of oxygen.

His hands trailed from her breast to her waist holding her close, while his lips sucked her neck. She moaned, shivers racking her body as she clutched him tighter. It was enough to send her into an orgasm on sensation alone.

She had never really been consumed with sex. Her ex hadn't even bothered to get her off the few times they'd had sex. After that she had decided she was done, that sex was something she could live without.

Now, for the first time in her life, she wanted a man between her thighs, pounding deep inside her body. Not just any man. She wanted Damon. She'd bet he wouldn't have a problem getting her off.

His calloused hand cradled her cheek with a gentleness she didn't expect from a man his size. She turned, nuzzling his palm. Their gazes locked. He swiped his thumb across her bottom lip. Her lips parted, sucking his thumb into her mouth, moaning at the saltiness of his skin.

He groaned. "Fuck, baby."

"That's what I'm trying to do."

His mouth came down hard across hers, his tongue invading her mouth. God, he tasted good, like hot alpha male. She wanted more, she wanted to taste all of him.

His hands slid lower until he cupped her ass. He lifted and she wrapped her legs around his waist. He pressed her back against the wall, grinding against her, as he continued to assault her with his heated kisses.

Digging her fingers into his shoulders, she sucked his tongue. He growled and she ground against his erection. His body fit her perfectly.

Suddenly, he pulled away. Disappointment and frustration washed through her. If he was going to stop again, she was going to have to strangle him and have sex with him once he passed out.

"Take your shirt off," he commanded as his heated gaze bored into her soul.

Arousal spread from the pit of her stomach down between her legs. She went wet from the unmistakable lust flowing in his eyes.

Keeping her eyes on his, she reached for the hem of her sweater. His eyes followed the movement as she lifted the garment, revealing naked skin inch by inch. By the time she pulled it over her breasts, his breathing had grown ragged.

She let the garment drop to the floor.

"Take your bra off too." His gaze was glued to her breasts as he rocked his erection against her, making her pant.

"You do it."

He lifted his gaze to her eyes.

"My hands seem to be full at the moment." He squeezed her ass while thrusting against her.

"Then use your teeth." She licked her lips.

His nostrils flared. "I can't be gentle with you, Ava."

"I don't want gentle. I want you." She wanted him any way she could get him.

Growling low in his throat, he bent his head, his hot mouth covering her bra-clad nipple. His wet mouth engulfed her as he licked and sucked through the lacy material. He moved his head in the valley between her breasts and nuzzled.

"God, you smell wonderful, like honeysuckle." He moved his mouth to the bra clasp and bit.

She heard a snap before the cool air brushed across her heated skin. Shrugging out of her bra, it joined the shirt on the floor.

"You're so fucking gorgeous."

She grabbed his head and pulled him toward her breasts. "I want to feel your mouth on me." Her body was on fire, threatening to consume her alive.

Her head lolled against the wall as Damon licked her nipple before pulling the bud into his hot mouth. She cried out as he tortured her with his wicked tongue, stroke after stroke. Arching against him, she ground her hips against his thick erection trapped between her thighs.

"Take your shirt off." She wanted to feel his naked chest against hers.

With his hands still on her body, he walked over to the bed and laid her down. She let her hands slide down his muscled arms as he stood back. Shrugging out of his jacket, he tossed it. He reached behind his head and tugged off his shirt.

She pushed up to her knees, trailing her hands up every defined muscle of his stomach to his broad chest. He pulled her against him. She gasped as the sparse hair on his chest rubbed against her hardened nipples.

"You're making me wet," she moaned against his lips as his hand caressed her ass.

"This isn't a good idea." His voice was hoarse, like he'd been running a marathon.

She swallowed, hoping his lust would override whatever honorable bullshit that was running through his mind. "We are both adults. I think we can do whatever we want. I want this, and from the feel of it, you do too." She reached between their bodies and stroked his erection through his jeans. He buried his face in the crook of her neck and growled.

She palmed his cock, squeezing him as she ran her hand up and down the hardened length. He thrust against her hand.

Cupping her face between his hands, he forced her to look at him. Pleasure and pain danced across his handsome face. "You are the most beautiful female I've ever seen."

His declaration seared her to her soul as she fought not to let the sting of tears end their pleasure.

"Kiss me, Damon."

"Say that again."

"Kiss me."

"No." He growled. "Say my name while your hand is on my cock."

Keeping the steady pressure on his erection, she looked him directly in the eyes. "Damon."

CHAPTER FIVE

His lustful growl made her ache between her legs.

She sighed as his tongue danced and tangled with hers. She rubbed her body against him, growing restless to feel the rest of him.

Her hands slid up to the fly of his jeans. She fingered the button open and unzipped him. His hips rocked back as she pulled the sides down into a vee. He wore no underwear, commando style. She sucked in a deep breath as his large cock strained upward.

"Like what you see?"

She clenched her thighs together, stilling the ache between her legs. Excited and aroused, she couldn't wait to see how he was going to cram every inch of that inside her body.

"I'm very impressed." She took him in her hand and licked her lips.

"You won't be very impressed when I come in your hand." Despite his warning he wrapped his hand around hers, showing her how hard he wanted her to squeeze.

She gripped him harder and his breathing turning to a pant.

He pulled her hand away. "Enough. I want to see you naked."

Her heart jumped a little. Yes, this was definitely going in the right direction. Naked was good. Naked was really, really good.

Sliding off the bed, she stood. Keeping her eyes on him, she unzipped her jeans as she kept her gaze on his body. His cock twitched against his belly.

Biting her bottom lip, she forced herself to go slow, to give him a little show. She wanted anything but slow right now. She wanted to be naked and underneath him. She didn't want to rush this moment, this memory that she would have forever. It might be the only moment they had in this crazy adventure she'd found herself.

He seemed to drink her in, an inch at a time, like he was worshiping her body with his eyes, making plans of how he wanted to use his hands and his mouth on her.

As she pushed her jeans over her hips, his breathing hitched. She was glad she had spent the extra money on the lace thong in the casino boutique. When her jeans reached her feet, she slowly stepped out of them and kicked them to the side. She hooked her thumbs on either side of her thong.

"Stop."

"What?" Her heart nearly stopped. He wasn't changing his mind, was he?

"I want to take off those off."

"Be my guest." She shivered and lifted her hands.

He tossed his jeans and stepped toward her, a feral look etched into his dangerous features. She grew wetter.

He pulled her against his body, the tip of his cock tickling her belly.

He bent and picked her up. Very carefully he laid her on the bed, his hands tracing down her body like he was memorizing every curve. His gaze and hands traveled across her body, claiming every inch of her. She knew this was more than sex. At least, for her, it was more.

With this revelation, she blinked away the tears that burned the back of her eyes.

"What's wrong?" He traced a finger down her cheek.

"It's the way you're looking at me." She swallowed. "It's like you want to eat me alive."

His grinned. "You have no idea."

He slid down her body, licking every curve as he traveled to her flat stomach. When he sucked the delicate skin beside her belly button she moaned and arched off the bed.

He chuckled and moved his mouth lower. "It's only going to get better, baby." When he reached her thong, he hooked his fingers on either side and tugged. The thin material broke, tearing in his large hands.

"Do you know how much those cost?" Breathless, she leaned up on her elbows, eager for what he'd do next.

"Actually, I have a good idea since it was my money." He glanced up and grinned. "I'll make it up to you."

"What are you...?" Her words turned into a deep moan as Damon buried his head between her thighs and licked.

She fell back on the bed, the sensation of his mouth too much to handle. She was going to die from the intense pleasure.

"Don't stop." His tongue was relentless, licking and stroking her until she was arching toward him. Leaning her head to the side, she looked down. The sight of his mouth on her sent erotic shivers coursing through her body. She grabbed his hair and pulled him closer, demanding he finish her.

He watched her with those wicked blue eyes of his, knowing exactly where she wanted him to lick, to stroke, to pleasure.

"That feels so good." Her voice was but a whisper and it seemed to only intensify his lust. Feeling the pleasure slowly start to build, she ground her pussy against his mouth. As her orgasm approached, she let go of his hair and dug her nails into the bed unable to control her own body. White-hot pleasure exploded through her as she cried out his name. He didn't stop until she was a quivering mass of nerves and breathless words.

When the tremors subsided, she reached for him.

She smiled and pushed him over. "My turn."

Damon heard a groan and realized it came from him. She was going to burn him alive until there was nothing left but ashes.

He pulled her down to his mouth, lust flowing through his veins like lava.

Without breaking the kiss, he pulled her over to straddle him. He threaded his fingers through her silky black hair, as he held her against his mouth, kissing her like tomorrow wasn't promised.

She pulled away and beamed that sexy smile of hers. She pressed her lips to his shoulder, gave him a lick and then sucked his flesh into her mouth. Without warning, her teeth sank into his shoulder. He jerked and ground out a curse. She pulled back, looking unsure.

"I'm sorry." She cringed. "I'm not sure why I did that."

Cupping her face, he shook his head. "The male usually bites, the females don't."

"Sorry."

"Don't be sorry. I liked it." He liked it way too much.

She smirked. "Let's see what else I can do with my mouth to make you feel good." She bit her lip.

He was in so much trouble.

She kissed her way down his chest. She ran her hot tongue across his nipple. He hissed, cupping her head to his body. Keeping her eyes on his, she sucked his nipple into her mouth and then bit.

"Fuck, yeah. That feels good." She was going to make him come before her mouth even got to the important parts.

She licked around each defined muscle of his abdomen, taking her time and savoring him like he was dessert. She moved further down until the tip of his cock brushed the bottom of her chin. His body ached as he grasped for control.

She looked up and grinned.

"Baby, you're killing me." He wound her silky hair in his hand.

"I thought you liked what I'm doing."

"I do, but I'd love it if you put that sweet mouth on my cock."

"My pleasure."

He was pretty sure it would be his pleasure, but without a coherent thought in his brain at the moment, he could only groan as he watched her mouth move closer to his dick.

Opening her mouth she licked, swiping the glistening tip and tasting his arousal seeping out of the slit with her tongue.

"Fuck."

"You like that?" She gave him her best innocent look. It didn't work. There was nothing innocent about Ava.

Ava reached for his large cock as it jutted up, hard and swollen.

She wrapped her hand around his velvety hardness. She was rewarded when his hips jerked up, pumping his cock into her hand. She tightened her grip and slowly slid her hand down before squeezing up. A pearly bead of arousal leaked out the tip.

She took the head into her mouth and sucked. His taste spilled onto her tongue, hot and wild. He groaned and tightened his hold on her hair. She knew that he was struggling not to grab the back of her head and pump into her mouth.

She sucked more of him into her mouth, her lips stretching to accommodate his size. As she teased him with her tongue, he cupped her cheek before threading his hand in her hair. She cut her gaze up at him. The look of ecstasy on his face was enough to almost make her come again.

"That's it, baby. Suck my cock."

Gripping him tighter at the base, she sucked him hard. His hand tightened in her hair, setting the pace he wanted.

She reveled in every groan, every pant she dragged out of him. She reached down and fondled his balls until they were tight.

"If you don't want me coming in your mouth, you need to move."

She had never let her ex-boyfriend do that. She didn't want him to. But with Damon it was different. She wanted to taste him.

Locking her lips around his cock, she sucked, tasting his seed as it hit the back of her mouth. She swallowed his hot and salty release, savoring the taste of him as he quivered until he was spent.

His hand came around the back of her neck, urging her up.

When he pulled her down, he kissed her hard and deep. From what she thought, guys didn't usually like to kiss a girl after she'd gone down on them. Damon didn't seem to mind. He seemed to like it.

She kissed him back, their scents merging and mating, and loved the way they tasted together.

She straddled him and slid her hand between their bodies. Her hand locked around his already hard erection.

"I'm impressed."

"I have a quick recovery time."

"Because you're a wolf?"

"We are known for our sexual marathons." He shot her a heated grin.

"Really? Let's put that to the test." She raised herself up, guiding him to her slick entrance.

He gripped her waist and flipped her onto her back.

"I'm always on top."

"Yeah, well, I like being on top, too." She wrapped her legs around him and pushed him to his side.

He narrowed his eyes. "Baby, the male is always on top." He flipped her on her back and imprisoned her there.

"Do females always do what they're told?" She gritted her teeth.

"The submissive ones do."

"See, there's our problem. I'm not exactly the submissive type." She struggled under his weight, but he held her tight.

"Neither am I." He growled near her ear. It sent delicious shivers down her spine.

Bam!Bam!Bam!

"Son-of-a-bitch." Damon reached for his gun as he leaped off the bed. With his free hand, he pulled her to the floor while keeping his gun pointed at the door.

"Stay down."

For once she obeyed him. He angled his body, making himself a shield between her and whatever danger lay on the other side of the door.

He was quick to put himself in harm's way to keep her protected. Her heart tugged with affection for her Guardian.

Her eyes wandered down his muscular body, a grin playing at the corner of her lips. He was still sporting an erection, like she was still on his mind and on his lips

Damon slowly lowered his forty-five after he looked through the peephole. He looked back at Ava.

"Who is it?" She had her eyes locked on his erection.

Her gaze met his and she blushed. She stood up and wrapped the sheet around her.

"It's Jayden." He blew out a breath. Fucking Jayden. Turning back, he cracked the door, keeping the security chain in place. The second Jayden's face popped between the crack, Damon growled.

"What do you want?"

"I just got some Intel on that group of rogue wolves that kidnapped Ava."

"I'll meet you in your room." He tried to shut the door, but Jayden stuck his foot in the opening.

"I think you better bring Ava, too."

"Meet you in ten minutes." He kicked Jayden's foot out of the way and shut the door. Turing around, he bumped into Ava.

"I'm coming."

"No, you're not. You're staying here." He walked around her and reached for his jeans.

"What happened to 'You can't leave me alone'?" She arched a brow.

He tugged his shirt over his head. She was right. "Shit."

She reached up on her tiptoes to gently kiss his lips, but he was having none of that. He wrapped his arms around her. The sheet slipped. He brought his mouth down to hers and kissed her, hard and long.

"You need to get used to the idea of me riding you." She stepped back and let the sheet drop to the floor. She bent over and picked up her clothes, giving him the most amazing view of her ass.

Rising slowly, like a temptress, she stood, walked past him, and into the bathroom, making him seriously reconsider his opinion on who exactly was on top.

He ran his hand down his face. What the fuck had he done? If Jayden hadn't knocked on the door and interrupted them, he would be inside Ava, right now.

If that had happened, he would have ruined his career. The Arkansas Guardians had given him a home when Louisiana kicked him out. Ava was the General's daughter. He couldn't ruin her life because he had a raging hard-on for her. If he didn't start thinking with his head instead of his dick, he was going to lose everything.

Damon glanced around Jayden's room and sneered. No typical room décor for his friend. He was willing to bet Jayden had charmed the casino management into letting him decorate his room to his own style.

Jayden sat hunched in his overstuffed recliner, his elbows resting on his knees as he clasp his hands together.

"I got a call from Barrett. There's been another kidnapping." Jayden looked right at him.

Damon's head jerked up, a little more than irritated. Barrett and Jayden knew each other from when Damon was transferred into the Arkansas Pack, other than that he hadn't realized Barrett knew Jayden so well. "Why didn't Barrett call me?"

"He knows you've got your hands full with Ava. He told me to help out." Jayden glanced at Ava before looking back at him. "The kidnapping took place in Lafayette."

Damon scowled. Was it the same rogue wolves that had kidnapped Ava? Had the kidnappers been brazen enough to jumped state lines? "That's a little over three hours from here."

Jayden nodded, as he reached for a brown folder on the stainless steel coffee table. "The victim is a female werewolf, Haley Guthrie, who lives in Baton Rouge. She told her roommates she was going over to Lafayette to visit her boyfriend. She never made it. At midnight, the boyfriend called the Louisiana Pack to report her missing. They found her car abandoned on the side of the road with no sign of her."

The couch shifted as Ava slid closer. Damon reached for the folder and wrapped his free arm around Ava. The picture of the victim was paper-clipped to the top. Haley Guthrie was beautiful, with blond hair and blue eyes. She looked like she should be getting ready for some beauty pageant, not getting kidnapped to become a sex slave for rogue red wolves.

"She's the same age."

Damon looked at Ava. "What?"

"She's twenty-four. She's the same age as me." He felt her shudder against his chest.

"Which seems to indicate that Ava's kidnapping wasn't an isolated incident. Haley went missing the same night as Ava." Jayden's expression was grim.

"This probably means there are other girls out there." Her eyes widened in terror as she looked up at him.

"Possibly. But the only one we know for sure is Haley." He gave her shoulder a reassuring squeeze.

"Then we'll start with Haley." Ava stood.

"What do you mean, 'we'?" Damon eased to his feet, already hating where this conversation was heading.

"I mean, *we* are going to go find this girl."

"There is no '*we.*'" He growled. "You aren't going anywhere."

"I won't just sit here and do nothing. Especially since I know what they're planning on doing to her." Sparks built up behind her emerald gaze.

"I won't let you put yourself in danger to save someone you don't know." His heart pounded between his ears as he curled his fingers into fists.

"Why not? You did." Ava cocked her head to the side.

"That's different. I'm a Guardian, a soldier. It's my job. This is what I do."

"There's been no trace of Haley, no sightings, no credit card activity. It's like she vanished." Jayden frowned and took the folder.

"I guess that means we've got to start from the last place she was seen." She stuck her hands in her pockets and met his gaze.

"They searched her car and found nothing. Besides, they already towed the vehicle so the scene has been compromised." Jayden rubbed his neck.

"We start with where her car was found, back on the highway." Damon shrugged into his leather jacket. He had to figure out what to do with Ava before they took another step.

"I'll get the coordinates off the computer." Jayden called over his shoulder as he headed into the next room.

"If you're going, I'm going." She raised a beautiful eyebrow at him, as if daring him to stop her. Now he remembered why he never dated women like her. He liked a woman who wouldn't defy him at every turn.

"Fine, but you're going to have to do exactly what I say."

Her lips trembled, as she fought back a smile.

He gritted his teeth. "I mean it, Ava. You listen to me, or you're staying here. Even if that means I have to tie you to the bed."

"While that sounds fun, I suggest you save that entertainment for tonight when we get back." She winked, sauntered to the door and opened it.

He slammed his hand against the door, closing it, and scowled. "I'm not kidding. I won't have you out in the open unless you agree to listen to me. I want your word, or we both stay here."

She huffed and turned around to face him. "Fine."

"Swear it to me."

"I swear I'll listen to you, Damon." She gave him a smartass salute. "Happy?"

"Ecstatic. You know what would make me even happier?"

She propped her hands on her hips and narrowed her emerald gaze. "I'm not staying here, so you can forget it."

"I wasn't going to say that."

She gave him a doubtful look. "I can't image what else would make you happy."

"I can. Tying *you* to the bed."

Her lips curled into a sexy smirk. "If anyone's tying anyone to a bed, it's going to be me doing the tying."

"I don't think that's going to happen." He reached out and ran his finger across her cheek. He couldn't seem to stay away from her, even if it cost him everything.

"I think I might persuade you, especially if I tied the knots with my mouth."

His smile slide off his face like hot butter. His gaze drifted down to her mouth.

"As I recall, you seem quite fond of my mouth, or was it my tongue you liked so well?" She took a step forward. Her warm breath tickled his face. He briefly entertained the thought of taking her up against the door before Jayden came back.

"If you two are finished sniffing around each other, we need to hit the road." Jayden stuck his head in between them.

"We're done, for now," Ava said. Why he found her sarcastic tone such a turn-on, he had no idea. What he did know was, this female put him in a constant state of arousal.

That was a very dangerous place to be.

"Where do you get your Intel?" Ava leaned forward from the backseat of the black Mustang.

"A lot of it comes from Facebook, Twitter, social media." Jayden and Damon spoke in unison.

She snorted, "You're kidding me, right?"

"No. You'd be surprised how much information people are willing to share. It's like they think life is one big reality show. It's really pretty pathetic." Jayden pushed the CD button, and Emimen filled the interior of the car.

"Are you on Facebook?" She looked at Damon.

"Yeah."

"I can't imagine you posting much." She wished she had her phone. She was dying to see what kind of profile picture he had.

"He doesn't. He's a lurker." Jayden drummed his fingers on the steering wheel to the beat of the music.

"Oh, one of those." She eased back in her seat and grinned.

Damon twisted in his seat to scowl at her. "What do you mean, 'one of those?'?"

She shrugged. "There's nothing wrong with being a lurker."

"You make me sound like a stalker." He shook his head. "Just because I don't post every insignificant detail of my life doesn't mean I'm a lurker."

Jayden smiled. "I believe your quote was, 'I don't feel the need to post every time I take a shi–.'"

Damon slugged him in the arm.

"Hey, man." Jayden made a face and rubbed his arm, pretending great injury.

"It wasn't that hard." Damon snorted.

Jayden glared and slowed the car to the side of the road.

"What are you doing?" Ava angled forward.

"We're here. This is where Haley's car was found." Jayden killed the engine and opened his door. Ava crawled out and arched her arms over her head stretching out her back as she inhaled the crisp autumn air.

Immediately, an overwhelming sense of dread hit her in the pit of her stomach. Frowning, she looked around trying to find some visible sign of danger to confirm her fears.

It was an isolated stretch of blacktop with barbed wire fence and trees framing both sides of the country road. Past the row of trees lay pasture land where cows grazed. It looked peaceful enough, yet something felt off.

She looked back at the guys. Damon and Jayden stood at the hood of the car discussing something in the folder.

The eerie sensation didn't ease. Something was very wrong about this place. She didn't want to be here anymore. She wanted nothing more than to run to Damon and wrap her arms around him, so she could feel protected.

She shook her head and sucked in a deep breath. She knew if she started depending on Damon, she would be devastated the day he left. And, he *would* leave. Men like Damon didn't stick around. He'd made it perfectly clear what his intentions were and they didn't include a future with her.

She shoved away that feeling of dread and focused on the reason she was here. Haley was out there somewhere. Ava wasn't going to stop looking until she found her.

She glanced down at the withered, yellowed grass and tried to find a trace of the girl who had been here only a few days ago.

She wandered down the shoulder of the highway as bits of dried grass clung to her boots while her gaze swept the ground. Occasional bits of dirty cigarette butts and wrinkled gum wrappers littered the grass like unwanted confetti. Out of the corner of her eye, she saw something shiny. Dropping to her knees, she combed her fingers through the grass.

"Did you find something?" Damon crouched down beside her.

She picked up a tube of lipstick.

"Someone probably chucked it out the window." Damon shrugged and stood.

"I don't think so." She frowned, turning the tube over in her hand.

"Why is that?"

"Because it was placed standing up and from my brief knowledge of physics, I don't believe a tube of lipstick that's tossed out the window will land on its end." She cut her gaze up at him.

"Did you find something?" Jayden came up behind them.

"She found an old tube of lipstick."

"Actually, I think I found a clue." She stood and held out the lipstick.

Jayden took it from her. "Why do you think that?"

"One, it's not a cheap lipstick, it's a very expensive brand. Two, it's not old. This color just came out a few weeks ago. Three, not only did I find it standing on its end, but it was also dug into the ground by someone. All this makes me believe Haley knew she was in danger and wanted to leave a clue."

Both men gave her doubtful looks.

She sighed. "A woman never leaves behind an expensive lipstick she's barely used." She took the tube out of Jayden's hand and pulled off the top and twisted. A full length of lipstick shot up. Smiling, she reversed the twist and replaced the cap before tossing it to Damon who caught it in midair.

She called out over her shoulder as she made her way to the car. "And then there's the biggest clue of them all."

"Yeah? What's that?" Damon called after her.

"The name of the lipstick."

As Ava walked away, a surge of pride washed over Damon. Smart and beautiful, Ava would definitely make the perfect mate for... someone else. Thick, hot jealously spilled into his gut. He would never be okay with the idea of Ava with another male. Never.

"Well?" Jayden looked at him expectantly.

"Well, what?"

"What's the name of the lipstick?"

Damon turned the tube over and groaned. "Lethal Red."

"That could mean she was kidnapped by the same group of rogue red wolves that kidnapped Ava." Tossing the lipstick to Jayden, Damon headed for the car. He crammed himself into the backseat next to her.

"What are you doing?" She narrowed her eyes at him.

"Sitting."

"There's not enough room for both of us back here." She pushed against him, but he didn't budge.

"You were right. It's a clue."

"Really?" Surprise spread across her face.

"You have excellent instincts." He cocked his head as he studied her.

"Thanks."

"I was thinking we need to head back up the interstate to the last gas station we passed and see if the clerk remembers seeing anyone with Haley."

She reached for his arm and looked at his watch. "If it's the same clerk, he should be getting there soon."

Ten minutes later, they were pulling into the country gas station. As Ava climbed out of the back seat, Damon kept his eyes on her tight ass. He remembered the feel of her in his hands and he craved to touch her all over again. God, he was pathetic. He couldn't keep his mind on his job for three minutes without thinking about taking Ava to bed.

That could not happen. Not again.

Shaking his head, he slid out of the car, a little more than irritated for letting a woman cloud his thinking when it came to a case like this. He needed to be focused in order to keep her safe. Ava was his responsibility and his job, nothing more.

Inhaling the crisp, cool, fall air, he forced his thoughts back to finding the kidnapped girl.

Damon opened the door of the convenience store. He let his eyes briskly roam the interior of the sparse store before letting Ava walk across the threshold. He walked in behind her and let the door slam in Jayden's pretty face.

"Nice manners you got there, asshole," Jayden yelled through the glass before tugging the door open.

There was one customer at the register buying cigarettes and three teenage boys hanging out at the beer cooler trying to build up the nerve to buy a six-pack with a fake ID. The teens spotted Damon. He shot them a glare and they immediately forgot their beer and headed for the exit.

He waited until the paying customer left before he approached the counter. The tall, lanky clerk in his early twenties had a textbook spread open beside the cash register.

The clerk's startled expression when he saw him made Damon want to shake his head. He knew he was big and intimidating and the ugly scar across his cheek didn't exactly look like Mr. Sunshine. It was the same response he'd gotten from countless humans over the years. He'd never known a human or wolf to not seem uneasy around him. Well, that was until he'd met Ava. She didn't seem scared of him, in or out of bed.

"We're looking for someone." He narrowed his eyes at the young man. "A young woman who came in here last night."

The clerk gave him a wary look and stuck his hands under the counter. Damon growled at the sudden movement.

"Oh, for goodness sake." Ava shoved him to the side. "You sound like something out of a mafia movie." She gave him a warning glare.

"I do not." He gave her an offended look. It was how he did his job. "I'm asking questions."

"You really need to work on your people skills." She smirked.

Jayden clamped his hand on his shoulder. "The lady is right, my friend. Your social skills are lacking."

Shaking off Jayden's hand, he turned his attention back to the clerk, but the guy's focus was pointed elsewhere. On Ava.

She gave the clerk a smile. "Sorry about that. He's not really a people person."

Damon grimaced. "I'm not that bad."

"Of course you are. But that's how I like you." Ava winked.

She turned her attention back to the clerk. "I'm hoping you can help us. Did you happen to work last night?"

He nodded, obviously eager to help her. "I came in after my Anatomy and Physiology test. I got here late, a little after nine."

Her smile widened. "A&P is hard. You must be going into the medical field."

The clerk relaxed and placed his elbows on the counter. "I am. I want to be a cardiologist."

"Wow, that's really ambitious. I bet you'll make a great doctor."

The clerk blushed and shrugged.

Damon scowled. Was there a male Ava didn't affect? Probably not.

"We're looking for a friend." Her expression became serious. "She was on her way to visit her boyfriend and never made it. Her car was found a few miles from here."

The clerk straightened. "The cops showed up here at lunch. Chet, the guy who works the day shift, said they were in here asking questions about a missing girl. They showed him a picture, but he didn't recognize her. He said they'd be back tonight to see if I recognized her." The clerk narrowed his eyes on Damon. "Are you a cop?"

"Do I look like I eat fucking donuts all day long?" He scowled. A cop was the last thing he wanted to look like.

Jayden laughed. The sound echoed through the empty store.

She shook her head. "No, we're not cops, but she is a friend of ours. The cops aren't putting much effort into looking for her, so we decided to look ourselves." She shrugged. "If they knew we were here, we'd probably get in a lot of trouble. But I don't care. She's out there, alone and scared."

He could hear the fear in Ava's voice. The fear she had for Haley was the same fear she'd experienced the night she was kidnapped.

Damon cupped her cheek. "We will find her, okay?"

She looked up at him and nodded. Even if they found the girl she might not be alive, and if she were alive, what kind of condition would she be in? He wasn't sure how he could tell her if that happened.

"You guys got a picture of her?" The clerk looked between him and Ava.

"Right here." Jayden stepped up and pushed a photo across the counter with his finger. The clerk's eyebrows shot up.

"I remember her." The clerk tapped the photo with his finger and looked up at Ava. "She came in around ten. She was by herself."

"Did she seem okay?"

"She seemed fine, nothing out of the ordinary."

"Did she talk to anybody?" Damon cocked his head.

The clerk shook his head and stopped.

"What is it?" She leaned across the counter.

"Well, I remember she was in line to pay for her gas because the debit machine wasn't working on the pump. In fact, it got kind of backed up in here because people had to come in to pay for their gas. The guy in front of her was kind of an asshole, griping about how I wouldn't accept his check because it was an out of town check. He even asked your friend if he could borrow some cash. She said she didn't have enough, even though she was holding a hundred-dollar bill in her hand."

"Do you remember the name that was on the check?" he asked.

"No, but I do remember it was an out-of-state check."

"What state?"

"Arkansas."

CHAPTER SIX

Damon snaked his arms around Ava as she paled.

"Are you sure?" He spoke to the clerk but kept his gaze on Ava.

"Yeah. When I didn't accept his check, he said he had some cash out in his truck." The young boy raised an eyebrow. "I knew that was a load of crap, so I went to the door to get his tag. He sped off without paying."

"Did you call the cops?" Jayden asked.

"Sure did. By the time they got here he was long gone. In fact they didn't even bother writing down his license plate." The clerk snorted. "The police force here is like an army of Barney Fifes. You wonder why people make fun of the South."

"You got his license?"

"Yep. Got it right here." The clerk flipped a couple of pages in his college textbook until he reached a florescent note. Peeling it off the page, he handed it to Damon.

He glanced at the note before handing it to Jayden. "Is there anything else you can remember about the truck?"

"It was an older model blue Ford. The handle must not have worked on the driver's side because he stuck his hand through the open window to open the door. Does that help?"

"Yeah, it does. Thanks." Ava gave him a grateful smile.

"Thanks, kid." Damon nodded at the clerk before they headed toward the door.

"I hope you find your friend." The clerk's voice drifted out to them as they walked outside.

Ava spoke just loud enough for Damon to hear. "I hope we find her too."

Ava sat in the backseat as Damon and Jayden stood outside the convenience store, each on their cell phones.

A chill ran down her back, like a single bead of water from an icicle, and oozed down her spine. Wrapping her arms around herself, she fought the disturbing images she conjured about what could have happened to the missing girl. Dread, deep and dark, filled her chest until there was no empty space.

She shook her head. She couldn't do this. She had to stay positive or she would go insane with worry.

Rubbing the ache that had been building at her temples, she closed her eyes and tried to find some semblance of calm. She needed to focus. Worrying didn't help anything. Opening her eyes, she found herself looking straight into Damon's hardened gaze through the windshield.

She smiled tightly and nodded, letting him know she was okay. Jayden said something to him. Damon's gaze never wavered from her as he answered back.

She glanced out the window and sucked in a bitter breath.

Haley was out there somewhere, and at the moment, she was alive. She could feel it. They just needed a little bit of luck to find her before it was too late.

It was well past dark by the time they got back to the casino. As they walked through the brightly lit lobby, Ava's stomach growled.

Damon cringed. He was such a selfish bastard. He had been so consumed with trying to find the missing girl that they hadn't bothered stopping for lunch.

"Why don't we grab something to eat before we head up?" He looked over at Jayden.

"You guys go ahead. I'm going to run up to my room and call my contacts to see if anything new has turned up. I'll order room service." Jayden pushed the elevator button. "The steak is really good here." Jayden motioned with his hand. "Head down that way past the slot machines until you see the restaurant."

Damon rested his hand on the small of Ava's back and led her through the casino. More than one male craned his neck to get a better look at her. Instinctively, he pulled her closer. When she gave him a quizzical look, he covered her lips with his. He needed to make it clear to any male watching, she was not available.

She laughed, the sound shooting straight to his heart. "What was that for?"

"I just felt like kissing you." He always felt like kissing her. That was the problem.

"I didn't peg you as the kind of guy who was into public displays of affection." Her lips quirked up. "Not that I'm complaining."

He ran his thumb across her beautiful mouth. She wrapped her fingers around his wrist and gently bit the tip of his finger.

"Just wanted to make sure those two guys at the blackjack table knew who I was with, in case they didn't see the kiss." She gave him a heated look.

"You are like no other female I've ever known, Ava."

She was beautiful, intelligent and strong. He doubted she would ever be the kind to live her life on the safe side or do what she was told. No, not Ava. She would squeeze every last drop out of life and never regret her choices.

Her eyes softened. "I like it when you look at me like that."

"Like what?"

"Like I'm standing here without any clothes on. Like you wouldn't hesitate to take me on the floor, right here in front of everybody."

Lust stirred in his gut and his cock hardened. "Don't tempt me."

"Really?" She shifted, pressing herself intimately against him. "You'd do that? In a room full of people?"

Her scent filled his head, wrapping around him until he couldn't think straight. He grabbed her ass with both hands. Her breathing turned to a heated pant. Her scent of arousal flooded his head as he brushed his lips across the shell of her ear. "There are always dark corners, Ava. I could have your jeans down and be inside you before anyone saw it."

"Oh, God." She dug her nails into his biceps and moaned.

Her stomach let out another growl.

Shaking his head, he reluctantly pulled away. "Come on. You're hungry."

"I'm not hungry." She shook her head. "I want to find a corner." She grabbed his hand as she scanned the busy room.

He laughed. "Come on."

Inside the restaurant, they were quickly seated at a table for two near one of the large windows that looked out over the water. The attentive waitress took their orders and had their beers on the table in a matter of minutes.

Damon leaned back and studied her. "I talked to Barrett and gave him that Arkansas license plate. He ran it through the system and came up with a name. David Jenkins, resident of Little Rock."

She sat forward. "Are we going to his house?"

He shook his head. "No, it's too far. Barrett is sending some men over there to check it out."

Ava picked up her longneck beer and took a drink. "What do you think they'll find?" She picked at the label from her bottle with her fingernail.

He shrugged. "No clue. If it's the same guys who took you, they've probably made sure to cover their tracks and haven't left anything incriminating in their home."

"Haley is alive."

He reached for her hand. "Ava, the odds of finding her alive go down every second."

"I don't care what the odds are." Her gaze locked on his. "I can't explain it but I know she's alive. I feel it."

He frowned and cocked his head.

"Don't look at me like that. I'm not crazy." She tried to tug her hand out of his, but he wasn't letting go.

"It's your animal instinct. That's why you feel she's alive."

She snorted.

"Don't dismiss what you are. Animal instinct has saved my ass more than once."

"Really?" She paused, holding the beer halfway to her mouth. "For example?"

He took a long pull on his beer, the cool liquid quenched his thirst as his memories of that night rushed to the surface. "I was on my way to South Carolina to meet up with some of my bike-riding buddies. I pulled into a gas station near Augusta, Georgia. It was late, and there was only one other vehicle parked outside. By the time I filled up my tank and made a phone call, the car was still there."

"So?"

"Well, I wouldn't have thought much about it, except I kept getting a feeling that something was off." Damon shrugged. "I even got back on my Harley and tried to ignore that feeling. But I couldn't leave. That feeling wouldn't let me leave. I got off and made my way to the store. As I walked closer to the convenience store I noticed the clerk was gone and there were two guys hanging out near the beer cooler, watching me."

"You went in anyway?" She leaned forward in her seat.

He nodded. "I went in, walked over to the coolers, and grabbed a bottle of water. One of the guys stepped up to me and said the clerk was in the bathroom and that they didn't know how much longer he'd be."

"What did you do?"

"I said I'd wait." He grinned. "They didn't like that answer. They suggested I leave the money on the counter. I said okay and walked over to the counter. I heard them come up behind me. I slammed the cash down and turned in time to see the bigger of the two men swinging a bat at my head."

"Did he hit you?" Her eyes widened.

"I ducked and then tackled him. After I knocked him out, I saw the other guy pointing a shotgun at me. He must have gotten it from behind the counter."

"A crashing sound from the beer cooler startled him and the gun went off. I ducked. The full impact missed me and I was left with only a few buckshot in my shoulder." He touched his scarred cheek. "And, here."

"I was wondering how you got that." She frowned. "I thought werewolves could heal. Why do you have a scar?"

He snorted. "When I rushed the guy with the gun, we ended up toppling a shelf-full of salt. Once you get salt in a wound it won't heal. There will always be a scar."

"I like your scar. It makes you look even sexier." Ava grinned and took a drink.

He blinked a couple of times. She actually thought his scar was a turn-on not a defect.

"Go on. What happened next?" She folded her hands under her chin.

"It didn't take much to subdue him. After making sure both guys were restrained with some zip ties, I went over to the cooler. Opening the door, I looked past the broken beer bottles to the very back of the cooler where they stock the shelves from the inside. There was the missing clerk, gagged and hogtied."

"Was he okay?"

"Yeah, he was just shaken up. The two thugs were trying to get the security code for the owner's safe in the office. He said he'd seen me come in and knew if I left they would have killed him. He managed to scoot close enough to the beer shelves and kick the bottles off."

"Did you call the cops?"

He nodded. "I didn't stick around. I'd already lost too much time by stopping, so I kept going."

She shook her head. "You didn't stick around because you didn't need the recognition of being a hero."

He grimaced. "I'm no hero, Ava."

"You're my hero. You're that clerk's hero, too. Without you, we'd both be dead." She reached out for his hand and held it between her palms. "You're going to be Haley's hero, too."

He swallowed down the ache that had suddenly developed in his throat. Things didn't always work out like you wanted. He knew that all too well.

Ava was busy brushing her teeth when Damon poked his head in the bathroom.

"Jayden called. I'm heading over to his room for an update on what they found at David Jenkins's house."

She turned. "Did they find Haley?"

He shook his head. "No. I didn't expect her to be there."

Her heart shuttered and fell.

"It doesn't mean she isn't somewhere else." He gave her a determined look.

"Wait and I'll come with you." She knew they were up against the clock. They could be torturing that poor girl right now, while she was safe and comfortable in her hotel room with Damon as her guard.

She pushed past him to grab her jacket.

He shook his head. "No, Ava. It's late and you're exhausted."

"But..."

"No buts. Stay here and get some rest. If there's anything new, I'll let you know." He pulled down the comforter and sheets and motioned for her to climb in. "I put the do not disturb sign on the door, so no one should bother you. Jayden has rerouted the hall camera to his computer so I can keep an eye on you from his room." He reached in his jacket pocket and handed her his cell phone. "Jayden's number is programmed in. Call me if you need me." He handed her the phone before leaving the room.

Ava plopped down on the bed, not bothering to stifle the yawn that rose up in her throat. Damon had been doing all the work. He was the one who was exhausted. Not her.

She placed the cell phone on the nightstand and slid between the soft covers. Guilt surged in her chest as her mind wandered back to the kidnapped girl. She knew what those wolves wanted to do to Haley. She squeezed her eyes shut, trying to block out the vivid images that rose like ghosts in her mind. How fair was it that an innocent girl should be caught in the clutches of animals so evil?

She curled herself into a ball as the tears fell. She cried for the injustice of the whole fucking situation, for Haley's stripped innocence and for what tomorrow would bring. A short while later, with her body exhausted and her heart heavy, she drifted off to sleep.

She didn't look at the clock later that night when the door eased open. The bed shifted as Damon slid in behind her.

She smiled as his large hand wrapped around her waist and pulled her against his chest. Safe and content, she drifted back to sleep.

Ava blinked open her eyes and arched as the light of dawn spread into the room. When her hand landed on the empty mattress, she froze. She glanced at the clock. 9:00 a.m.

Weird; she'd never slept this late.

She threw off the covers and headed to the bathroom door.

"Damon?"

No answer. She opened the door and stared into the empty bathroom. Great, he was probably in another meeting with Jayden, leaving her out of what was going on.

She grabbed her clothes and turned on the shower. She wanted to be dressed and ready when he got back.

She had just finished drying her hair when Damon pushed the door open with his shoulder while balancing two large cups of coffee. He let the door slam behind him.

"I wondered where you had gone." She smiled and took the steaming cup. "Thank God. I was beginning to get a caffeine headache." What she wouldn't give for a cup of her own coffee versus hotel coffee.

"Were you worried?" He gave her a devastating grin, the kind of grin that made her go wet.

"Maybe." She took a tentative sip, hoping he couldn't see how badly he affected her. "What did you find out last night?"

"Not much. Jenkins didn't even own the house, only renting it. Our guys retrieved a computer. They spent all night scouring the data, trying to recover any detail that might be of importance. We're on our way over to Jayden's room to see what they found." He handed Ava her jacket and ushered her out of the room.

Five minutes later they were sitting around Jayden's living room, finishing their coffee, and eating an assortment of glazed and jelly-filled doughnuts, compliments of their host.

"Did they find anything on the computer?" Damon handed her another lemon-filled doughnut. She grinned. She'd already eaten three. Guys were not known for encouraging cellulite growth. Yet, here he was, encouraging her to eat.

Taking the doughnut, she settled back on the leather couch. Damon rested his hand on her knee. His larger-than-life presence calmed her, like her own personal fortress against a raging storm.

"We found something that was very interesting." Jayden swiped a glazed doughnut and took a huge bite. "Haley wasn't kidnapped at random. According to what was recovered on the computer, David Jenkins had been doing his research on her."

"What kind of research?" She licked the sugar off her fingers. When no one spoke, she looked up. Both men were watching her with unveiled interest as her tongue swirled around her fingertip.

Damon cut his gaze at Jayden and growled.

"Sorry, man." Jayden held his hands up defensively and looked a bit worried. "I will *so* keep my eyes off your girl."

"I'm not above ripping your throat out." Damon's voice sounded more animal than she'd ever heard. Her heart sped up, as excitement blossomed in her chest.

She placed her hand on Damon's muscled arm. "I can think of a better use of all that testosterone and it has nothing to do with fighting."

Damon jerked his head back to her, his expression a mixture of surprise and desire.

"Jayden, please continue." She gave a wave with her hand.

He cleared his throat. "Jenkins kept a file on Haley, everything, from where she lived to her hobbies. He'd even followed her around during the day to get a fix on her daily schedule."

"Why Haley? Why target her specifically? I mean if he wanted to kidnap a girl, surely there would have been easier targets. According to her file, she comes from a well-known family. He'd have to know people would be looking for her." She reached for another doughnut.

Damon nodded. "Ava's right. He specifically wanted Haley. Just like they specifically wanted Ava. We need to find out why."

"Well, there is something else, something odd." Jayden looked from Damon to Ava.

"What?"

"They found a link to a website for a family tree."

She shrugged. "So? Lots of people research their ancestors."

"It wasn't on him. It was on Haley."

The room grew silent, the tension pressing down on them like an anvil.

"They also ran tests on Jenkins's DNA from his toothbrush. He's a wolf, a red wolf."

She swallowed hard and set the half-eaten doughnut down, her appetite suddenly gone. A cold dampness seeped into her very marrow. She'd suspected this from the lipstick. But hearing the confirmation brought her fear to life.

Shivering, she wrapped her arms around herself against the invisible chill.

Damon's hand squeezed her knee, assuring her without words that he was going to protect her, even from the unseen force that seemed to scare her with each new vital piece of information.

She wished she could turn back time and never answer the door that night. If only she'd been more cautious.

"They would have come for you, no matter what you would have done, Ava." His gaze bored into hers.

"Can you read minds, too?" Her stomach cramped and she regretted eating so many doughnuts.

"No. I can smell your fear. It's not your fault. None of this is your fault." He cupped her cheek as he forced her to meet his intense gaze.

She blinked back the tears and nodded, not trusting her voice.

"Do we have a copy of Haley's family tree?" Damon stretched his neck side to side as he looked at Jayden.

"Not yet. I asked the Guardians to send me a copy."

"How the hell did you get them to agree to that? You're not even employed at the compound." Damon's voice was harsh and Ava could detect a hint of resentment in his tone.

Jayden's grin split across his handsome face. "I may not be employed as a soldier like you, my friend, but I do have my connections."

"You mean you blackmailed someone." Damon snorted.

"It helps to be one of the few in the world who can erase an entire night of debauchery that's been caught on Facebook." Jayden shrugged.

Ava narrowed her eyes. "That's impossible. Even if you erased some pictures someone else posted, someone would have already seen them."

"That's when you replace what they think they saw with a subliminal message that makes them forget what they saw."

"You're serious. You can actually do that?"

"Thanks to technology, our information is limitless." Jayden stood. "I've got to check on some things down in the casino. I do have a job, you know."

"I was beginning to wonder. You seem to have a lot of time on your hands to be hanging with us." Damon walked Ava to the door.

"Just trying to keep Ava entertained." Jayden shrugged. "Wouldn't want her to think all wolves are as uncivilized as you."

Walking through the casino, Ava stayed close to Damon. He'd not touched her since they were interrupted in the room, and since then his mood had changed for the worse. He'd grown more distant. It was probably for the best. She didn't want to get him in trouble with his job. He'd told her many times that his job was his life, his everything. She couldn't take that away from him. Besides, she wanted to be first in a man's life, not second best.

Her gaze swept the casino as the flashing lights and the rhythmic sounds of the slot machines lulled her into a sense of normalcy. Despite having her world turned upside down these last few days, she thought she had handled it pretty well. Discovering she was a werewolf hadn't shocked her as much as it should. In some odd way, she'd always known she was different.

An older blue-haired lady pulling an oxygen tank hurried to pass them to a recently vacated slot machine. Easing herself up onto the stool, the old lady held her bucket of coins in one hand while feeding the machine with the other, all the while oxygen pumped into her lungs via tubing attached to her nose.

Ava grinned and watched with interest as a second elderly lady walked up to the blue-haired lady and accused her of stealing her slot machine. A few heated words were exchanged and security was called. Jayden, dressed in his black security uniform, arrived at the scene and tried unsuccessfully to diffuse the situation. The woman with the oxygen refused to move, arguing it was empty when she sat down. The other lady said she had to go get more money and had intended to come back.

"Do you want to wait and see if they end up slugging it out?" Damon's breath tickled her ear.

Looking up, she smiled and shook her head. "No. My bet's on oxygen lady."

He grinned. "Yeah, she's tenacious. Plus, she had a cane stuck beside her oxygen tank. I'm willing to bet she wouldn't hesitate to use it."

"Well, look what the dog dragged in."

She felt Damon stiffen behind her.

A sense of foreboding crashed over her as Ava came face-to-face with a stunning blonde with beautiful brown eyes. The woman was dressed to the nines in an expensive white pantsuit and red heels that matched her smirk.

"Lorry." Damon's voice spat out the woman's name like a curse.

Ava's heart sunk.

"Damon, you're looking well." Lorry glanced at Ava with evident surprise in her eyes. "I see you have a new plaything. Odd. You always preferred blondes."

Fury and anger pitted in Ava's gut until she wanted to pound Lorry's pretty little face into the floor. She forced a smile and looked directly at the rude woman. "Damon's tastes have changed. For the better."

Lorry's smile faltered, her façade of perfection cracking as she uncrossed her arms and clenched her mouth.

He chuckled. "What's wrong, Lorry? Did you think I would be pining away for your sister, unable to get on with my life?"

Lorry narrowed her pretty brown eyes at him.

He snorted. "Of course you did. You both probably did."

"You were mated," Lorry spat out, her beautiful features turning vindictive and bitter.

Ava stilled and couldn't breathe. Her heart melted like a crayon under the heat of an Arkansas sun.

Damon was mated.

"You can't mate someone who tries to kill you. A mate would never do that." He took a step toward Lorry, anger flashing across his face like lightning.

Ava felt like she'd been punched in the chest with a steel hand as she stared up at Damon. Why would any female try to kill him? He was magnificent and powerful and protective. It was in that second she realized something else about Damon. He was also hers.

"You don't understand, Damon. She would have lost everything. She didn't know they were going to try to kill you." Lorry crossed her arms and fixed him with a stare.

"We both know how attached Laura is to her money."

"You don't know what it's like to grow up poor, to have the other kids make fun of you because your mom didn't have enough money to buy decent clothes." Lorry snarled. "For once we had money and her lifestyle was threatened. She didn't know what to do."

"My money. You mean, you both had my money. Because if my memory is correct, Laura never worked a day in her life after she met me. In fact, you moved into my house the week after Laura did."

"We're family. Family is supposed to take care of each other." Lorry stuck out her chin. Ava changed her mind. She didn't think Lorry was so pretty after all.

"Actually, I think that's called being a gold digger." Ava took a step forward. For once she was grateful for the difference in height so she could look down at Lorry.

Lorry's lips turned upward in a very unattractive snarl. "Well, it looks like you're doing the same thing, so you're one to talk."

Damon growled and Ava reached out and touched his arm reassuringly. "Damon doesn't take care of me financially. I work and have my own money, just so we're clear." She raised her eyebrow. "Now, the bedroom is something completely different. In fact, he takes really good care of me in the bedroom."

Lorry's mouth dropped open and pumped like a trout before she slammed it shut. Turning on her expensive heels, she stomped away, elbowing the elderly gamblers out of her way.

Ava gave Damon a disbelieving look. "You actually dated someone related to that bitch?"

"I'm afraid so."

CHAPTER SEVEN

Damon itched to get his hands on the information. Jayden dumped the contents of a black folder on the bed and pointed to a document containing a list of names. "This is the family tree that David Jenkins was keeping on Haley." He looked up at Ava. "Do any of the names sound familiar to you?"

She studied the paper and shook her head. "I don't recognize any of these people."

Damon picked up the document. "Jayden, scan this and send it to this number."

"Who is it?"

"Zane. He's one of our Pack members in Arkansas. He's a genius with genealogy. If there is something significant about these relatives, he'll find it."

Jayden averted his eyes. "Does Zane happen to have a sister named Katy?"

"Yeah, how did you know?" Damon cocked his head and frowned. "Please tell me you didn't bang his sister."

Jayden gave him a pained look. "Didn't have time. Zane showed up, armed to the teeth. I managed to escape out the window, buck-ass naked. It was dead of winter and I almost froze my balls off before I made it to my car."

Zane was very protective of his only sister. Hell, the dude didn't even let you look in her direction without threatened to castrate you. The fact that Jayden made it out alive was a miracle.

"Don't tell him who you are then. Just tell him you're a friend of mine."

Jayden nodded and headed back to his room.

"I'm going to call and check in with Barrett. He should have a safe house ready for you." Damon slid a glance to Ava.

She shook her head and crossed her arms. "Hell, no. You're not taking me back until we find Haley."

"Ava, this is not a game." He gave her his fiercest scowl, but she didn't bother looking the least bit intimidated.

"You're not the boss of me."

"No, I'm not. I'm just the person responsible for keeping you safe and alive." He narrowed his eyes.

"That's not why you're so eager to get rid of me."

"What?" A flicker of irritation flashed through his eyes.

"You want to get rid of me because you don't trust me." Her voice carried a note of surprise.

"This has nothing to do with trust."

"It has everything to do with trust." She reached out and cradled his scarred cheek. Her touch nearly took him to his knees.

He closed his eyes, forcing himself to remain in control of his emotions. He needed to focus on the job.

"I'm not like her. I'm not like Laura."

His eyes sprang open. "God, I know that, Ava. I never said you were."

"You didn't have to. Sometimes when I look at you, I see it in your eyes, the distrust. At first I didn't understand why, but now after seeing Lorry, I do. I want you to know that I would never hurt you like Laura did. Never."

No one had ever said that to him and actually meant it. Words were lies, easily spilled and quickly forgotten.

"Damon, what did she do?" She took his hand in hers.

The memories of that night were too painful. Hell, it had been painful for years. It was the reason he never came back to Louisiana. His stomach clenched as he watched her emerald eyes. If Ava knew the details, would her opinion of him change?

He eased down onto the bed.

Ava eased onto the opposite bed and waited patiently for him to speak.

Sucking in a deep breath, he held it a second and blew it out. "I suppose I need to start from the beginning, before I even met Laura. That might explain why we ended up together in the first place." He swallowed. "You remember me saying that I grew up in an orphanage?"

"Yes."

"Well, that part of my childhood was pretty uneventful until my last year there."

"What happened?"

"I was going through puberty. You know, voice changing, mood swing, hair developing in all the right places, all the typical teenage stuff." He shrugged. "Anyway, one night after dinner, I broke out in a fever and my muscles started aching, really bad. The nuns put me in bed thinking it was the flu. My bed was facing the window and as I lay there shivering, I watched the moon come out from behind the clouds. I was drawn to it and couldn't keep my eyes off it. It was mesmerizing." He averted his gaze to the floor.

"Instead of my symptoms getting better, they started getting worse. For three days I stayed in bed, one of the nuns always at my bedside. Sister Mary actually sent for the priest thinking I was going to die." Damon laughed ruefully. He remembered the pain. At the time, he had actually wished for death so the pain would finally end.

"On the third night, as I lay there, alone, in my own sweat and screaming in pain from the muscle aches, my eye caught the full moon coming out from behind the clouds. The instant I saw it my pain intensified. It was so much worse than those three days of agony I'd experienced."

"Were you shifting?"

He looked up and nodded.

"That first time it took me an hour to make the transformation. And at midnight, when I was fully wolf, the priest decided to finally get off his ass and arrive. You can't imagine the look on his face when he came through the door.

"He called me a demon and started throwing holy water on me."

"Did it hurt?"

"No, but it did piss me off."

She chortled.

"I jumped through the window and kept running until I reached the woods. The next morning I tried going back to the orphanage, but they'd locked the doors and wouldn't let me in. They said I was evil and of the devil." He glanced away. At the time, he had thought maybe they were right.

"You were just a child."

"I wasn't just a child Ava, I was a wolf."

"Where did you go?"

"I was homeless for a while." Damon bit his cheek as his past washed over him.

"How did you survive?" Her brows furrowed together as if she were reliving the pain right along with him.

"I slept where there weren't a lot of people, like cemeteries. Sometimes, I managed to sleep in churches that were unlocked. Finding food was the hard part. A lot of times, the only way I could eat was to steal it." He hated admitting that desperate part of his life.

"One night, I got into a fight with some guys over some bread I had stolen from a restaurant. It was at night and there happened to be a full moon. Of course you can guess what happened next."

"I thought you didn't need a full moon to shift?"

"You don't. But you are more likely to shift if you don't know how to control it. I was still young and hadn't learned how to control it." He shrugged. "Anyway, the guys freaked and ran away. I was in the city so trying to hide was almost impossible. To make a long story short, a couple of rednecks spotted me in an alley and captured me."

"What happened next?"

"They shipped me to South Carolina where they entered me in an underground dog-fighting ring."

"They made you a slave? Even after you shifted back?" Her eyes held a pain for him that he'd never experienced from another person.

He nodded. "There are some humans who will do anything for money."

"Could you not escape?"

"I tried once, when they forgot to chain me."

"They chained you?" Her voice was tight with rage.

"They'd always chain me around my neck, like the other dogs. They never knew when I was going to change, so they made sure I was secured."

"That's why you don't like anything around your neck."

"Yes." Shame burned through his gut as he looked away. He didn't want to see the pity in her beautiful eyes.

"How long were you there?"

"One year, three weeks and thirteen days."

"Oh, Damon." She reached for his hand.

He sucked in a deep breath. He needed to finish the story before he chickened out. "One night, I managed to finally break my chains. I escaped and didn't stop running until I got to Louisiana. Jayden was the first friend I made. He'd caught me out behind his grandmother's house one night digging through the garbage, looking for something to eat. I knew the minute he got close enough to catch his scent, that he was a wolf. Granny took me in, cleaned me up and fed me. I ended up living with them for a while."

He chuckled. "Granny was the one who explained to me what I was. She said I wasn't a freak. She actually contacted the commander from New Orleans when I needed a job. It was the first time I was ever in a Pack and working as a Guardian."

"Is that where you met Laura? In New Orleans?"

"Yes. She was a waitress at a restaurant near Bourbon Street. She always waited on me when I came in. I didn't go out much other than to eat. Even then I was usually alone, unless Jayden happened to be in town. Laura found out that I had recently bought a remodeled loft downtown and asked to see it." He grimaced. "Anyway, she ended up coming back to my place and..."

"You two got it on. Understood. No details please." She flinched.

It had been nothing like being with Ava, and they hadn't even had full on sex.

"After that, Laura started coming by, bringing me meals, checking on me. For the first time in my life I felt like I mattered," he continued. "I thought I was in love and asked her to move in with me. It was the worst mistake of my life."

"Laura's a wolf?"

"Yes."

"How does that work, being wolves and being a couple? I mean did you guys shift and go run together at night?"

He grinned. Ava made it sound so simple, so right. So completely unlike Laura and how she viewed being a werewolf.

"Laura never shifted in front of me the whole time we were together. I'm not sure she shifted at all. She said she despised being a wolf."

"Can you do that, prevent shifting?"

"There is something you can take to stop yourself from shifting, but the side effects are too dangerous."

"Why did Laura despise being a wolf?"

"She said it was uncivilized. She liked herself in human form where she could show off her beautiful clothes and jewelry that I bought her." He shook his head. "Laura always worried about what others thought of her if she didn't wear the very best."

"How did she try to get you killed?"

"I came in late one night after having busted some werewolves making crystal meth. I walked into the kitchen to grab a sandwich when Laura called to me from the bedroom. The lights were off, which I thought was weird because Laura always kept a nightlight on."

"The second I walked through the bedroom door, a baseball bat hit me across the chest. I dropped to my knees and two guys jumped me." He looked down at Ava's white-knuckled grip on his hand. He held her hand against his scarred cheek.

"Right before I passed out I looked up. Laura was standing there looking down at me with nothing in her eyes. Not love, not hate, just emptiness. Later, I found out that the two guys were looking to collect on a very large debt she'd run up at the jewelry store owned by an Italian guy who happened to be connected to the mob."

"I assume you had no idea she'd done that."

He snorted. "I had no clue. She was given a choice of returning the jewelry or they would take my life. She chose to keep the jewelry."

"What a fucking bitch." She growled.

"I was harder to kill than an average human. After they left me for dead, I lay on the floor for days, my body knitting its bones back together. It took about a week until I was able to walk, another month to be completely healed."

"Where the hell was Laura?"

"I found out later she had been shacked up at her lover's house waiting for me to die in order to inherit my stuff. When I didn't die, it put a kink in her plans."

"Why the hell didn't you kill her?" She jumped to her feet. "I would have."

Damon stood, a little surprised by her anger. "It wasn't worth it. When I was healed, I found out my Pack had kicked me out for not showing up for work."

She jerked her head, her emerald eyes flashing with rage. "They fired you? You were left for dead in your own home! Did you tell them that?"

He laughed and pulled her closer. "It didn't matter. Being kicked out meant one less tie to Louisiana. I left

New Orleans and moved to Arkansas. I found a job with Barrett, the Arkansas Pack Master. Despite what the Louisiana Pack master told Barrett about me, Barrett still hired me."

"You let Laura have the loft?"

"I was willing to pay whatever price to get her out of my life, for good."

"I understand that." Ava nodded against his chest. He tightened his arms around her. Talking about his past hadn't hurt as bad as it once did. This time, it felt like he was finally ready to let that part of his life go.

"Is this the first time you've been back to Louisiana?"

"Yes. I should have come back sooner to see Granny." He ran his hand through his hair. "She was the only one who took me in and cared for me. She didn't expect anything in return."

"She seems like a great judge of character." She picked up his hand and kissed his palm. Immediately, his dick went on alert and hardened.

He rested his forehead against hers and closed his eyes. "Why hasn't a male claimed you?"

"I'm too hard to hold, I guess." She sighed. "I've been told I'm stubborn."

"You're fucking perfect."

"That's because you're the only male that is strong enough to handle me. Maybe this whole kidnapping thing is fate's way of bringing us together." Her breath was warm against his lips as pleasure curled low in his belly.

"You keep talking like that and I'm going to show you how good I can handle you."

She rubbed her body against his. "Promise?"

Oh, yeah. He was definitely good and hard now with her lush curves pressing into his body.

She parted her lips as he covered her mouth and thrust his tongue between her lips. She was sweet and sexy and he knew he was never going to get enough of her taste, even if he lived a million years.

Her fingers threaded through his hair and rested at the nape of his neck as she clung to him. Digging his fingers into her hips he ground himself against her sweet spot. She moaned into his mouth.

"Ava." He dragged his mouth away, licking and kissing a trail to her neck. He had long silenced those voices in his head telling him this was a bad idea.

"I want you inside me." She jumped and wrapped her long legs around his waist.

"Anyone else touches you, I'll kill him. You got that?" He held her face in his hands as his possessiveness burned through him.

※ ※ ※

"Housekeeping!" The female voice on the other side of the door was followed by three sharp knocks.

"Fuck," Damon ground out between his clenched teeth. It looked like fate had other plans for them.

"Doesn't look like we're going to get to." Ava rolled off him.

Damon stomped to the door and threw it open. "We don't need anything, thanks." He tried to shut the door, but the pudgy housekeeper put out her hand and stopped him.

"It's after ten o'clock."

"So?"

"Checkout is ten o'clock. I have to get this room ready for our next guest." She lifted her chin and propped her hands on her ample hips.

"We're not checking out."

The housekeeper kept her eyes on him as she retrieved her clipboard off the cart. Glancing down, she nodded and thrust the clipboard under his nose.

"This says you are."

"That's wrong." Damon glanced at the clipboard and shook his head. "We'll go downstairs and straighten this out."

The housekeeper nodded and pushed her cart to the next door.

"I've got to go downstairs."

"I'll go with you." Ava grabbed the key and followed him to the elevator.

Damon frowned at the long line winding toward at the front desk. He tried walking up to the front of the line, but all that earned him was a, "You'll have to wait your turn," and a glare from the clerk.

After fifteen minutes of waiting, he finally reached the clerk.

Ava patted his arm. "Be nice."

"I'm always nice." He scowled.

"You're never nice." She gave him a wide smile.

"Yeah, you're right. Maybe you should handle this."

She winked and patted him on the butt. "Will do, sweetheart."

"How may I help you, miss?" The desk clerk identified as Sam from his white name badge gave Ava a weary smile. With his index finger, he shoved his glasses up his large nose and sniffed.

"I think there has been a mistake."

"Oh, well, let's see what we can do to make you happy." Sam smiled politely.

"We're in room 351 and the house cleaning lady said that we were checking out today and, you see, that's simply not the case." She batted her long eyelashes at Sam. If Damon didn't view the older man as a threat, he would definitely be pulling some alpha shit right now and ripping the man's liver out.

Sam's eyes hardly left Ava's as his fingers clicked along the keyboard at lightning-fast speed. His smile faltered as the computer screen drew his full attention.

"Well, it says here that you two paid cash for two nights when you arrived. If you would like another night, we could definitely arrange something." The man looked at Ava and his smile returned.

Ava turned to Damon and he dug his wallet out of his back pocket. "How much?"

"One hundred and sixty-nine dollars."

His head jerked up. "One hundred and sixty-nine dollars? I paid that much for both nights we stayed."

Sam gave him an apologetic look. "I understand, sir, but that was our weekday rate. The one-hundred-and-sixty-nine dollar rate is our weekend rate. They are having some kind of erotic writer's convention down the street, and we've almost got the whole hotel booked." Sam looked over his shoulder. "You know, you two were lucky. In fact, the majority of the people behind you are probably not going to be able to get a room."

"I don't have that much cash." He frowned.

"What about a credit card? I saw where you reserved the room with a MasterCard. If you'd like us to run it, I'd be happy to do that."

Closing his wallet, Damon shoved it back into his jeans pocket and grabbed Ava's hand. "I'm going to have to say no. We're trying to get out of debt, and I hate using a credit card. Who knows, maybe I'll get lucky at blackjack."

"Yes, sir, but there might not be a room available if you wait any longer." Sam frowned, looking from them to the computer screen.

"We'll take our chances." Damon spoke over his shoulder as he pulled Ava through the crowded line.

Once they were alone on the elevator, she turned. "Okay, what was that about?"

"I can't use a credit card. It can be traced to our location." He stepped off the elevator and hurried down the hall. The housekeeper's head popped out the door a few rooms down, and she gave them the stink eye before they disappeared into the room.

Damon pulled out his duffle bag and began shoving all of their stuff into it.

"What do we do now?" She gathered their toiletries from the bathroom.

Damon was already dialing his cell phone when she came out of the bathroom.

"I'll call Jayden to see if we can crash in his room tonight." After a few rings, it went straight to voicemail. Cursing, he left Jayden a brief message.

"We can't stay here." Damon grabbed her jacket and handed it to her. "Let's go get something to eat while we wait on Jayden to call back."

Ava peeked over her plastic-cover menu at Damon. He had been silent since they sat down at the diner.

Biting her lip, she lowered her plastic menu. "Damon?"

"Yeah?" He didn't take his eyes off the menu.

"Do we have enough money to eat?"

"Yes, Ava, get whatever you want. I should have brought more money with me for the room, but I hadn't anticipated some unexpected expenses."

Her stomach fell at the tense tone of his voice. She was the unexpected expense. She shoved her menu away, not even hungry anymore.

"It's because I had to buy some clothes, isn't it?"

He lowered the menu until their eyes met. "This isn't your fault so don't start blaming yourself."

"Then you stop blaming yourself for not having enough cash."

He stared at her for a couple of seconds before his lips twitched, breaking out into a grin. "Deal."

He reached for her hand across the table. "When Jayden calls back, I'll see about us staying with him. Although I don't know how he'll feel about sleeping on the couch in his own room."

"You're kicking him out of his bed?" She gave him a droll look.

"Yep, so I can get you in it." He brought her fingers to his sensual mouth, kissing each fingertip, making her stomach purr with desire. It amazed her that a man could have so much control over her body.

"Can I take your order?"

Damon slowly looked up at the waitress. "Fuck."

Damon couldn't believe he was looking into the pale blue eyes he'd once thought he'd loved. Oh, how wrong he'd been. Now, it was like looking at a perfect stranger.

"Hello, Laura." He could smell Ava's possessiveness pouring off her as she glared at Laura.

"Damon." Her voice was but a whisper as her hollow eyes shone with surprise. Something similar to pity swirled in his stomach at her gaunt appearance. What had happened to the vivacious girl he had once known?

"I didn't know you were back in Louisiana."

"I'm not. Just passing through." He shrugged and turned his gaze back to Ava. His heart softened. She sat there, her dark green eyes sparkling like emeralds with banked anger.

"Laura, this is Ava."

"You've mated." If it were possible, Laura paled even more.

"Yes." Ava threaded her fingers through his.

He stilled. Though it was a lie, Ava spoke it with such conviction that he almost let himself believe it might happen.

He wanted nothing more than to jump the table and mount Ava, right here in front of everyone.

"I'm glad to see you happy, Damon." Laura's voice brought his attention back to the situation and away from the throbbing erection in his pants.

"What are you doing here, Laura? Why aren't you living in New Orleans?" He scowled.

She shrugged her thin shoulders and he wondered if they'd snap like twigs with the slight motion.

"I had some trouble."

"Really? I thought you and your lover would be living it up in my loft." He didn't bother keeping the sarcasm out of his voice.

"I got kicked out."

"Of your own home?" He narrowed his eyes.

"The neighbors got upset when I couldn't pay the light bill. I had no way to keep the food cold and it spoiled. They complained about the smell and said I was running the place into the ground. They got together, got an attorney, and had me evicted."

"Why couldn't you pay your bills? I would have thought with your all your jewelry, you'd be set." The jewelry he had bought.

"Jimmy stole my jewelry to buy drugs."

"Jimmy is your boyfriend?" Ava was watching Laura as if waiting for her to attack. From the looks of Laura, she didn't have the strength to fight her way out of a potato chip bag.

"Not anymore." Laura shook her head. "He ran off and I never saw him again."

"What about a job? Didn't you work? Couldn't you have paid your own bills?" Ava raised her eyebrow. It was clear Ava had no sympathy for the girl.

Laura didn't speak and he knew exactly why. "After she moved in with me, Laura quit working." He expected the anger and resentment to still be there after such a bitter memory. Surprisingly, those emotions were long gone.

"Why the hell did you do that?" Ava snarled. She was definitely not giving Laura any slack.

"Damon took care of me. Why should I have to work?" Laura shrugged.

"Every woman needs her own money. She shouldn't have to depend on a man to support her." Ava narrowed her eyes at Laura.

"That's easy for you to say. I'm willing to bet he bought the clothes on your back and a lot more." Laura looked from Ava to him, and he saw something wistful, longing toward him. Laura was out of her fucking mind if she thought she had a chance with him now.

He looked over at Ava, expecting a witty comeback, like always. Instead she didn't speak. She looked a little uncomfortable and tried to pull her hand away from his. He tightened his grip. Their gazes met for a brief second.

"I had to move back to Shreveport after I left New Orleans. I've been here for four years." Laura hefted the pad out of her apron pocket along with a pen. "I'm sorry. I should have taken your order by now." She shook her head and laughed a little. "It's just seeing you again was a real shocker."

"No problem." Damon waited for Ava to order before placing his own. They both watched Laura head back into the kitchen for their drinks.

"She's changed a lot."

"I hope she doesn't spit in my food." Ava looked at him under her lashes. "She's still pretty."

"She looks like death warmed over." Laura paled in comparison to Ava.

Ava met his eyes as he kissed the back of her hand.

Laura returned with their drinks. Ava pulled back away as the plastic glasses were placed on the table.

"Thanks," Ava mumbled.

He nodded his thanks at Laura, who lingered a little longer than necessary.

"Lorry said she saw you."

He looked up at Laura. "She didn't mention anything about you living in Shreveport."

Laura's lips parted under the force of a weak smile. "She probably didn't want you to know that I wasn't doing well financially. She always did care what people thought about her."

"I guess you two were a lot alike in that area." He arched his eyebrow at her.

Laura's smile faded. "I've changed, Damon. I really have."

"Laura, you got another customer," a plus-sized waitress with hair that looked like a brown football shouted from behind the counter.

Laura turned. A strange metamorphosis occurred as her gaze landed on her customer. She stood up straight and stuck out her nonexistent breasts. Her face brightened as she stretched her lips into a wide smile. In the space of a few seconds Laura transformed back into that same selfish person he'd known so long ago.

She hurried over to the table where an older man dressed in a suit and tie sat. He greeted her with a smile and a wink.

Apparently, Laura hadn't changed.

She should go into acting. He shook his head, feeling a small amount of pity for the older man.

For the rest of lunch, Ava didn't say much despite his attempt at conversation. He sucked at making conversation. Hell, he didn't even like to talk. When she didn't engage him back, he finally gave up.

After a painfully silent lunch, he motioned Laura over to get the check while Ava excused herself to the bathroom. He thought about not leaving a tip, since Laura didn't deserve it. In the end his softer side won out and he left a ten-dollar tip.

As soon as Ava exited the bathroom, he stood, grateful to leave.

Ava strode to his bike. His eyes were glued to her sexy little ass and he suddenly couldn't help himself. Coming up behind her, he wrapped his arms around her waist and buried his face in the crook of her neck.

She let out a low moan. Damn, he wanted to bite her right there on her sensitive flesh.

She laughed softly, her ribcage trembling under his hands. "What's gotten into you?" She caressed his scarred cheek. Her touch was cool and soothing against the jagged flesh.

"I love the way you smell." He kissed the curve of her neck. He closed his eyes, inhaling her scent into his lungs, into his very soul. He might not have forever with her, but he had this moment. He didn't want to waste a minute.

She tugged his hand upward to her mouth where she kissed it. She turned in his arms and smiled up at him. "Do you have a plan?"

"Well, first, I'll take your clothes off and then mine."

"No, not that." She swatted his arm and laughed. "A plan about where we will spend the night since we have no money and can't use a credit card."

"I'll try calling Jayden again. I'm sure he's finished breaking up the brawl between the two blue hairs by now." He plucked his cell phone out of his pocket and punched in Jayden's number. After a few rings it went straight to voicemail. Again.

"Shit." He ran his hand through his hair.

"What?"

"Jayden's not answering."

"He's probably still working."

"He always carries his phone. And he always answers it." He thrust his hands through his hair. Something was off.

His phone rang.

"Hello?"

"I've got an informant that might have some info on the missing girl." Barrett's voice came over the line slow and steady. His voice, just like his personality, never seemed to waver.

"There's a bar off the highway that caters to bikers. Do you know the one I'm talking about?"

"I know the one." It was more than a bar. It was a strip club. It was the last place on earth he wanted to take Ava.

"Figured you did. Be there tonight at ten o'clock. Go to the far end of the bar and order a shot of vodka, Grey Goose. This is the signal for the informant to talk to you."

"What about Ava?" He gritted his teeth.

"He knows you'll have company. Unless you find a safe place to leave her, you're going to have to take her with you. I told him you were with your mate so that should be enough for him to keep his hands off."

"If it's not, I'll be more than happy to rip his hands off for him." Damon gave Ava a pointed stare. "You make sure to tell him I don't share. You got that?"

Barrett's laughter rumbled through the line. "I think he'll get the message loud and clear when he lays eyes on you, Damon. Besides, I've warned him. You know the rules."

"Yeah. The first time is a warning. The second time is death." Damon grinned a little. "Because you hate to repeat yourself."

"That's right."

"I've found a couple of options for a safe house for Ava. They won't be ready for a couple of days, so you'll have to keep her a little while longer."

He said nothing, his stomach tightening at the thought that soon he'd have to let Ava go.

"Damon, you know you've got to let her go, right?" It was more of a command than a question. Directions were one thing. It was ultimatums he didn't respond so well to.

"Damon, you do right by that girl. We clear?"

Damon growled, holding onto his rage by a thread. Without a word, he ended the call.

"You okay?" Ava touched his arm.

"Yeah." He pulled the helmet off the bike and handed it to her. "We need to get going."

"Where?"

"You'll see."

CHAPTER EIGHT

Ava clung to Damon as he sped down the interstate on his Harley to their next destination. She hadn't pressed him about where they were going. Frankly, she didn't want to know. Wherever their destination, it might be the place he would leave her. She wasn't ready to tell him goodbye, just yet.

Rubbing her hands across his washboard abs, he shivered under her fingertips. She loved how he responded to her touch. If only they had more time together. The minutes seemed to be siphoning away, their days rushing by with no way to slow down and enjoy the short time they had left.

He pulled into the parking lot of a decrepit-looking building with no windows and steel bars on the door.

"What is this place? It looks condemned." She wrinkled up her nose.

"It's a bar that caters to our kind." He turned and scanned the nearly empty parking lot. There was only one other bike parked near the entrance. She assumed it was someone who worked there.

"A werewolf bar?" Her eyes widened. It still seemed weird to say. "Is it dangerous?"

"Only on a full moon and then hardly anyone comes in unless they are looking for trouble. Humans rarely come here."

"Sounds like you know from experience."

"Maybe."

The closed sign hung limply on its side like a broken arm. Instead of going through the front door, he led her around to the side of the building.

He rapped on the backdoor.

"We're closed. Can't you see the damn sign?" A deep voice roared from the other side of the door. She took a cautious step back.

"No shit, you senile old fart. Get off your lazy ass and open this goddamn door," Damon thundered.

The back door flew open and a man with shoulders as wide as a dump trunk stomped out. His bald head resembled Mr. Clean and was the only part of him that wasn't covered in hair. He towered over Damon, which was a feat in itself.

"Damon? What the fuck you doing here?" Mr. Clean on steroids looked over at her and blushed. "I mean, what the hell are you doing here?"

"Looking for a favor. Think you can help me out?" Damon's expression grew serious as he shook hands with the giant of a man.

"Come on in." He motioned them inside.

Despite the run-down appearance of the outside of the building, the inside was very clean. As they wound their way through the kitchen, her nose was assaulted by the tempting smells. By the time they reached the bar, her mouth was watering.

"Can I get you two something to eat? I was just putting the finishing touches on my crawfish etouffee for tonight's customers."

"We just ate." Damon shook his head.

"That sounds great." She gave the man a grateful smile.

"I like a girl with an appetite. You better treat her right, Damon. Mates like her don't come along that often." He disappeared into the kitchen.

"Why didn't you tell me you were still hungry?"

"I wasn't until I walked in here." She shrugged. When she was nervous she ate a lot.

The guy came back through the kitchen doors in a much better mood. "That's one fine mate you got there, Damon. If I was twenty years younger I'd fight you for her." He smiled broadly and set the bowl in front of her.

"Ava, I'd like you to meet Jeff. He's the owner of Romulus and Remus."

She narrowed her eyes. "You named your bar after the founders of Rome?"

"Beautiful and smart. I agree with your choice of a mate." Jeff gave Damon an appreciative nod.

Damon sighed loud enough to irritate her. "We're not mated."

"Humph. That's what you keep saying." Jeff lifted his eyes to the ceiling.

"Keep saying? Who've you been talking to? Jayden?" Damon narrowed his eyes.

"Nope. Granny told me. Ran into her while I was picking up some groceries." Jeff squeezed his brows together marring his perfectly round head. "She said she was picking up some hors d'oeuvres for some kind of party. Did she say anything to you about having a party?"

Ava almost choked on her etouffee. Damon's face turned bright red and he quickly shrugged. "Nope, not a word."

"This is the best etouffee I've ever tasted." She pointed to the bowl with her spoon.

Jeff's face broke into a large smile. "Thank you, Ava."

"No, really." She spooned another bite into her mouth and sighed. "I've already had a burger for lunch, but for some reason I can't stop eating your food."

"You said she's not mated." Jeff looked at Damon as his lips curled into a wicked grin.

"If you want to keep your arms attached to your body, I'd squash that idea right now."

She glanced between the two men. Although Damon seemed offended when everyone assumed they were mated, he didn't hesitate when it came to keeping other men away from her. Just like a man. Damon didn't want her, but didn't want anyone else to have her either.

He was really starting to piss her off.

"Tell me, since I'm new to the whole werewolf thing, does the female ever get a voice in this whole mating thing? Because it sounds to me like a bunch of testosterone bullshit." She shoved a bite into her mouth and glared.

Jeff grinned. "Are you kidding? The female has all the power in the relationship."

She raised a doubtful eyebrow at him. "Doesn't sound like it to me."

"Oh, believe me. The female holds more power in the relationship than the male, especially when it comes to mating." Jeff gave her a wink.

"Really?"

Damon shook his head and looked at Jeff. "Look, we're not here to have a lesson in mating. We're here looking for information on a kidnapper."

Jeff propped his elbows on the table. "A kidnapper?"

"One of the Louisiana females was kidnapped. Right after Ava was kidnapped."

Jeff turned concern eyes on her. "Darling, did some asshole hurt you?"

She averted her eyes. "You mean assholes; there was more than one."

Jeff's face went red with rage.

"No one hurt me." She gave Jeff a reassuring smile. "Damon got there in time and rescued me."

"You killed them?" Jeff's question seemed more like a statement than a question, his back arched in a protective gesture. Ava's heart warmed. Jeff didn't even know her and he was actually genuinely concerned. How many human men had she been around who would have been worried about her? Jeff, like Damon, saw her as something more than just a pair of boobs.

Wolves may be animals, but they certainly took care of their kind, more than humans did.

"I thought you might have some Intel on David Jenkins who kidnapped the second girl." Damon's deep timbre drew her attention. She couldn't help the fact that every time he spoke, or looked at her, or touched her hand, it had her heart spinning in her chest.

Desire heated her face as he turned and met her eyes. She reached for the bottled water on the wooden table to quench her sudden thirst. With just one look at him, all her years of being in control of her life and not taking shit from any man sent her steel resolve flying out the window. For him, she would almost relinquish complete control.

Almost.

The consequences shook her to the core.

"You okay?" He reached for her hand. She fought against the urge to place his fingertips into her mouth and suck.

"Yeah. Etouffee's just a little spicy." She sipped her water, pulling out of his reach and out from under his spell.

"I wish I could help, but I haven't heard of the guy." Jeff shook his head, obviously frustrated. "You might try the Beaver Tail. They get lots of wolves, especially near the full moon."

"What's the Beaver Tail?" She pushed away her empty bowl.

"It's a strip club," Damon answered without looking at her. "It's the reason I need a favor from you, Jeff."

"We get to take a field trip. Nice." She rubbed her hands together. "I've never seen the inside of a strip club before."

"You're not starting today." Damon narrowed his eyes on her.

"What do you mean?"

"You'll be staying here with Jeff while I check it out." He cut his gaze to Jeff.

Jeff grinned. "Is this where you ask if she can stay here? Or were you just planning on telling me?"

"Nope, no way." Ava sat up in her chair. "You sure as hell aren't leaving me out of this now, Damon. If you go, I go."

"Ava, it's too dangerous. You're not going to a strip club. Do you know how many guys would be on your ass the second you walked through the door?" He glared at her.

"Then I guess you're just going to have to watch my ass." She shrugged.

"You sure you're not mated?" Jeff arched a hairy brow.

"I'm sure." They both answered in unison.

"You know she's probably right, Damon." Jeff's smirk disappeared. "I'm short on bouncers since Jayden went to work full-time at the casino. With the full moon coming up, having her here would not be a good idea. She needs someone covering her all the time."

She shot Jeff an encouraging smile before looking back at Damon, whose face was buried in a scowl so deep she thought it would leave permanent lines.

Damon cursed as he ran his fingers through his hair, his muscles ripping under his tight T-shirt. She licked her lips and swallowed hard. Suddenly, she was struck with the image of him, naked in bed, with his huge strong body covering hers as he pounded himself into her body.

"You okay?" Damon's scowl was gone, replaced with concerned.

"Yes, why?" She looked away and swiped her hand across her brow.

"You're flushed and your eyes are glossy. Do you have fever?" He pressed his palm to her forehead. "You feel hot."

Hell yeah, she was hot, and wet too. How could she not be all hot and frustrated with him touching her?

She pushed his hand away. "I'm fine. It just got kind of warm in here." She rubbed her sweaty palms on her jeans-clad thighs. "When does the strip club open?"

"It opened hours ago." He cocked his head as he looked into her face, still searching for some signs of illness.

"I thought they only opened at night."

"Nope. They open before noon, for the lunch crowd." Jeff stood and picked up her empty bowl.

"They serve food?" She wrinkled her nose. "Wouldn't that be a health violation or something? How the hell could you eat with all that in your face?"

Jeff barked out a laugh. "Damon, I like your girl! I think she's got some Alpha in her." He disappeared through the swinging door into the kitchen

"What?" She cocked her head. "Don't tell me you haven't thought the same thing. Would you be eating while some girl is shaking her naked ass over your BLT?"

He leaned in close, his eyes darkening and his breath grazing her cheek. "Only if the naked girl was you. And I wouldn't be eating a BLT. I'd be eating you."

Damon pulled up to the Beaver Tail, careful to park away from the front door. It was just getting dark and the security lights were blinking awake, illuminating the quickly approaching darkness.

Securing her helmet to the bike, he took the opportunity to assess for danger. Inhaling deeply, he scanned the parking lot, relaxing only when he didn't sense a threat. Grabbing Ava's hand, he walked toward the front door. As much as he hadn't wanted to, he'd brought her along.

"Will they even let me in?" Ava whispered as they drew near the entrance.

"Of course. Why wouldn't they?" He glanced down at her. Damn, she was fucking beautiful. If he lived for eternity, he would never get tired of looking at her.

She shrugged. "I don't know. What if I'm some irate wife looking for her husband? I could be dangerous, you know."

He grinned. Hell yeah, she could be dangerous. It's what he liked about her, that and her stubbornness. And the way she looked at him. And the way her body fit under him. And the way...

"I'm telling you right now, you go in there and let some tramp touch you, there's going to be trouble. For her and you."

His chest swelled with pride. He especially loved how possessive she was.

"Just letting you know before we walk in." She batted her eyes and smiled sweetly.

He grabbed her and pulled her into a hug. Burying his face in her neck, he inhaled deeply and rubbed his scent across her body. He let his hands run down her back until they rested on her tight little ass.

When he finally let go, she looked up into his eyes.

"What was that for?"

"Insurance." He was making sure the other males knew she wasn't available. He didn't give her time to ask any more questions as he herded her through the entrance. He nodded at the bouncer, making a mental note that he, too, was a Were. The bouncer nodded back as they walked farther into the club. The stench of drugstore perfume and the smog of cigarette smoke hung heavy in the air.

"Would you two like to be seated at the bar or a table?"

He jerked his head toward the deep feminine voice, a result from years of cigarette abuse.

"Do you have a table that is non-smoking?" Ava spoke up before he could answer.

"We do have a non-smoking section, but it's not going to be completely free of smoke." The waitress pointed to the location across the room. He noticed there weren't as many men sitting in that area.

"That's fine." He followed the waitress, making sure to keep Ava in front of him. The men in the club were too busy watching a blond stripper wrap her legs around a pole to notice Ava.

Good. He hated having to kill someone this early in the day.

They settled into a corner table. He reached over and pulled Ava's chair closer until she was nestled against his side.

"Damon, I don't think someone is going to jump up and try to take me right here."

"You're right. I'd kill them first."

Absently, he ran his fingers up and down her arm as he looked around. Men in suits sitting at tables near the stage, while blue-collar men huddled around the stage itself. The stripper finished her performance, and a brunette entered the stage wearing nothing but cowboy boots and a G-string. She was pretty enough, but she didn't do a thing for him.

"I bet I could do that." Ava nodded as the stripper gripped the pole with both legs, allowing gravity to spin her downward, landing in a split.

"You're not going to find out." Letting Ava get on a stripper pole would be like igniting World War III.

"Why not?"

"Can I get you something to drink?" The waitress's name badge read Sherry Pie and she was dressed in a yellow apron with cherries splashed across the material. Her brilliant red hair was bumped up high on her head like a Jersey girl. Her eye makeup was black and heavy, making her resemble a raccoon that had lost a fight. What amazed Damon the most was the fact that her lipstick matched her blazing red hair to perfection.

"Can I ask you something?" Ava nodded toward the stage. "Do you have to go to school to do that?"

The waitress followed her gaze to the stage and grinned. "No, honey. All you need is core strength."

"Are you a dancer too?"

"Yes, but I don't dance until the ten o'clock crowd comes in. That's where the money is."

"Is that when the CEO types come in, after work?" Ava propped her chin on her hand.

"Don't I wish? The CEOs are tight with their money, although they don't mind spending on themselves."

Sherry laughed. "The big money is those rough-looking bikers, like that guy over there at the bar."

They both turned. Perched on a barstool and wearing a scarred leather jacket was a huge guy. The second the dude glanced in their direction, Damon caught his scent and knew he was a Were.

His nostrils flared as he picked up the scent of danger. The Were's eyes landed on Ava.

Immediately on guard and defensive, Damon angled his body, blocking the arrogant male's view. The male grinned, his white teeth gleaming under the lighting of the club.

Damon growled. Slowly, the male turned on his stood until he was facing the bartender, keeping his eyes on Damon in the reflection of the mirror behind the bar. From this distance he couldn't scent if the wolf was a red or a gray.

"What are you doing?" Ava shoved at his chest.

"Aw, honey, don't be too hard on him. Men who are that protective over their women are few and far between." Sherry Pie snorted. "Every guy in here wouldn't hesitate to let another man have you if the price was right."

Damon grimaced. "Are you saying they allow prostitution in here?"

Sherry narrowed her eyes at them. Her expression changed and he could feel her clamming up. "Hey, you're not some kind of cop are you?"

"Hell, no."

Sherry snorted as her face relaxed into a smile. "You never can tell these days."

"True. But I can assure you we're not cops. With his temper, he wouldn't last a week." Ava jerked her thumb at him.

"Me? What about you? You've got a temper as well."

"You are confusing temper with confidence."

Sherry Pie roared with laughter. "Girl, you'd make a fine dancer. I bet you wouldn't take shit off anyone."

"Really?" Ava's lips stretched into a glowing smile. "You really think I could dance?"

"Yep, there's not much to it. Why look at Shania Vain up there on stage." The waitress waved her hand in a dismissive gesture. "She isn't doing nothing but prancing around and humping the pole every few beats."

He turned his attention to the stage. The stripper in question must have been between beats because she wasn't humping the pole but sashaying around the stage as she cupped her tassel-clad tits. She paused and bent down to shake her boobs dangerously close to the male customers sitting along the edge of the stage.

"I could do better than that. At least I know how to dance."

He jerked his head toward Ava. "Your little ass isn't going to be stripping."

"Who said anything about stripping?" She shrugged her slim shoulders. "All I said was that I could dance better."

"This isn't a dance contest; it's a strip club." He narrowed his gaze. "The girls that work here are strippers, which you are not. Besides, we won't be here long enough for you to get into this line of employment."

"Actually, we do have an amateur night once a month." Sherry Pie popped her chewing gum.

"Do you get paid?" Ava looked at Sherry.

"Not by the club, but you do get to keep the money you get from the customers. The really pretty girls can make a killing." She gave Ava a cool once-over. "Why hell, I bet you could make over three hundred dollars."

Ava turned a hopeful smile on Damon. "It's a way for us to get some money for a room."

Damon's eye twitched. "No way in hell." He slapped his hands on the table and Sherry retreated two steps back to safety.

Ava gawked at him and he could tell she was struggling to keep silent. Biting her lip, she looked back toward the stage. "Fine, whatever."

We / we've gone

He ran his hand over his face. "We've are completely off track here." He glanced over at Sherry who'd edged closer to Ava.

"We were wondering if you knew anything about a guy named David Jenkins. We heard he hangs out here."

The waitress stopped chewing her gum, and her eyes hardened around the edges. He knew they had struck gold.

"Sherry, do you know David Jenkins?" Ava prodded.

"Yeah." The waitress swallowed hard, her eyes darting nervously between him and Ava.

"Sherry, we really need your help in finding David. We believe him to be a suspect in a kidnapping."

Sherry's eyes grew wide. "I thought you two said you weren't cops!" She took a step back.

"We're not. He took a girl, a friend of mine, and I'm not going to sit around on my ass and do nothing while the girl is in danger."

"Oh, God. He actually kidnapped a girl?" Sherry pursed her lips. "That asshole. I knew he was dangerous, but nobody ever listens to me." Sherry shook her head.

"So, you *do* know him."

Sherry nodded. "He comes in here every Saturday, you know, to watch amateur strip night. We get a lot of college girls coming in trying to earn a little extra money. Heard him tell the bartender he doesn't like the regular girls, said they were beneath him." Sherry snorted. "Like we could ever be lower than that piece of dog shit. The truth is none of the girls would give him the time of day. Didn't matter how many hundreds he would throw at them, no one ever left with him. He gives off this bad vibe, this evil that seems to cling to him."

"So, he only comes in to watch the college girls." Ava looked at him and gave him a knowing look. "Like LSU college girls?"

"Yeah, how'd you know?"

"Because the girl he kidnapped goes to LSU."

After leaving the strip club, they headed to the nearest coffee shop down the street.

Although it was Saturday night, it was relatively empty, which gave them plenty of time

to talk privately.

As Ava secured a corner table, Damon placed an order for two coffees and a couple of pastries he'd seen Ava drooling over.

Sitting across from Ava, he handed her a coffee and the plate of sweets.

"You are quickly using up your funds on my eating habits." She shook her head.

"You want me to take this back?" He reached for the plate, but she batted his hand away.

"Never mind. I don't mind sleeping under a bridge." She took a sip of her coffee and grimaced. "I was hoping this coffee was better than the hotel. I guess I'm just used to mine." She glanced at the sweets and licked her lips. "How'd you know I was lusting after these?"

Damon imagined tracing his tongue over her lips and he froze. His jeans grew uncomfortably tighter as he stared at her mouth.

She looked up and smiled.

"I saw you looking at them when you came in." The corners of his lips curled up into a grin. "So you have a sweet tooth, do you?"

"I usually don't like sweets that much. I don't usually eat like I've been doing today." She sighed. "Must be all this nervous energy." She cut the pastry and forked a bite into her mouth.

"That's really good." She closed her eyes and moaned.

"Keep that up and you're going to make me jealous of a pastry."

Her eyes opened. "You have no competition. I'd much rather be tasting you right now."

Lust licked deep in his belly. He wanted to be inside her this second. He gazed at the restroom door.

"Oh, no. I refuse to have sex in a bathroom." She wrinkled up her nose. "So unsanitary."

"Even if I hold you up?" He grinned at her.

"Yes." She arched her brow. "Plus, the next time I get you naked it's not going to be quick. I want you all night, for hours."

He held up his hands. "Okay, okay, stop. I'm seconds away from ruining my jeans if you keep up the dirty talk."

She laughed low and took another bite.

"What's the next step? We know David will be heading over to the Beaver tonight."

"No, we don't. He only shows up on amateur night." He opened his mouth when she offered him a bite. The pastry melted on his tongue.

"Yep, and guess what tonight is?" She waggled her eyebrows. "Amateur night."

"How the hell did you find that out?"

"Sherry told me when you went to the bathroom. She said they had a lot of girls signed up and said I should do it too."

"No fucking way."

She gave him another eye roll. "The point is Jenkins is probably going to show tonight. And we need to be ready."

"You're not going anywhere near that bastard." He curled his fingers into fists.

"Where do you suggest I go? We don't have a room or any money to get a room."

He took his cell phone out of his jacket. "I'll call Jayden. I'm sure we can stay with him, if he'd bother to ever answer his fucking phone." He punched in redial and waited. After going to voicemail, he left another message and disconnected.

"Do you mind if I used your phone? I'd like to call my father." Ava pushed her plate away and sipped on her coffee.

He shook his head. "It's not safe. Barrett is the only one with a secured line and I don't want those rogue wolves tracing us here."

"Now what?"

"We'll just head back to the casino and I'll ask Jayden if he can watch you while I go back to the club."

"You don't need to go after him by yourself." She frowned at him

"I'll call Jeff and see if he can lend me one of his bouncers and a van. Once I grab him, I'll take him back to Jeff's and question him. The quicker we find Haley the better."

She looked at him. "In my heart I believe she's alive. I can't explain it. I don't know if it's rational or not, but I don't want to lose hope." She looked away. "And if she's dead, I hope that it was quick and that he didn't torture her. Because if he did, I'm going to kill him myself."

He reached across the table for her hand.

"Doesn't matter if he killed her or not, he's on my radar which makes him a dead man walking.

"Good." She picked up his hand and kissed his knuckles. At that very moment, Damon Trahan's heart swelled. An unfamiliar emotion swamped him and his chest tightened. He'd never felt a bond, a closeness with another person in all his years. It was like being in a cold, dark hole for years and finally escaping to be engulfed with the warmth of the sun. It filtered through every cell in his body, touching places that had been long dead.

He swallowed, admitting what he'd already known. He was in love with Ava Renfroe. Loving her would be the end of him.

Ava stood at Damon's side while the front desk clerk at the casino paged Jayden.

"What's keeping him?" Damon growled. The passing hotel guests were smart enough to give him a wide berth. "Jayden should have shown up by now."

"Maybe he had to go to Granny's house."

He pulled out his phone and called Granny.

"Well, do you know where he is?" He finally asked halfway into an obviously lengthy conversation.

After a few more seconds, he hung up.

"I take it he's not there." She threaded her fingers through Damon's.

"No." He grimaced. "But, Granny did mention she was having another sex party tonight and invited you."

"That sounds fun." She gave him a big grin.

"There's going to be male strippers." He narrowed his eyes.

"Sounds even better. I should bring the chip and dip."

"This automatically counts you out."

She stuck out her tongue. "You're no fun at all."

"Baby, I'm a lot of fun." His intense stare melted her insides, making her feel all hot and gooey.

"I bet you are." She stuck her hands in the back pockets of her jeans. A couple of guys stumbled as they walked by, too focused on looking at her.

She didn't struggle when he wrapped his arms around her waist and pulled her into him. His hard chest muscles teased her nipples, making them pebble and ache.

"You're going to cause those guys to get their asses beat if they keep looking at you." His hot breath tickled her ear and she shivered.

"What? I'm not doing anything." She gave him her best innocent look.

"You don't have to. All you have to do is stand there." His hands caressed up and down her back.

She couldn't resist. Leaning in, she kissed him hard and deep. When she pulled away, she nipped at his bottom lip.

"You keep that up, I'll throw you over my shoulder and find the nearest corner." He playfully slapped her on the ass. "Besides, we've got to find a place for you to stay while I get David Jenkins."

"There's always Granny's." She smiled wide.

"No."

"Can I hang out at Jeff's bar?"

He shook his head. "Jeff's bar is too dangerous."

"You keep forgetting that I work in a bar."

"You're a bartender at a restaurant. This is a biker bar. A Were biker bar. Two totally different things."

She gave him a droll look. "I also worked at the Mule." The Mule was the only bar near Jonesboro that catered strictly to bikers. No Harley meant no admittance.

"Are you kidding me?" He looked horrified. "Do you know how dangerous it is to work in that bar?"

"That's why I keep a sawed-off shotgun behind the counter. And the Judge. That sucker will put a hole through you the size of a melon."

"You ever use it?"

"One time."

"You've killed someone?" His eyes widened.

"Not exactly. He dove under the pool table, and I ended up shooting the door." She grimaced. "My aim was off. The owner had to order a whole new door and took it out of my pay."

"What did he do to make you shoot him?"

"He put his hand on one of the waitresses."

He grinned and pulled her close. "That's my girl."

"I'll be perfectly safe at the bar, as long as Jeff gives me access to a weapon."

"Come on, Sarah Conner. Let's get you weaponed up."

The parking lot of Remus and Romulus was already crowded and it was only nine o'clock. After a scan of the area, Damon led Ava up to the front door. A large Were stood blocking the entrance, arms crossed. Damon nodded once at the bouncer and he moved aside, allowing them entrance.

Holding Ava's hand, he pulled her beside him. "Stay close."

A couple of humans stared at Ava until he let out a lethal growl.

"Easy there, boy." Ava ran her hand up and down his arm.

"They're looking at you."

"Lots of men look at me."

"Doesn't mean I have to like it."

"Damon, I can take care of myself." She kissed him. Before he knew what he was doing, he had her tight, crushing her into his chest. He thought she might fight him, or pull away, embarrassed by the public affection. God knew Laura had done that plenty of times. Laura always told him kissing in public wasn't appropriate behavior. Looking back on it now, it was probably because she didn't want her lover catching her.

Not Ava. She already had her arms locked around his neck. He waited for the panic to set in, but it didn't.

Her lithe body rubbed against his, her curves pressed into his muscles. She moaned into his mouth and male satisfaction surge through his veins, knowing she wanted him just as much as he wanted her.

"Damon, do you need to use the room in the back, boy?"

Jeff's booming voice had him slowly pulling away from Ava and turning to face the man.

"Don't call me 'boy.'" He grimaced at Jeff.

"I'm older. That makes you a boy." Jeff looked from him to Ava. "Hello, beautiful. Is this boy treating you all right?"

"He could be treating me better if we could use your room in the back." She waggled her eyebrows.

Jeff blinked and then roared with laughter. "Damn, Damon, you lucky son of a bitch."

He shot Ava a look. She just shrugged, her attention snagged by a waitress passing by carrying a huge cheeseburger. She licked her lips.

"Are you hungry?" He frowned.

"Yeah. It seems those pastries I ate didn't stick."

He reached for his wallet and pulled out a twenty.

"No. You've already spent too much money on me. Besides we need money to rent a room." She shoved the twenty back at him.

"Ava, I'm not going to let you starve."

She huffed. "I'm not going to starve. I've eaten enough for a hibernating bear."

"Don't say bear!" Jeff's brows knit together in frustration.

"Don't tell me, there are Were bears?" She gave him a droll look.

"Yeah. And a couple of them from New Orleans came in a few months back. There was a huge fight, tore the place up pretty good. Just got it looking nice again." Jeff puffed out his chest.

"This is nice?" She scanned the interior walls. Old car tags from around the world were nailed on every inch of space. She gave Jeff a doubtful look.

"I was wondering if Ava could stay here while I go handle some business." He kept his voice low.

"Here? You want to leave her here? In a wolf bar?" Jeff raised an eyebrow.

"The way you say that, Jeff, is not making me have warm fuzzies about your fine establishment." She looked between him and Jeff.

"I can't take her to the Beaver Tail."

"More like he won't let me go to the Beaver Tail." Ava crossed her arms over her chest and proceeded to pout.

"She'd probably be safer at the Beaver than here, Damon." Jeff shrugged.

"Are you fucking kidding me?"

"Well, yeah. I mean, have you seen the security they got over at the Beaver? If a male says something wrong to a female they get their asses kicked out in a hurry." Jeff swept his hand across the room. "I don't have enough bouncers here tonight, and I'm stuck behind the bar since the damn bartender called in sick."

A slow smile crept across his face. "Well, you just happen to be in luck because Ava here is a bartender."

CHAPTER NINE

"Is that right, honey?" Jeff asked.

She nodded and smiled.

"Well, why didn't you say so? Sure she can stay." Jeff's face broke out into a smile.

"Good, I should be back around midnight. If I'm lucky, I'll be bringing a guest." Damon let out a breath. At least he knew she would be safe with Jeff watching over her.

Jeff nodded. "The workers know not to go in the back room."

"Good." He turned his attention to Ava, who snagged a French fry off a passing tray. She gave him a sheepish smile after she stuffed the evidence in her mouth.

"Stay behind the bar with Jeff."

"What if I have to go to the bathroom?"

"Then Jeff will wait outside the door." Damon gave Jeff a heavy stare. "Feed her before she starts working." He handed him a twenty, but Jeff waved it away.

"All my employees get a free meal when they're working."

He nodded, but handed her the twenty anyway.

"I'll be okay. I can handle myself."

"Just like with those kidnappers."

She scowled at him. "They drugged me. It wasn't a fair fight. If it was, I would have ripped their dicks off and shoved them up their asses."

"Nice visual." He cringed.

"Thanks." She slid closer. "Be careful."

"I always am."

"And no lap dances." She stuck a finger in his face for emphasis.

"Only if you're doing the dancing."

"And no slipping money in a G-string." She narrowed her eyes.

He smiled. He liked her being jealous, not that she would have any reason to be. After her, no woman would ever mean anything else to him.

"You have nothing to worry about." He held her close and kissed the side of her neck. Opening his mouth, he let his teeth graze her shoulder. He wished they were alone so he could run his mouth down the rest of her body.

Her hand skated under the front of his T-shirt as she trailed her nails down his skin. He growled against her neck. "Female, you're driving me crazy."

"This is nothing." Her deep sultry voice was making it hard to concentrate.

Reluctantly, he pulled away from her. For once in his life, he really didn't want to do his job. For once, all he wanted was to stay with Ava.

"Jeff will look after you."

"I'm going to take care of her, Damon. Don't worry." Jeff slapped him on the back as he passed by.

He kissed her hard before turning toward the door. He grinned as Ava spoke to Jeff.

"So, Jeff, what kind of gun do you carry behind the bar?"

Damon shouldered his way through the crowded strip club and eased onto a corner bar stool with his back to the wall.

The club reeked of smoke and sweat, making his stomach turn. Hopefully, he could get what he wanted and get out.

He glanced at the stage and frowned. There were still professional strippers dancing. He glanced at his watch. Amateur dancing should have started by now.

He ordered a shot of Grey Goose. The bartender with sleeve tattoos and spiky, blue-tipped hair met his gaze. His informant. The bartender turned away as he filled Damon's order. It gave him a moment to think about Ava. He ran his hands through his hair, irritated at himself for leaving her alone in that damn bar.

She wasn't exactly alone. Jeff was there and had promised to look after her. But still, he didn't like it.

Shaking his head, he pushed away his irrational worries and scanned the bar, looking for David Jenkins.

The strippers had more rhythm than what he and Ava had seen earlier that day. The club probably saved their better dancers for the night crowd.

A group of college-aged guys lined up around the end of the stage waving dollar bills as the voluptuous stripper jiggled her huge tits in their faces.

"I bet you don't usually order Grey Goose. I bet you're usually a Jack Daniels man." The tattooed bartender slid him the shot of vodka across the counter.

Damon narrowed his gaze. "I heard you got some information for me."

A drunken frat boy wearing a purple LSU sweatshirt stumbled into Damon before slamming his hand down on the table. "Give me a round of tequila shots."

Damon flinched, fisting his hands to keep from punching the guy. Now was not the time to cause a scene.

The bartender ignored the guy and continued drying a glass with his bar towel. "I think you've had enough, son."

"Look here asshole, you're not my mommy. I got money and I want my tequila shots." The frat boy slapped a hundred-dollar bill on the bar.

Damon turned toward the college guy. "I think you better listen to him and walk away."

The frat boy faced Damon, looking him up and down before turning his lip up in disgust. "Do you know who I am, Scarface? My father is Senator Harris."

Rage boiled over in his chest, and he grabbed the kid's hand and wrapped it behind his back. Frat boy screamed like a little girl.

Leaning near his ear, he growled. "That shit doesn't fly in here. I could rip out your fucking throat and disembowel you before you take your next breath. And no one in here would ever breathe a word about it. Your little daddy would never find enough of you to bury, you piece of shit."

The scent of fear rolled off the boy, fueling his rage.

"I'm sorry! I'm sorry! I didn't mean anything by it, man!" The guy's breath was coming in small pants and he appeared to be on the verge of passing out.

"Here's what you're going to do. You're going to apologize to the bartender for calling him names because I know your daddy didn't raise you to be a dickhead, now did he?"

"I'm sorry! I'm sorry, man. I didn't mean what I said. It's the alcohol; it makes me act like an asshole." The kid turned his panicked gaze on the amused bartender.

"Now, you're going to get your college buddies and get the fuck out of here because I know you dickheads have a curfew."

"Okay, okay, just let me go." His voice turned into the whine of a child.

"You guys aren't coming back in here, are you?"

"No! I won't, I swear! Hell, the only reason I came was to see amateur night."

Damon slowly let go of frat boy. The guy bolted and ran headlong into a waitress, sending alcohol and glass flying across the floor. He tried to stand up as another waitress came with a towel to help clean, but ended up slipping and busting his ass. He sent out a yell that even made Damon cringe.

His buddies pulled him up and escorted him out.

Damon turned back to the bartender.

"Appreciate the help, man." The bartender slid a shot of Jack Daniel's in front of him. "Here, on the house."

"Thanks." He tossed the amber liquid back, letting it burn a fiery trail down his throat.

"No problem. The name's Braxton." He stuck out his hand and Damon accepted it.

"Damon." He nodded toward the door where the college group exited. "He's too fucking young to even be in here."

"Tell me about it. I told the bouncer to make sure and check for IDs. I'm sure that little prick and his gang slipped the bouncer a hundred to get in." Braxton shook his head in disgust.

"I'm not surprised." Damon shrugged.

"The sad thing is he only came tonight with his buddies to see his girlfriend strip."

His head jerked up. "His girlfriend's a stripper? Aren't they a little old for him?"

Braxton shook his head. "She's not regular dancer. She's a college girl. His girlfriend was going to strip for amateur night. It got canceled until tomorrow night and he ended up staying anyway."

"Wait. They canceled amateur night?"

Braxton narrowed his eyes in suspicion. "Don't tell me you were here to watch the college girls strip for money."

"I was waiting on someone to show up. Apparently, he only shows up on amateur night." He gritted his teeth.

"Let me guess. This guy isn't a friend. Is this Pack business?"

Damon bowed up. Damn, this guy was a wolf. How the hell had he missed it?

Braxton smiled. "Relax. The only reason you couldn't smell me is all the damn smoke in this building. I swear I think I've got black lung. Besides I'm not in a Pack, too damn many rules for me."

"You work in a strip club. Why not work at Jeff's and bartend there? At least you wouldn't be around so many humans."

"Actually, I used to work at Jeff's, until . . ." The bartender looked away.

"Until what?" Damon cocked his head.

Braxton looked pained. "Until he caught me banging his daughter in the kitchen."

Damon's mouth fell open. "Jeff has a daughter?"

"I know, right! I had no idea he was ever mated. When this hot-looking blonde came in one night, we got to talking and one thing led to another, and the next thing I knew..."

"You were in the kitchen on the butcher block."

"Well, not me. She was the one lying on the table." Braxton shook his head. "Anyway, the next thing I know I'm looking down the barrel of a sawed-off shotgun aimed at my dick."

"Damn." He shook his head and grinned, looking into his empty shot glass.

"I ended up getting a job here. You'd be surprised how wolves are more ethical than humans."

"Actually, I wouldn't." Not after the hell he had gone through when he was younger.

"These young girls coming up from LSU, just to strip for money on amateur night, well, it's pathetic. When we had to turn them away because it was postponed until tomorrow, you would have thought someone had died."

"Why did they postpone it?" He clenched his shot glass.

"There was a football game tonight, and they figured it wouldn't be much of a turnout."

"Shit."

"Are you going to let me know exactly who you're looking for? Or, do you want to play twenty questions?"

The bartender seemed to have his moral compass set in the right spot, the question was, could he trust him? He knew from experience people could turn on you in a second, human or wolf.

"Look, man. I'm just offering. No pressure." Braxton held his hands up defensively before turning his attention back to fill a drink order. He filled two mugs with beer and placed them on a tray for a waitress to pick up. The waitress gave him a wink and Braxton shook his head.

"I'm looking for a guy named David Jenkins. I don't have a picture, but I was hoping you might remember him."

Braxton straightened, recognition filling his eyes before his mouth turned into a straight line. "Yeah, I know that asshole. You better hope you get to him before I do."

"Why is that?"

"Fucker took a baseball bat to my Harley."

"Are you shitting me?" Damaging someone's Harley was like fucking someone's mate.

"He came in here one night messing with one of the dancers. When she told him she was a stripper and not a hooker he slapped the shit out of her. I took his ass out back and beat the shit out of the bastard. The bouncers had to pull me off him. He threatened to sue the club."

"What happened?" He tensed and leaned in. If David Jenkins was brave enough to slap a stripper in a room full of witnesses, then he wouldn't hesitate to torture a female in private.

"The club thought about firing me, but all the dancers said they would all walk out if they did. They said I was the only one here looking out for the girls. So, they put me on probation." Braxton shrugged his tattooed shoulders.

"And your bike?"

Braxton snorted. "Here's the kicker. He came in one night while I was working the bar. Didn't say anything, in fact he didn't stay fifteen minutes. When I got off work, I walked around back and that's when I saw my bike had been beat to shit."

"Why didn't the police get him?"

"I called the cops and made a report, even told them he did it. But they said there wasn't enough evidence to support my claims." Braxton shook his head. "Total bullshit."

"How do you keep from killing him when he comes in?" He almost hit a guy for touching his bike one night at a bar in Fayetteville.

"For one, I need this job. The Packs in Louisiana won't hire me as a Guardian since Jeff threw his weight around. Right now, this is my only option."

"Leave the state."

"My mom's here and I can't leave her, not now." Braxton averted his gaze.

"Bring her with you."

Braxton shook his head and grimaced. "My mom won't leave my father."

Understanding dawned and Damon realized more about the situation than Braxton was voicing. "Is he abusive?"

"Yes." Braxton scowled.

"I take it you try to set the bastard straight?"

"Multiple times. All that did was get my mom upset. I don't say anything to her anymore about her leaving. I can't leave her, not yet."

Damon's respect for the guy grew tenfold. Sticking around to protect his mother without killing his father took a lot of patience.

"I take it you're not with any of the Louisiana Packs."

"How'd you guess?" He gave a wry smile.

"You don't seem like the ass kisser sort," Braxton added dryly.

He barked out a laugh. "You're right, I'm not. In fact, I got kicked out of the Louisiana Pack a few years back. Now, I'm in Arkansas."

"Really? You like the Arkansas group?"

To be honest, he hadn't really thought about whether he liked the members of the Pack, or not. He never really made an attempt to join in whenever they all went out. Maybe he should have made more of an effort.

"It's as good as any, I guess."

Braxton nodded. "Barrett Middleton is over the Arkansas territory, isn't he?"

"Yeah. You know him?"

Braxton grinned. "I know his reputation. He doesn't tolerate a whole lot of bullshit."

He snorted. "No, he doesn't. I wouldn't want to cross him."

"Maybe if my situation ever changes, I'll look you guys up."

"Do that." Damon nodded and shoved his glass back.

"Since Jenkins didn't show, I'm assuming you'll be back tomorrow night."

"Count on it. Will you be here?" He arched an eyebrow.

Braxton shook his head. "I'm not supposed to be working when Jenkins comes in. It's part of my probation. That's why they let me work tonight. They knew he wouldn't show when amateur night was canceled."

Damon nodded and stood. Pulling out one of his last twenty-dollar bills, Damon stuffed it in Braxton's tip jar before leaving.

"This is like porn for your mouth."

Ava smirked and stood a little taller as she looked at her customer sitting at the bar. The guy in a black wife beater, leather vest and jeans carefully held his chocolate martini glass in both hands. He was the size of a Mack truck and looked totally out of place drinking a girlie drink.

"Yes and it would be even better if Jeff carried Grey Goose." She cut her gaze at the owner.

"You know how much that shit costs?" Jeff slapped his towel on the bar and propped a hand on his hip.

"You can't make a decent chocolate martini without Grey Goose." She turned and faced him, mimicking his stance. "It's blasphemy."

"Seagram's is cheap and Seagram's is what I got."

She breathed out a sigh of frustration.

"It tastes like the bomb to me." The biker sighed in delight.

"Thanks, I think." She shook her head. "What's your name?"

The biker set his martini glass down. "Rusty."

She rested her forearms on the smooth surface of the counter. "Rusty, what if I said I could make a better martini if I had some Grey Goose. Would you be willing to pay the extra money?"

"Hell, yeah." His bushy eyebrows shot up, and his goatee did a little excited shake when he grinned. "I don't see how you could make a better drink than this right here." He looked at the martini with reverence in his eyes.

She turned toward Jeff. "See, Rusty's willing to pay extra for the good stuff."

Jeff rubbed the back of his neck. "I don't know, Ava. Chocolate martinis in a Were biker bar just doesn't seem right."

Ava arched her eyebrow. "You know, I'm surprised you even had the chocolate liqueur."

"It was left over from a bachelorette party a few weeks back."

"All I'm saying…" Her words trailed off to a whisper as a delicious sensation hit her deep in her stomach.

Damon.

She didn't have to turn around to know he'd just walked through the door. Closing her eyes, she inhaled. His male scent of sandalwood and leather seeped through every cell in her body and made her tingle in the most inappropriate places.

"Hey." The deep timbre of his voice had her turning around.

"Hey." She opened her eyes and cleared her throat. "You're back early. Did everything go okay?" Damn, he looked good. Real good. Good enough to eat.

He eased himself onto the bar stool with that dangerous air that seemed to surround him. She bit her lip thinking about how he didn't wear underwear under his tight jeans.

He gave Jeff a nod and the owner slid a whiskey over to him. Damn, she should've been the one to do that.

"Jenkins didn't show. It seems amateur night got canceled."

Rusty nodded his large head. "Yep, LSU is playing tonight. Can't do amateur night when LSU is playing. It's the law."

"There isn't no damn law about LSU and amateur night at the strip club," Jeff snarled.

"Might as well be in these parts. People take their college football very seriously in the South." Rusty nodded.

Damon watched Rusty as he took another sip and sighed.

He studied Rusty's glass. "What the hell are you drinking?"

"Chocolate martini." Rusty held out his glass. "Want a sip?"

His lip curled up in a sneer. "Hell, no."

"Don't dismiss a drink because of its name." She narrowed her eyes.

"We could name it something else, like orgasm." Rusty sighed.

"I think that name's already taken." She reached for her shaker and rinsed it off under the faucet.

"I take it there were no problems tonight?" Damon's gaze landed on her and seemed to linger a little too long. All of a sudden it was sweltering in the bar. She grabbed the bar towel with her trembling hands, then quickly proceeded to dry the tumbler, hoping Damon hadn't seen her reaction.

"Nope. Some males tried to get close but quickly realized she was scented. After that they kept a respectful distance."

She frowned. Lifting her arm above her head, she turned her head and discreetly sniffed.

Nope. No body odor. She smelled like soap.

"What do you mean scented? Is that some kind of wolf thing?" She looked between the men.

Rusty barked out a laugh. "It means you have a male's scent on you, warning the other males that you are taken." He jerked a thumb in Damon's direction. "And the scent they smelled belongs to your mate here."

"We're not mated." Even though she answered in unison with Damon, it hurt a little that he was so quick to not link himself with her.

"Whatever." Rusty pushed his large frame off the stool and stood. He reached in his wallet and pulled out a couple of twenties, sliding them across the counter to her. "Thanks, Ava. Will you be back tomorrow?"

"No, she won't" Damon answered a little too quickly.

Rusty gave her a serious stare. "It's a shame. You need to teach Jeff how to make them martinis before you leave tonight."

"I am not making any damn chocolate martinis. I told you I don't do pussy drinks." Jeff's voice boomed from the kitchen.

"Sounds like you handled yourself tonight." Damon reached across the counter. When his fingertips wrapped around her wrist, she sucked in a breath. Absently, his thumb began to rub tiny circles at her pulse point at her wrist. She was sure her heart was going to jump out of her chest.

"Did you eat?"

"Yeah, Jeff fed me before I started bartending. Did you?"

He shook his head.

She pulled out of his grip and walked back into the kitchen. She reappeared a few minutes later with a hot bowl of chili, and a thick slice of Italian bread and placed it in front of him.

Ignoring the food, he pulled her between his legs as he kissed her. The kiss began gentle but soon grew more urgent as his tongue licked the seam of her lips.

She wrapped her arms around his neck, clinging to him as her body came alive. She parted her lips, letting his tongue possess her mouth. His tongue darted and licked every inch of her mouth until she could no longer fight back a moan.

"All right, all right. Cut that out." Jeff's voice had them reluctantly pulling away from each other.

She opened her eyes and tried to catch her breath. He always did that to her, stole her breath, stole her mind, stole her soul.

Silence filled the bar. Looking around, she saw all the werewolves in the place looking at her with glowing yellow eyes.

Damon stood, his muscles straining through the thin long sleeved T-shirt. He pushed her behind him, trying to block the other werewolves view. He growled as one Were took a step towards them.

"Damon?" She pressed against his back, as dread pitted in the base of her stomach.

He didn't move. His growl grew louder and for once, she was a little afraid of him.

One werewolf wearing a sleeveless leather jacket took a step forward. She cringed as Damon pushed her further behind him until the bar counter pressed into her back.

Damon's menacing growl seemed to go on and on.

"What's going on?"

"They are challenging Damon for rights to you."

Jeff moved to her side holding the sawed-off shotgun.

She pressed her cheek against Damon's T-shirt, trying to keep from trembling. Standing on her tiptoes, she peered around his shoulder. The group of werewolves stood shoulder to shoulder, craning their heads to see her, their eyes glowing a strange yellow color.

She narrowed her eyes on the closest male. When she met his gaze, his nostrils flared and he reached down to stroke himself through his jeans.

Disgusted and scared, she snarled.

"You both need to get the hell out of here." Jeff's voice was strained, the shotgun aimed at the nearest werewolf.

"I'm going to kill you all for even looking at what is mine."

Ava felt the raw anger in Damon's voice. Unexplainable excitement quivered through her body, and she pressed herself more tightly into his strong back.

For the very first time, he was publicly claiming her.

And, now, they'd probably both end up dead.

He had perfect timing.

"Damon, you need to get her out of here, now." Jeff moved to stand beside him, his shotgun sweeping the room, ready for one of the werewolves to take another step.

Without looking away from the motley crew, Damon reached for her hand and placed it directly across his cock.

Her breath caught in her throat. He was hard, his erection straining against the zipper of his jeans.

Her fingers gripped his erection through the denim and she squeezed.

Something was so desperately wrong with her to be so turned on by Damon's possessiveness.

The other werewolf's eyes locked on her hand and they all let out a wail.

"It's bloodlust." Jeff answered her unasked question. "When wolves fight, it excites them sexually. He's making it clear that he is willing to fight to the death to keep the other wolves away from you."

She should have moved her hand away. After all, it was the decent thing to do. It was uncomfortable having all these males staring at her touching Damon so intimately. For some reason she couldn't stop.

She glanced at Jeff, making sure he wasn't watching her with those same yellow eyes as the others. Jeff faced straight ahead, obscuring her view.

"Tell him you want to leave, Ava. He won't listen to anyone other than his mate."

"I'm not his mate." She bit her lip.

Jeff snorted. "A male would only fight to the death for his mate. There are too many for us to fight and survive. If you don't get him out of here now, this will be the last night he walks this earth."

The thought struck her like a hot knife in her stomach. If she hadn't been sandwiched between the bar counter and Damon she would have fallen to her knees.

Swallowing back the pain in her throat, she pressed her lips to Damon's neck. "Damon, take me out of here."

She'd been prepared to argue with him, but his reaction was immediate.

He swiveled, and in one graceful motion swung her up into his arms. The werewolves slowly advanced.

"Ava, tell him you want to leave now." Jeff's voice was calm as he took a step in front of them, leveling his shotgun at the nearest werewolf.

Urgency hit her like a ton of bricks. Tightening her arms around Damon's neck, she pressed her lips to his ear.

"Baby, I want to leave, right now." She caught the lobe of his ear between her teeth and nipped.

He growled and looked at her.

She gasped. His blue eyes were gone, replaced by the same startling shade of yellow as the other werewolves.

He looked away and took a step toward the kitchen. A werewolf tried to follow them, but Jeff slammed the butt of the gun against his head. The guy stumbled to the ground.

Damon growled and carried her across the threshold to the kitchen. In the next moment, she heard the shotgun blast.

She screamed and buried her face into Damon's neck, clinging to him.

Once outside, she expected Damon to set her down, but he didn't. Instead, he carried her to his bike and set her on it.

The Harley roared to life as they peeled out of the parking lot, sending loose gravel flying behind them. She wrapped her arms around his waist and held on tight.

His hand covered hers and gave her a reassuring squeeze. He turned off the highway and headed out of town until the streetlights grew fewer and fewer.

"Where are we going?" she yelled over the roar of the motorcycle. "The casino is the other way."

"We're headed to Granny's."

"Is Jayden there?"

"I have no idea. He still isn't answering his cell phone. All the calls are going straight to voicemail. The casino said they haven't seen him for hours."

Her stomach felt like heavy mud. Something was very wrong.

"If anyone knows where he is, it will be Granny."

CHAPTER TEN

Damon pulled into Granny's driveway after midnight. Her powder-blue Oldsmobile was parked in the carport, but Jayden's Mustang was nowhere in sight.

Killing the engine, Damon helped Ava off before hopping off the bike himself.

"What if she's asleep?" The moonlight illuminated the worry etched on her beautiful face.

"Even if she is, I don't think she'll mind a late-night visit. Especially from you."

Ava wrinkled her brow. "From me?"

"Yeah, Granny likes you. I can tell."

"Really? How do you know?"

He hesitated for a second. "You're the first female she's ever claimed was my mate."

He watched Ava's brow relax, her lips curling up into a sexy grin.

"Who's out there?" Granny called out from the front door. The flick of the outside porch light lit up the yard.

"It's Damon and Ava." He waited a second before stepping further into the light. For all he knew Granny was pointing her late husband's rifle at them.

The screen door opened and Granny stepped out onto the porch wearing a purple Muumuu and fuzzy pink slippers, her hair wrapped in some kind of scarf. "Well, why didn't you two say so? Come in." She held the door open as they stepped across the threshold, pausing to give them each hugs.

"What are you two doing here at this hour?" Granny asked as she locked the front door. Damon frowned as he counted five locks on the door, two of them deadbolts.

"We're looking for Jayden."

Granny turned toward him, concern creasing her already wrinkled brow. "Isn't he at the casino?"

"We tried calling his cell phone, but it goes straight to voicemail. The casino says they've not seen him for hours." He shrugged. "Is he dating someone, Granny? Someone he might be with right now?"

Granny shook her head in quick, short jerks. "No, no one. This isn't like Jayden to not answer his phone." Her eyebrows shot up. "I'll call. He always answers when he sees it's me." Granny headed into the kitchen, her slippers making scuffing noises against the black-and-white linoleum.

He nodded in agreement, but deep in his gut he knew something was wrong.

A minute later, Granny returned wearing a grim expression. "I didn't get an answer."

"Okay, let's not start worrying until we have something to worry about," Ava said.

Granny worried her chest with the palm of her hand as her brows knitted together. Ava took her by the elbow and led the old lady into her worn recliner. "Damon, why don't you go into the kitchen and get Granny a glass of water." She looked over her shoulder at him and knelt at Granny's knees.

His heart warmed at Ava's compassion.

Granny turned toward Ava, a slight smile playing on the corners of her lips. "You are a good girl, Ava." She cupped Ava's cheek in her palm. "I hope Jayden can find a female like you."

Ava patted Granny's hand, brushing aside the comment. Looking back over her shoulder, her eyes met his. "Damon, the water?"

"Forget the water. Get me a shot of Wild Turkey. It's in the cabinet behind the sugar bowl."

He returned with a double shot of her favorite Kentucky bourbon in a crystal wineglass when he couldn't find a shot glass.

"Oh. This is much nicer than a shot glass, more sophisticated."

He grimaced as the old lady took a bigger drink than he would have without blinking.

He sat down on the floor by Ava and wrapped his arm loosely about her shoulders.

"When was the last time you heard from Jayden?" Ava looked up at Granny as she leaned back and rested against his chest. She never failed to steal his breath with just her touch.

"This morning. He calls every morning to check on me." Granny frowned before taking another sip.

"That means we were the last ones to see him." Ava turned her face up to him. "Do you know who he was going to meet with regarding the kidnapping?"

"Kidnapping? What kidnapping?" Granny sat forward so fast her Wild Turkey sloshed across her wrinkled hand.

"Granny, I don't think you need to know the details."

"Damon Trahan, don't you try to leave me out of this. I know you want to protect me, but Jayden is my grandson, and I want to know what's going on." She pursed her lips and scowled as she dotted her hand with a tissue she'd miraculously pulled out of her sleeve.

Damon blew out a breath, debating how much to reveal.

"It all started when I was kidnapped by some rogue wolves." Ava frowned and looked at Damon. "Didn't you say they were red wolves?"

Okay, so much for keeping things on the down low.

"Red wolves? That's impossible." Granny shook her head and frowned.

"Damon rescued me and now I can't go home because they bombed my house in Arkansas. That's how we ended up here in Louisiana. Soon after we arrived we discovered another female wolf was kidnapped by someone named

David Jenkins. We've been trying to locate her before something horrible happens." She took a deep breath.

Yep, so much for being invisible. He nudged her with his knee.

Ava gave him an innocent look. "What?"

"Remind me not to tell you anything top secret."

"You think these wolves knew Jayden was helping you and snatched him for some Intel?" Granny's face took on a look of hardened determination. She took another gulp of her Wild Turkey.

He shook his head. "Maybe he just hooked up with a stripper from the Beaver and went down to New Orleans for the weekend."

"Nope, not my Jayden." Granny pursed her lips together.

He gave her a disbelieving look. "Right. What was I thinking? Jayden wouldn't do something like that." Jayden got more pussy in a week than most men got in a month.

Granny scowled. "Okay, maybe he would, but he wouldn't have left and not said anything to me about going out of town. That much I'm sure." Granny drained her glass and slammed it down on the scarred rectangular coffee table. The old lady hoisted herself out of her chair and stood, her balance better than what Damon was expecting.

"Maybe if we find David Jenkins we'll find Jayden. And Haley." Ava stood, keeping her hand on Granny's arm.

"So where do we start?" Granny and Ava both looked at him.

He held his hands up. "Now hold on a second, neither of you are going anywhere near David Jenkins."

"Who says we're going anywhere near him? We could be your eyes and ears," Granny pleaded.

"Hell, no." He shook his head until it felt like it would fall off. "Look, we don't even know where to start."

"Yes we do. You said Jenkins was going to show at the Beaver tomorrow night." Ava raised an eyebrow at him.

"The Beaver. Why those girls are my best clients!" Granny clapped her hands and gave them a hopeful smile.

"Your clients?" Damon was afraid to ask.

"Clients from my sex parties. Why those girls were dropping three hundred dollars apiece at the last party. I sold out of my crotchless edible panties." Granny frowned in concentration. "Several of the girls had items on backorder. They just came in a couple of days ago. I need to deliver their orders and the Beaver is the perfect place to do that."

Ava turned to Granny. "Are those things really good? The edible panties?"

"The strawberry and the green apple are quite tasty. I don't really like the grape flavor, tastes too much like cough syrup."

He cringed. Holy shit. There was an image he could do without. "There's nothing we can do tonight."

"You and Ava will stay here. It's too late to be out on the roads on that death trap."

"It's not a death trap. It's a Harley," he grumbled.

"Hit a deer with that thing and tell me it's not a death trap." Granny waved for them to follow her down the hall.

"This room used to be Damon's when he lived here." Granny flipped the light switch.

He was surprised that everything still looked the same, except not. His twin bed sat in the middle of the room with a different comforter of soft floral colors instead of the blue and white plaid he remembered. The supermodel posters were gone, replaced with paintings of birds and flowers. But one thing stayed the same. She hadn't moved his model cars off his dresser. There they sat, perched on white crocheted doilies.

It meant a lot that Granny hadn't tried to erase him out of her life.

"How are we both going to fit in that bed?" Ava was trying hard not to grin.

His dick hardened. "I'll show you."

"Absolutely not." Granny propped her hands on her hips.

"We're adults." He scowled.

"And according to you, you are not mated to each other." Granny lifted her chin.

He took a deep breath. "Wait a minute. Are you're telling me I can't share a bed with Ava?"

"Yep."

"But you sell sex toys."

"Honey, sex toys aren't immoral. I have testimonies that women have claimed my toys have brought them closer to their husbands. In fact, one woman, and I won't mention her name, but she's a member of the Baptist church, said her husband didn't know where her G-spot was until..."

He clamped his hands over his ears. "Fine, Fine! I'll sleep in the other room as long as you don't ever say that word again."

Granny gave him a questioning look. "What? G-spot?"

He cringed and hurried out the door. "I'll see you in the morning."

Damon awoke to the aroma of coffee and the scent of Ava. Her warm body curled into his chest. He smiled and tightened his arms around her.

"Morning." She pushed herself up on her elbows, her eyes drifting from his face to his bare waist. "I'm guessing you're not wearing any underwear underneath this." She hooked her finger on the sheet and threatened to tug.

She was beautiful, hair tousled, eyes shining and sleepy, lips soft and kissable. He wrapped his arms around her, pulling her back onto his chest. "I wear underwear." His hands skimmed her back underneath the thin T-shirt she'd worn to bed last night. He recognized it as one of his when he'd been a teenager. Granny must have dug it out of a drawer.

His hands went lower until he cupped her naked butt and his breath hitched. "You didn't tell me you weren't wearing any panties." His eyes widened.

"I *am* wearing panties. A thong." She giggled.

He didn't think he could get any hotter with her sprawled on top of him, but once again, he was wrong.

With one hand on her ass and the other cupping the back of her head, he twisted his body, pinning her underneath him.

"I told you, I like to be on top." He pressed his lips to the soft skin underneath her chin.

She gasped. He could feel her pulse racing against his mouth.

"Must be a wolf thing." Her voice was low and breathless, just like he liked it.

"It's a horny thing." He grinned, his tongue darting out to lick the crook of her neck. He was rewarded when she arched her hips into his erection.

"I bet you'd like it if I was on top." Her tongue darted out and licked the corner of his ear as she dug her fingernails into his scalp.

"Not as much as me riding you." If he didn't get inside her he was going to have an aneurysm. Between his legs.

"Is Granny up yet?" Sex would have to be quick, before the old lady woke up.

"I'm right here." Granny's voice was like a bucket of ice water being dumped on his crotch.

He scrambled for the sheet, tugging it across his naked ass.

"Get off her and let's eat before the food gets cold." He made sure he heard Granny's slippers shuffling down the hall before rolling away from Ava.

Running his hand across his face, he let out a frustrated breath. Yes, he was definitely going to have an aneurysm.

She crawled over him and he caught her around the waist.

She grinned down at him. "Better be careful. I think I hear Granny coming back."

"I don't care. I need to taste you." He cupped her face between his hands. When her lips rubbed against his, he was lost, floating on an emotion he never thought was possible.

When she moaned his name against his lips, his chest tightened.

He couldn't imagine a day without her.

"Damon let go of her." Granny's stern voiced echoed from the doorway.

"She's on top of me," he said defensively.

"But, it's *your* tongue in *her* mouth." Granny's slippered foot tapped against the hardwood floor, waiting for him to obey.

"Fine." He sighed and let his arms fall to his sides.

He waited until Ava and Granny were heading into the kitchen before climbing out of bed and sliding his jeans over his erection.

"That was great, Granny." Damon pushed the empty plate away.

"Thank you." Her brittle smile attempted to hide the worry she was carrying around about Jayden. Truth be told, he was starting to get a little worried himself.

"Can I have your recipe for the pancakes, Granny?" Ava licked the last of the syrup off her fork. She looked over to the platter where there were two pancakes left, as if deciding if she wanted another one.

He smiled and pushed the platter toward her. "Take it."

She shook her head.

"It's just going to get thrown away," he taunted.

Her eyes grew large. "Well, in that case, I don't want to waste food." She forked the remaining pancakes onto her plate and began bathing them in thick syrup.

He shook his head. He had never known a female to eat so much, yet stay so slender.

"So what's the plan?" Granny's hand trembled as she picked up her green-and-pink cup and took a sip of her coffee.

"I'm going to go back into town and see if Jeff has heard anything about Jayden."

"Oh, I hope Jeff's okay." Ava's fork froze halfway to her mouth.

"Why wouldn't Jeff be okay?" Granny's cup made a clinking sound as she set it in the saucer.

"A bunch of werewolves started acting crazy at the bar last night. Damon put himself between me and the wolves. Jeff had to bring out the shotgun in order for us to get away.

"That's weird. Last night wasn't a full moon." Granny frowned at Ava.

"I'm sure Jeff's fine. I'll call and let you know how he is when I go by there today." He finished his coffee and stood.

"You're not going without me." Ava scrambled to her feet.

"Or me." Granny was right behind her.

He gritted his teeth, hating where this was going. "Now look . . ."

Ava stepped into his space. "No, you look. Jayden is my friend, too, and I think it would look less conspicuous if we were with you. Besides, Granny has to go by the Beaver anyway and drop off her orders."

He opened his mouth, but Granny leveled a look so intense it made him rethink it.

Damon pinched the bridge of his nose. If he tried to stop them, they'd find a way to come. They would be in more danger without him there to protect them.

Opening his eyes, he looked between the two women. "You can both come, but on one condition."

"Okay."

"If you go, you both have to do exactly what I say." Ava crumpled up her nose like she smelled something bad. "I'm serious, Ava. Do what I say or you're not going."

She sighed and gave him half a salute. "Okay, okay. Whatever you say."

He gave Granny a pointed look. "You, too."

"Boy, I'm older than…"

"Granny." His voice, serious and low, had its affect. Granny slumped a little and nodded her head. He knew it was the best show of submission from the old lady he was going to get.

Damon, Ava, and Granny were all piled into Granny's powder blue Oldsmobile. Damon drove while Granny sat up front and Ava sat in the back.

"How are we going to play this?" Granny clutched her white plastic purse in her lap while looking over at Damon. "Are we going to play good cop, bad cop?"

Ava snickered and then slapped her hand across her mouth. Though she couldn't see his eyes, she knew Damon was doing that irritated look where his brow crinkled up. He really shouldn't do that, or he was going to need some Botox soon.

Did wolves even get wrinkles? She mentally added that to her list of questions to ask Damon later when people weren't suddenly disappearing.

Granny certainly had some wrinkles, but there was no telling how old the lady actually was. Yet another question she would have to ask.

"We aren't going to *play* this. I'm going to do all the talking while you two sit in the car." He turned toward Granny.

"Humph. We'll see about that," Granny muttered under her breath.

"What?"

"Oh, nothing." She pointed through the front windshield. "Look, we're here."

Jeff's tin building bar came into view. As Damon pulled into the parking lot, her gaze swept over the building trying to see how much damage had been done to the bar from those crazy werewolves. From the outside, she couldn't see any signs of a fight.

The front door of the bar flew open and Jeff stepped out pushing a broom. Ava let out a relieved sigh.

Jeff seemed surprised to see them. His bushy eyebrows shot up and his mouth dropped open. Before he could say anything, Granny was rushing to his side, pulling him into a tight hug. His broom hit the sidewalk with a clack.

Ava grinned as she watched Jeff blush.

"Well, thank goodness you're not hurt." Granny released Jeff and took a step back, her head traveling up and down his body, looking for injuries.

"Why would I be hurt?" Jeff looked from Granny to Damon.

Damon propped his hands on his hips and shook his head. "Wasn't sure how things ended last night. I shouldn't have left you to face those werewolves alone."

"You did exactly what you should have. You know the Were law. Protecting a female is top priority. Nothing supersedes that."

Ava's heart warmed and melted like caramel.

"How much damage did they do?" She tried to look past Jeff and into the building.

Jeff turned his head toward her, a slow grin crossing his face. "Come in and see for yourself."

She followed behind Granny as Jeff led the way, with Damon bringing up the rear. A tingle ran down her spine, and she wondered if Damon was looking at her ass. Biting her lip, she put a little sway in her step.

He groaned.

She grinned to herself. She was right: he was watching her ass.

"Wow." Ava followed Granny's gaze upward. In the center of the ceiling was a sixteen-inch hole.

"Yeah. I shot a little too soon." Jeff shrugged.

"You mean you did that?" Granny gave him an incredible look.

"They were getting a little too close to Ava. As soon as Damon got her out of here, they all calmed down."

"Calmed down?"

"Yeah, they were all very…" Jeff rubbed the back of his head, clearly uncomfortable talking about this with Granny.

"You mean they were sexually aroused," Granny said in a matter-of-fact shrug.

"Damn, Granny." Jeff grimaced.

"Wait, I know I'm new to the whole Were thing. But why did that happen last night?" Ava looked at the group, but no one answered.

Damon scowled while Jeff shifted his weight from one foot to the other.

"It sounds like bloodlust, Ava," Granny said casually, as if they were talking about the weather.

Almost afraid to ask, but too curious not to, Ava opened her mouth. "What's bloodlust?"

"It's what happens when a male Were smells an unmated female. They are willing to fight to the death to have intercourse with her." Granny gave her a smile.

"Sweet Jesus, she said intercourse." Jeff scrubbed his hand down his face.

"Don't blaspheme." Granny narrowed her gray eyes on him. The large bar owner paled.

"I'd rather not talk about it," Damon spat out.

"Why not?" She frowned.

"Because, it's going to piss me off all over again." He turned on Ava and a lick of pleasure flickered deep in her stomach at the depth of anger reflected in his eyes.

"What I don't understand is why all the males were acting like that." Jeff frowned, lost in concentration.

"What do you mean?" Ava dragged her gaze from Damon to Jeff.

"It's unusual for a group of males to fight over the same female. I've never seen it until last night." Jeff looked at her, his face relaxing, cocking his head to the side. "Only read about it."

Ava and Damon turned their attention back to Jeff, who was now exchanging a knowing look with Granny.

"Where did you read about it?"

"It was a history book, a Were history book."

"Books like that exist?" Ava arched her brow.

Jeff smiled. "Not in America. It's kept in the Temple of Romulus."

"In Rome." She nodded.

"I didn't figure you for a history buff." Damon's eyebrows shot up.

She smirked. "I'm used to people underestimating me, especially men." Ava turned her attention back to Jeff. "So what did this book say?"

Jeff looked from her to Damon before he spoke. "Well, the only time it happens is when a new werewolf Queen is looking for a mate."

She snorted. "I'm not a Queen. I'm not even sure I'm a werewolf."

"Why would you say such a thing, dear?" Granny looked highly offended.

"I've never even turn...ah... shifted." She jerked her thumb in Damon's direction. "I didn't even know I was a werewolf until Damon told me."

"What's your last name Ava?" Jeff asked.

"Renfro." Damon volunteered.

"Actually, that's my adopted name."

Damon took a step closer. "What do you mean adopted name? The General is your father."

She shook her head. "No. He's my adopted father. My biological father died in a car accident."

"What kind of car accident?" Jeff took a step closer.

"He ran up under an eighteen-wheeler on his way home one night. They said he was killed instantly." She wrapped her arms around herself, suddenly chilled at bringing up that painful memory. "My mother died when I was born so the General adopted me."

Damon grabbed her by the arms, his grip uncomfortably tight. There was something urgent in his voice and the way he was staring at her that scared her. "Ava, what is your last name?"

Wrenching out of his grip, she looked from him to the others. "It's Romanelli. Ava Romanelli."

Fuck.

Romanelli was as blue-blooded as you could get when it came to werewolves.

If what Jeff was saying was true, then Ava was somehow destined to be Queen, which put a kink in any kind of future with her. She was destined for someone else, a pureblood male.

Damon's stomach hit the floor. He actually glanced down, making sure his intestines weren't lying out like last week's road kill.

He looked away. He could feel Jeff and Granny's sympathetic stares burning into him. Everyone knew he would never be with Ava.

The silence was deafening.

"Well, maybe you're just a late bloomer. Maybe that's why you haven't shifted." Granny shrugged.

"Or, maybe I'm not a werewolf. Maybe I'm just ordinary." Her voice held a hint of disappointment. "I've never shifted. Surely I would have done that by now."

"You're a werewolf." He turned to her. "Make no mistake. You are far from ordinary."

"How do you know that for certain?" Her beauty took his breath away. He knew some other male would be waking up next to her every morning for the rest of his life. He also knew that male was not him.

"I can smell it on you."

She looked up at him with eyes so green they must have been cut from emeralds. If he stood there much longer he was going to throw her over his shoulder and take her into the kitchen where he would mate her, forever binding them together. The Were Law be damned.

"Fuck it." He stepped toward the back door. He swung, putting his fist through the sheetrock, leaving a five-inch hole. Flinging open the back door, he hurried outside, needing to put as much distance between him and Ava as possible.

He smelled her as she tracked behind him. He always smelled her. Whether in his sleep or awake, her scent haunted him.

"What's wrong, Damon?" She put her hand on his shoulder. He flinched. Did she not understand that she was putting him through hell by her touch? Of course she didn't. She didn't understand any of this.

"You used to like it when I touched you." His heart clenched at the hurt in her voice.

"That was before I knew you were a Queen."

She snorted.

"This is serious, Ava." He faced her.

Her expression changed, her smile gone, her eyes hardening. "I know it is and I want to know more. What does me being a 'Queen' have to do with us?"

He closed his eyes. "The Were Laws state that when a Queen arises, she will be mated to the strongest Alpha in the Pack."

Ava's lips turned upward into a devastating grin. "That would be you."

His heart broke, shattering and splintering into a thousand shards, each cutting as they made their downward spiral into the nauseating pit that was his stomach.

He swallowed back the lump in his throat. "You don't understand. There is already an Alpha in charge, the Pack Master." He watched her grin slip, the blood rushing out of her face.

"You are to be mated to Barrett."

CHAPTER ELEVEN

Ava's knees buckled. Damon's strong arms came around her, keeping her upright, preventing her from performing a face plant.

"Jesus, Ava. Are you all right?" His voice was warm against her ear and for a few precious seconds she let him take the weight of her body and the weight of the world off her shoulders.

She sucked in a breath

"I'm okay." She tried to keep her voice light as she chuckled weakly. "It's not every day that you find out fate has picked out a husband for you."

Damon's face grew stoic, that mask of indifference he always tried to wear. But Ava knew better. His emotions ran a lot deeper than anyone knew.

"Barrett is a good leader." Damon didn't bother looking at her when he spoke.

Hot liquid anger raced through her veins. She shoved him away. "So you're telling me I don't get a say in this? That I don't get to choose who I want to spend my life with." Her face heated.

He stood perfectly still, the muscle in his cheek working furiously.

"What if I told you I had already chosen a mate?" She crossed her arms.

His head jerked up, pure rage burning in his eyes. "Who?"

Some of the anger melted away. Did he really not know that she loved him? Of course he didn't. She'd never told him. He'd probably never heard those words in his whole life. She stepped closer and placed her hand on his chest.

"You."

His eyes widened with surprise. He pulled her against his hard body. She lifted her mouth to his, feeling his breath coming in hard pants. She closed her eyes, waiting for that moment when he would take her mouth.

But he didn't.

He grabbed her wrists and pushed her away. She tried to step closer, but he held her at arm's length.

"Don't say that."

"Don't say what? That I want to be with you?" She stopped struggling and looked into his eyes. "It's the truth."

They stood in silence, eternity thrust between them. He released his grip and let his hands fall to his side. "Barrett is a good leader."

"You already said that." She growled. God help her, she actually growled. And judging by the growing bulge she saw in his pants, he liked it. "I will not marry or mate someone I don't even know."

"It's the Were law, Ava." He looked away, grief etched into the corners of his eyes.

"Fuck the Were law." She turned and headed for the door. Damon grabbed her arm before she reached it.

Spinning around, she braced herself for an argument.

Her heart caught in her throat at the tender expression on Damon's face.

His fingertips grazed her cheek. "If you don't accept Barrett as your mate, you will be put to death."

Blood raced from her face down to her toes.

"That's murder."

"That's the law."

She narrowed her eyes. "As Queen, what am I expected to do?"

"Rule with your mate. Make decisions regarding the Pack."

"What about the bedroom, Damon? Am I expected to spread my legs for Barrett as well?" She wanted to needle him, wanted him to feel as bad as she did. Damn it, she wanted him to fight for her.

He stepped close, pulling her hips against his, all stoic expression gone. He opened his mouth, his white teeth looked a little larger than she remembered, but still she wasn't scared. Excited and aroused, but not scared.

"How would that make you feel, knowing I'm with another man?"

He growled. His entire body trembled against her. She traced his handsome face with her fingertips.

"I don't think you would like that at all." She licked his jawline.

He pressed his hips into hers, and she could feel herself getting wet. She wished he would pull her jeans off and unzip his own, and pound himself into her until they were both worn out.

"Do you know why I know you wouldn't like it, Damon?" She nipped the corner of his jaw. His breathing increased, ragged and fast.

He said nothing. She didn't need him to.

Licking her lips, she pulled back just enough to make sure he could see her eyes. "You wouldn't like it for the same reason I wouldn't like to see you with another female. If I ever saw you touching another female the way you've touched me, I would rip out her throat."

He rested his forehead against hers. "There will never be another female for me."

She smiled, but it quickly vanished as he pulled away from her. "After I get you back home safe, I'm leaving the Pack."

She stared longingly after Damon's retreating back. He was leaving the Pack. Worse, he was leaving her. He wasn't going to fight for her.

The reality of it hit her in the chest and she reached her hand to the area just above her breast, making sure there wasn't a hole.

It sure as hell felt like someone had ripped out her heart.

Damon strode to the front of the building. He knew for the rest of the mission, he was going to have to stay away from Ava. And that was going to be mission impossible.

Damn, he must be fucked up in the head to be making with the corny ironies.

He threw a hasty glance over his shoulder, making sure Ava wasn't following.

She wasn't.

His heart sank.

He leaned against the wall, the scratchy cinder blocks digging into his back as he closed his eyes.

Barrett. Ava was to be Barrett's mate.

The one male that he respected was to be bonded to the only woman he'd ever loved. Wasn't fate a fucking bitch?

His gut twisted painfully and his heart reacted the same. He palmed his left pec, trying to erase the pain. He knew better. He wasn't sure the pain would ever go away.

"Damon!"

He pushed off the wall in time to see Jeff rushing out the front door. He wanted to tell him to fuck off and leave him alone.

"It's Jayden."

"He called?" The hair on the back of his neck stood up as his senses went on high alert.

Jeff shook his head, his expression somber. "No. Someone else called using Jayden's cell phone. The caller sounded a lot like that bastard, Jenkins."

"What did he want?" He narrowed his eyes.

"They want to exchange Jayden for Ava."

Rage boiled in his gut and he clenched his hands. Every animalistic instinct came alive at that moment, wanting him to shift into wolf and kill.

"Damon, stay in control," Jeff warned.

It was no use. A growl started building until it came out of his mouth.

"Damon, you're in broad daylight. You can't shift. Not now."

He looked down at his fists clenched so tightly that his nails were biting into skin, leaving blood-shaped crescents on his palms.

"What's happening?" Ava came to a stop beside Jeff.

"It's Jayden." Jeff finally spoke, his tone tense, drawing Ava's attention away from him. It gave him the seconds he needed to force his body back under control. "Someone called from his phone."

"David Jenkins?" Ava's brow creased as she narrowed her green eyes.

"We think so." Jeff kept his gaze on the ground.

"Jenkins has Jayden." Ava's voice cracked as she looked at Damon.

He nodded.

"What are his demands?" She started at him, eyes wide, face pale.

He stayed silent, unable to force the words to come to the surface.

She nodded slowly in understanding. "He wants me, doesn't he?"

He didn't break her gaze. "I won't let him have you." He'd protect her with his life; he'd known this from the moment he set eyes on her.

"He's not going to let Jayden go without me."

"She's right, Damon." Everyone turned to look at Granny. "The second you walk into that bar without Ava, he won't hesitate to kill Jayden."

His expression changed from anger to sympathy. He had to choose between his friend and the woman he loved.

"Granny, I'm going to get Jayden out, okay? But, I can't risk Ava's life to do it."

"Why not?" Ava asked.

He gave her a stunned look.

"I said, why not?" Ava lifted her defiant chin, waiting for an answer.

"Ava." The breath left his chest as his lungs tightened. She wanted something from him, something he could no longer offer.

"You are under my protection until I can ensure your safety."

"Then what?" Ava kept her gaze glued on his.

"Then I will deliver you to Barrett." His stomach pitched as his heart dropped.

"Well then, I guess it's a good thing I'm here."

Ava's heart dropped as everyone turned at the sound of the male voice.

"Barrett?" Granny's eyes widened.

Leaning up against the corner of the building was a large guy. He was taller than Damon, but just as broad. His sandy blond hair hung down his back, and his eyes were hidden under dark sunglasses. He looked like a sex god.

So this was Barrett, the one they expected her to mate.

While Ava appreciated the package, he didn't make her body hum, not like Damon did.

Barrett pushed off the building and walked toward them in an unhurried swagger.

Ava felt her heart plunge like an out-of-control elevator. She reached out to steady herself against the wall just as everything started to tilt.

Just as her vision began to narrow, Damon's strong arms wrapped around her. Clutching his shirt between trembling fingers, she hid her face, refusing the reality of everything around her.

"Ava, are you okay?" Damon's tender voice made her heart break all over again.

"Get her inside." Jeff's barked out orders. Damon swung her up into his arms. She forced herself to release Damon's shirt when he set her down on the couch in the office.

Granny pressed a cold bottle of water into her hand. She took a long drink, letting the cold liquid slide down her throat.

"Are you feeling better?" Barrett knelt and whipped his Oakleys off. His green eyes searched her face. Damon sat beside her on the couch, holding his fingers on the pulse point in her neck.

"Your pulse is racing." Damon pained gaze made her heart catch.

She blinked at him, trying to slow her breathing. *Of course it's racing. It does that every time you're near, you idiot.*

"Maybe you should give her some room," Barrett commanded.

Damon let out a growl. Barrett stood, rising to his intimidating height and glared.

Her breath caught in her throat as Damon stood, meeting his Pack Master's unflinching gaze. Tension rose in the room as the two males looked ready to do battle.

She looked between the two men. Both were huge males and she didn't doubt if they actually got into a fight it would end in a death.

"Watch it, Damon. You seem to have forgotten your rank." Barrett's lips curled upward, revealing a set of blinding white teeth.

Damon didn't move, but held his ground. She could actually smell the musky scent of testosterone filling the room and from the corner of her eye she saw Jeff and Granny both take a cautious step back.

She scrambled to her feet. "Jayden's been taken."

Barrett spoke, but kept his narrowed eyes trained on Damon. "I know."

"The kidnapper wants to exchange me for Jayden."

Both males looked at her at the same time. She cleared her throat. "And since we know that David Jenkins—"

Barrett narrowed his eyes. "You know for sure it's David Jenkins?"

She shrugged. "He didn't say his name, but yes, I think it's the same guy who kidnapped Haley."

"Barrett, what are you doing here?" Damon hissed.

"Heard there had been some commotion at the bar last night." He shrugged his massive shoulders, his muscles cording at the motion. "Figured since the rest of the Guardians are busy trying to protect the state of Arkansas, I thought I'd come down myself and give you a hand."

"I don't need a hand." Damon growled.

"Sounds like you do, since Jayden's been captured."

"Does Jayden know you?" Ava cocked her head at Barrett.

"Jayden and I keep in touch." He winked. If she weren't head over heels in love with Damon it would have made her melt.

Damon shot a glare at Barrett. "Who told you there was trouble?"

"Word travels. Things seem to have gotten more complicated with the disappearance of Jayden." Barrett frowned and looked off into the distance.

"What are we going to do to get Jayden back?" She glanced between Damon and Barrett.

"We?" Barrett shot her a look so intense it should have scared her. All it did was piss her off.

Taking a step forward, she stuck her finger in Barrett's face. "Let's get something straight. I don't play this Alpha male bullshit you two got going on, so you might want to reconsider and start talking to me in a friendlier tone."

Damon snorted. She tossed him a glare over her shoulder, letting him know he wasn't off the hook.

Barrett's eyes grew round and she could tell by his scent he was equally pissed off. Her heightened sense of smell was something she'd noticed over the past few days.

Barrett's lips curved upward. "You didn't tell me she had a mouth on her, Damon." He chortled. "I like her."

"Well, that's good, dear." Granny patted Barrett's massive arm.

"Why is that, Granny?" Barrett gave the woman a puzzled look.

"Because, Ava is your mate."

"My what?"

"Ava is your mate. Didn't you know about Ava's bloodline?" Granny handed Barrett a bottle of water from the mini fridge.

Barrett's gaze zeroed in on her, first on her face then slipping downward over her figure, like she was some kind of juicy steak.

When Barrett's eyes finally drifted upward to meet hers, she smiled sweetly and flipped him the bird.

Barrett's eyes flashed in anger and she knew she'd gone too far.

"When did you figure this out?" Barrett looked at the others.

"Today." Damon's deep voice vibrated across her skin, making her shiver.

"How did you all come to the conclusion that the General's daughter is my mate?"

"She's not the General's daughter. The General adopted her after her father was killed."

Barrett slowly turned to look at her, surprise crossing his features. "Your last name isn't Renfro?"

"No, it's Romanelli."

Barrett sucked in a deep breath and turned away.

"You're right. Romanelli is the name of a royal bloodline." Barrett opened his mouth then quickly shut it. Nodding his head slightly, Barrett turned toward Damon. "I'm touched that you are so concerned about my future happiness, but right now we need to be planning how to get Jayden free instead of trying to get me mated."

"I'm helping." Ava lifted her chin, daring him to stop her. "Don't try to talk me out of it."

Barrett scored her with a warning glare before turning to Jeff. "I need to talk to the Pack Master of Louisiana. You wouldn't happen to have his number in your phone? Mine is dead."

"I have it on speed dial." Jeff pulled his cell phone out of his jeans pocket, hit a few buttons and handed it to Barrett.

Barrett took the phone and strode into the bar for privacy. Jeff and Granny headed into the kitchen to round up something for everyone to eat.

She didn't want to stay there, not in the same room with Damon after he practically served her up to Barrett on a silver platter. Too bad her feet didn't get the message.

"Ava." She looked up into those blue eyes she loved so much.

"I refuse to put you in danger."

Ava opened her mouth, suddenly finding the air too hot to inhale deeply. She licked her dry lips before looking at him.

"I'm not yours to command, remember?" She held her breath, her heart aching so bad she thought it would stop beating.

"You're not mine, Ava. You never were." Damon turned and walked away.

What Ava wanted from him was impossible. Didn't she know that?

Out of the corner of his eye, Damon caught Barrett talking on the cell phone with a determined look on his face.

The kitchen doors creaked open, drawing his attention. Granny and Jeff walked out balancing two trays of food in their hands. Without asking, he took the tray from Granny. He needed something to occupy his hands so he'd quit contemplating putting them on Ava.

As he set the tray down on a round table, Granny patted him on the arm. He didn't look at her, he couldn't. He was too afraid of the pity he would find lurking behind those old eyes.

Barrett handed Jeff his phone.

"Well?" Damon scowled. For the first time, he took in his leader's features. Despite his distant nature, Barrett was handsome, with long, sandy blond hair and green eyes. If he wanted to be honest with himself, Ava and Barrett would make a stunning pair and have beautiful children.

He looked away, running his hand behind his neck. Okay, so he wasn't ready to be honest with himself. He'd rather live in the land of denial. Denial, meet thy king.

"What's with you? You look like you ate some rotten meat." Barrett arched his brow.

"No, but the day is still young." Damon walked to the other side of the table away from Barrett and parked his butt.

Barrett glanced at his bowl. "This looks good, Jeff."

Jeff stuck out his barrel chest and smirked. "It's my grandmother's chili recipe."

Damon kept his eyes on the bowl in front of him, waiting to see where Ava would sit.

"Thank you." Ava's voice had him looking up in time to catch Barrett pulling out a chair for her. He narrowed his eyes, mentally warning Barrett not to sit beside Ava.

Too late. Barrett slid into the chair beside her. Damon clenched both sides of his seat to keep from punching Barrett in the face. He kept his gaze on Ava as Barrett leaned over and whispered something that made her smile a little.

He squeezed harder and the wood creaked under his hands.

He closed his eyes, trying to force the red haze of fury under control.

"What did you find out?" Granny asked.

Barrett slowly lifted his head, dragging his gaze away from Ava. "The Louisiana Pack knew of Jayden's disappearance from a snitch." He dipped his spoon in the bowl. "They suspect Jenkins is the kidnapper but can't seem to find the kidnapper or Jayden."

"So will the Louisiana Pack help us?" Ava looked at Barrett. Damon felt the green sludge of jealousy slide around his stomach. Why the hell was Ava even looking at Barrett? She should be looking at him, asking him for the answers. Not Barrett.

Barrett's eyes narrowed as his spoon clinked the side of the bowl. "They said they were already short-staffed since they are gearing up for Halloween."

Ava sneered. "What does Halloween have to do with anything? Is that some kind of wolf holiday or something?"

Damon shook his head. "Not a holiday. A full moon."

She paled.

"Does that mean I'm going to...?"

"Shift? Yes." Damon glanced around. Barrett's gaze was glued to Ava.

Bastard.

"Are you saying you've never shifted before?" Barrett cocked his head. He turned in his seat and gave Ava his full attention.

"Yes."

Damon's grip increased on the worn wood making the chair cry out in protest.

"You are sure you are lupine?"

"Lupine?"

"Wolf."

She looked at Damon. "Damon thinks I am."

"I didn't ask what Damon thought. I want to know what you think." Barrett touched a finger to her chin, forcing her to look at him.

Damon lost it.

A growl erupted so furious that everyone except Barrett jumped back from the table. Upturned chairs clattered to the floor. Damon sprang to his feet and slammed his hands down on the table, splitting the wood in two. Bowls of chili and utensils clattered to the floor as everyone backed out of the way.

Damon locked his eyes on Barrett. He wanted the Alpha to advance so he could sink his teeth into his throat.

Barrett stood and met Damon's stare with deadly intent. Damon knew that if he dared touch Barrett then he would die. An overwhelming urge to protect Ava drowned out all rational thought.

"Stop it!" Ava stepped between the two males and pressed her palms against Damon's chest. "What the hell is wrong with you?" Her face was tight with anger and her eyes flashed like lightning, her black hair spilling over her shoulders like a fierce goddess. She was mad as hell.

And she was the most beautiful creature that Damon had ever seen.

She was making him hard.

Laughter spilled out through the empty bar. Damon jerked his head toward Barrett.

In all the time he'd known Barrett, the male hadn't so much as cracked a smile. Now he looked like he was about to crack a rib laughing.

"We need to quit messing around. I need my grandson back." Granny scolded them with a look as she nervously rubbed her arms.

Barrett's laughter faded as he rubbed the back of his neck with his hand. "Granny's right, we need to get focused." He shot Damon a look.

"I'm focused." Damon growled.

"Are you kidding me?" Ava threw her hands up. "This isn't a dick measuring contest."

Barrett turned his back, smothering a smile, while Damon stared at Ava.

"We all know who would win anyway." Barrett sneered and then grew serious. "As amusing as this conversation is, Granny is right. We need to start planning how to get Jayden back." Barrett picked up Granny's overturned chair and motioned for her to sit. "When I said us, I meant Damon and myself."

"But..."

"No buts, Ava," Damon said.

Ava wasn't stupid. She knew when to talk and when to keep her mouth shut.

She blew out a breath and crossed her arms. "Where am I supposed to stay while you go after Jayden?"

"Granny's."

"I thought you didn't want me to stay out here."

"Plans change." Damon ran his hand across his face. "It's isolated, but safe. No one would think to look for you out there. It's too far off the main road."

"Fine." Ava looked at Granny, who gave her an innocent smile. As Damon's boots clomped toward the front door, she noticed Granny's expression change. The innocent old lady mask slipped, and underneath was a wicked wink of camaraderie.

"Granny?" Ava lowered her voice.

"You don't think I'm going to let those boys go after Jayden without me, do you?"

Ava grinned. "What do we do first?"

"We need to head home."

"Then?"

"We need to get us a plan together."

Ava smiled. "I've already got that covered."

CHAPTER TWELVE

"David Jenkins is more than just a frequent visitor to the strip club." Barrett tapped his lips with his fingertips, a gesture so refined that Damon often wondered about his leader's background. All he knew of the Alpha was that he'd been the Pack Master of Arkansas for years and that he had a reputation of being lethal when cornered.

Damon looked at the blueprints of the Beaver that Jeff had, somehow, delivered to Romulus and Remus less than an hour ago.

Damon turned to Jeff. "Where did you come up with these?"

Jeff heaved his brawny shoulders up in a casual shrug. "Friend at the courthouse. I called in a favor."

"Good to know."

"Look at this." Barrett pointed to a smaller room toward the back of the strip club.

"An office, maybe?" Damon narrowed his eyes. "That's weird."

"What?" Jeff leaned over his shoulder.

"There is no direct exit to the outside from the office. You want an easy escape in case there's trouble." Barrett finished Damon's thought.

"Yeah, like an angry boyfriend of one of the strippers." Damon ran his finger across the blueprints. "The nearest exit is right down that hall where the strippers enter the building." He straightened.

"With no direct exit, the office would be the only secured room where they could be holding Jayden."

"I need to get inside while Barrett covers that back exit. I'll locate Jayden and exit out that way." Damon glanced at his watch. "Tonight is Halloween and it's going to be pretty packed. That will work in our favor."

Jeff snorted. "Well yeah, especially since tonight is the costume party."

Barrett and Damon turned and looked at the man. "What?"

Jeff bobbed his head up and down. "Every Halloween they have a costume party. In fact, I don't think you can get in without a costume." Jeff paused and rubbed his chin. "I still might have my costume from last year that one of you could borrow."

"What is it?"

Jeff held up his hand. "Hang on. It would probably be easier if I just showed you."

When he reappeared from the back room a few minutes later, he was carrying a large box. He placed it on the ground and pulled open the top flaps.

"What's that smell?" Damon waved his hand in front of his face as a sulfur scent emanated up from the box.

Jeff shrugged. "Think I spilt something on it last year at the Halloween party."

Barrett wrinkled his nose. "Smells like rotten eggs."

Jeff lifted the bundle of fur to his nose and gave it a sniff. "I had it in the closet in the bathroom. That toilet always stinks."

"I'm not wearing a stinky bear costume." Damon shook his head.

"It's not a bear." Jeff drew his brows together in offense.

Barrett bent over the box and pulled out the head. "Fuck."

"What?"

"It's not a bear. It's a beaver." Barrett deadpanned.

"Oh. Hell. No." Damon stepped back, putting distance between himself and the stinky beaver. "There is no way in hell that I'm wearing that."

Damon skewered him with a look before turning back to Jeff. "This all you got? A fucking beaver costume?"

"I think Granny might have some of Jayden's old costumes at her house." Jeff's eyes ran up and down the length of Damon. "Besides, I don't think this would fit you anyway."

"Good." Damon pulled his leather jacket off the back of the chair. "I'm going to head out to Granny's and see what she has there." He checked his watch before glancing at Barrett. "You want me to pick you up something, too?"

Barrett nodded and then frowned. "Yes. But nothing stupid."

Damon snorted. "Man, you're standing next to a beaver costume that smells like shit. Anything would be better than that."

"I don't think this is going to work."

The older woman waved her hand in the air. "Of course it will work. We'll park around back of the Beaver. When I spot one of the girls that I have an order for, I'll talk her into letting me in the back way so I can deliver my other orders."

"Don't they have security guards in the back?"

"I don't know." Granny shrugged.

Ava sighed. "Granny, even if the girls could get you in, the security guard certainly isn't going to let you in."

Granny smiled, her face brightening like a sunbeam. "What if I tell them I'm a dancer?"

Ava's mouth hit the floor.

"What?" Granny's smile disappeared. "It's amateur night. They let anyone dance on amateur night." Granny's chin jutted out.

Ava's eyes sharpened. "Tonight is amateur night?"

"Yep, and since it's Halloween, everyone will be dressed up." Granny unpacked her large bag stuffed with edible undergarments. "Of course they'll let me in. Besides, I have to deliver these candy corn panties and licorice bra." Granny held up orange-and-yellow panties and a red bra that looked like it had been sewn out of rope.

Ava wrinkled her nose. "I don't like licorice."

"It's not black licorice, dear. Its strawberry licorice and it matches these candy corn panties."

Ava touched her right temple where a sudden ache was brewing. Rubbing the area with her fingertips, she closed her eyes. "Okay, so let's say you get in, then what?"

"I'll distract the girls with some of my latest sex toys. Like this one!" The old lady whipped out a pink vibrator the size of a baseball bat.

"Who in the hell can actually use that?" Ava straightened just as the front door creaked open.

Granny stepped into the living room still holding the obscene toy in her hand with Ava on her heels.

"Damon. What are you doing here?"

"I'm..." He stilled, his face paled and eyes widened on the weapon in Granny's hand.

Closing his eyes, he pushed the heel of his hand into his right eye socket, probably trying to gouge his eye out.

Ava knew just how he felt.

"I need to get a couple of Jayden's Halloween costumes." He grimaced and kept his gaze fixed on the ceiling.

Dropping her hand to her side, Granny patted the monstrous vibrator against her thigh as she gave him a pensive look. "Let me see." *Slap, slap, slap.* "I think I got rid of all his costumes."

Damon looked at her. "All?"

Granny shook her head. "No, I still have the one he was going to wear tonight. It's in my sewing room. Hang on and I'll go get it." She took two steps before hesitating. "Here Ava, hold this."

Ava took the vibrator and frowned, surprised by the weight of the thing.

"I'm not even going to ask." Damon looked up at some invisible spot on the ceiling and avoided looking at the vibrator.

"It's best if you didn't." Ava studied the floor.

After a beat, Ava cleared her throat. "So you need the costume for the Beaver?"

"Yeah, how did you know?"

"Granny told me about the costume party they have every year." Ava cringed. "I'm hoping she knows because she's heard about it and not because she's actually been there."

"Me too." He flinched.

Granny emerged from the hall with material draped across her arms.

"What is it?" Ava reached out and touched the material. It was made of leather and soft as butter.

"It's Spartacus." Granny held up the garment proudly.

"Well, fuc..." Damon didn't finish as Granny pursed her lips and shot him a warning look.

"Sorry, Granny." He grimaced. Shaking his head, he pointed at the costume. "I should have known that ass...idiot would want to dress up like Spartacus."

"It's his favorite TV show." Granny held up the costume so she could examine it.

"Fine." Damon held his hands out in front of him. "I'll take it."

Granny frowned. "Aren't you going to try it on?"

Ava grinned. "Yeah, I want to see it on."

"The fewer people that see me in this ridiculous thing, the better." Damon waited until Granny slid all the pieces of the costume into a paper bag before taking it from her.

He turned, piercing Ava with a glare. "Ava, I need to talk with you. Outside." He didn't wait as he exited through the front door. She'd started to follow when Granny grabbed her arm and whispered loudly. "Don't tell him about our plan. Don't let him break you!"

"I won't." Ava hissed and thrust the sex toy into the old woman's hands.

Damon leaned against his bike with his arms crossed, sunglasses in place, looking like sex on two legs.

Ava sighed, but it came out more like a purr.

She stopped a few feet away and tucked her hands in her back pockets. "What did you want to talk to me about?"

He moved so quick that it took her breath away. One minute they were three feet apart, the next, she was wrapped in his embrace, her arms trapped behind her.

His hand slid up from her back to the nape of her neck. Her heart drummed in her ears as her breasts crushed against his rock-hard chest. Ava rocked against him, loving the feel of how her body reacted to his, her nipples hardening against his solid chest.

He growled deep in his throat before he brought his mouth down on hers. He kissed and licked her mouth until she moaned. Ava arched her back, grinding her pelvis against his hard thick length.

One arm slid down her back, gripping her arms, while the other slipped between the tight spaces of their bodies.

"You aren't playing fair," he breathed as his fingers tweaked her nipple. Delicious licks of pleasure zinged straight to her core.

Ava moaned. "Neither are you."

His hand left her breast and slid downward until he cupped her through her jeans.

Well, if he was going there, so was she.

Slipping her hand free, Ava stroked his erection, the denim doing nothing to hide the heat against her fingertips, the very heat she wanted inside her.

"Damon. You forgot something." Ava froze at Granny's shrill voice. She quickly stepped away, leaving Damon standing there with a tent in his jeans.

"I found this in the bottom of the closet." Granny grinned as she held out a large sword and a matching sheath. Apparently the old woman was more focused on the sword in her hand than the sword in Damon's pants.

Damon breathed out a slow, weary breath as he took the weapon from Granny. His brows creased as his eyes drifted toward the old lady. "Is this real?"

"Of course it is. Jayden's friend, who happens to be a blacksmith, made it for him."

Gripping the handle, he unsheathed the sword and eyed the weapon with appreciation.

"Where are you going to put that? It's not going to fit in your saddlebag." Ava ran her finger down the flat side of the cool steel.

"I'll tie it to the side." Flipping open the saddlebag, he retrieved some small rope and black material. He wrapped the material around the sword before strapping it to the side of his motorcycle.

"Be careful." Granny whispered. "And bring Jayden back to me."

Ava looked at the hard ground and wrapped her arms around her chest, suddenly very chilled. What Damon was about to do was dangerous and could end with someone getting killed.

His calloused hand cupped her cheek. "I'll be back."

"What time?"

"I don't know. We're planning to go in around midnight when the crowd is the largest. It lessens the chance they'll spot us. The only place in the club that they could be holding Jayden is in the office in the back. If things go as planned, we'll be in and out."

"And if they don't go as planned?" Ava held his hand against her face.

"Then it will take a little longer." He shrugged.

"Come back to me."

His blue eyes flashed with unspoken emotion.

"Damon?"

"I'll be back, and I'll have Jayden with me." He kissed the top of her head before getting on his Harley. With a roar, the engine came alive and he was gone.

Ava stood in the yard looking at the flying dust he'd left behind, watching it settle on the ground.

"You're worried about him." Granny stepped to her side.

Ava snorted. "I know it's stupid. I'm not even his mate."

"This is true." Granny's voice trailed off.

"I don't like it. I'm sure as hell not going to mate Barrett." Ava turned, her gaze holding Granny's with determination.

"Barrett's pretty hot." Granny pursed her lips. "If I were younger I might have a go at him myself."

"I don't care how hot Barrett is. It's not him I want."

"I got something that will take your mind off that." Granny's thin lips slowly turned up into a grin. "We need to go get ready if we're going to help."

Ava nodded. "Let's get busy then."

Damon sat in Barrett's silver Hummer, his mind going over the plan. He had to get in and get Jayden out, and make it back to Ava. This might be the last night he had with her.

"They're not going to let you take that sword in there. Security's tight tonight." Barrett's voice brought him back to the here and now. Damon looked at the Alpha male who, despite the beaver costume, still looked lethal. But really. Barrett was wearing a beaver costume. That cheered Damon a little.

Barrett slid his gaze from the crowded parking lot over to him.

"I already thought about that. That's why I painted it." Damon reached in the backseat and pulled out the weapon. It shone bright yellow, like a child's toy. He'd even painted the tip of the sword red, mimicking drops of blood.

Barrett nodded. "Not bad. Just make sure when you walk up to the front door you have it sheathed on the opposite side of where the security guards will be standing. You don't need them bumping against it."

Damon grabbed the belt and sheath. Arching up, he secured the belt around his waist. "I'll make a sweep of the room before heading to the bar. The lap dance room at the end will be the closest to the door leading to the office."

Barrett's lips turned upward into an amused grin. "You're getting a lap dance. I don't think Ava's going to like that very much."

Damon pierced Barrett with a determined stare. "I'm not doing this to get off; I'm doing this to get Jayden out. Don't confuse the two."

Barrett gave him one last look before looking away. "You need to take out the bouncer watching that door to the office." Barrett reached into the console and pulled out a clear plastic bag. He tossed it to Damon.

"What's this?" Damon held up the bag and sniffed the white powder.

"It's Rophenol. Have the bartender put it in the bouncer's drink."

"The bartender is not going to give his co-worker a roofie." Damon frowned.

"*This* bartender will." Barrett turned his focus back on Damon

"Braxton?"

Barrett nodded.

"He's not supposed to be working on amateur night."

"The other three bartenders suddenly got sick."

"You wouldn't happen to have had a hand in that, would you?"

Barrett shrugged and looked away. "Braxton was the only choice left."

"Lucky for us." Damon tucked the package inside his belt. "I take it Braxton knows what's going on."

"I updated him this afternoon."

"At least there will be one more on our side."

Barrett grinned. "You ready, Spartacus?"

"Fuck off."

"I'll take that as a yes." Barrett grabbed the door handle and stopped.

"Don't forget your helmet." Barrett's eyes bore into him. "And be careful."

"I always am. See you inside." With that Damon was out of the vehicle and headed toward the front door.

After clearing his way through the bouncer, Damon entered the Beaver. The second he stepped through the gold doors of the lobby and into the main area, his senses went on high alert.

It was crowded, mostly men, but there were some women huddled together in groups at tables and lounging areas. The noise level was a constant drone as voices mingled with late nineties music. As he headed toward the bar, one of the strippers making the rounds reached out and touched him, raking her fingertips across his bare chest.

Damon grabbed her hand and pulled it away from his skin. Her eyes grew wide and he quickly shot her a grin while trying not to cringe at her touch.

Damon swallowed hard, forcing himself not to step away from the girl. She smelled of cigarettes and Mexican food.

"I've got to be on stage for my dance in a few songs. But after that I'm free if you're interested in a lap dance, honey."

"What's the price?" Damon focused on controlling his breathing. He couldn't stand for someone to be so fucking close to him. Unless it was Ava.

"Fifty bucks." She purred while entangling her fingers with his. He forced himself to stay still.

"For one dance? That's a lot of money for a five-minute dance."

She pulled back and looked into his face before letting her eyes travel downward toward his crotch. When she lifted her gaze back up to his, she grinned. "How about I make you a deal?"

"What kind of deal?" Damon looked away as a prettier stripper walked past, ignoring the one holding on to him. The less interested he seemed the better deal he'd get.

"For one hundred dollars I'll give you a lap dance for thirty minutes."

Despite the confident smile she wore, he could see the fear brimming in the back of her eyes at the possibilities of his refusal.

"I don't know; that's a lot of money." He started to look away, but she grabbed his hand and held it to her chest.

"I'll use the lap dance room at the end. It's more private so if there's anything else you might be interested in, I'm sure I can accommodate you."

It was exactly the room he wanted, but he didn't want to seem too eager. He stared at her for few seconds as if considering. Then he grinned. "I think you've got a deal."

Her eyes lit up before fixing her face into a sexy pout. He doubted she'd made that kind of money in thirty minutes with just dancing.

"I'll be at the bar. When you're done dancing, come find me."

The stripper pressed herself flush against his body before strutting away.

Damon winced. If Ava caught that girl's perfume on him, she was going to give him hell. He made a mental note to run by Jeff's and grab a shower before going out to Granny's.

The last thing he needed was to catch Ava's fury on the last night he could be with her.

Ava whipped the Crown Vic into the parking lot at the back of the Beaver Tail. She circled the place a few times, but finally found a parking space. Unfortunately, it happened to be two spaces away from the back entrance, not exactly inconspicuous.

Granny straightened her pink velour jumpsuit before reaching for her white plastic purse. She looked like a geriatric Easter Bunny.

"Are you ready?" Granny gave her an encouraging smile.

Ava nodded and glanced down at her white sweater, jeans and boots. "I suppose." She tapped her thumb against the steering wheel.

"Remember, we're just making a delivery." Granny reached down and pulled up a black bag from the floorboard.

"As soon as we get in, I'll distract them. You go find Jayden and get him out." Granny handed her the large white purse. "You take my purse. I've got a knife and some bolt cutters. Didn't know if they would tie him up with ropes or chain him." Granny's face creased, worry marring her usually serene expression.

Ava reached over and patted her hand. "It's okay. We're going to get him out of there."

Granny gave her a brave smile that didn't exactly reach her eyes. Who knew what kind of situation they were about to walk into? Ava knew with werewolves it was best to expect the worst.

With the white plastic purse slung across her shoulder, Ava walked beside Granny to the back entrance. She wrapped her arms around her as the cool night air brushed against her skin.

Ava hesitated as she drew near the backdoor. Standing in front of the door was the bouncer, a huge man with his bald head shining against the security light. Granny grabbed her elbow and urged her forward.

"Can I help you ladies?" The bouncer didn't budge.

Granny smiled wide. "I'm here to drop off some orders for the dancers."

"Sorry. This entrance is not for visitors."

"I don't think you understand." Granny's lips pulled into a pucker while her eyes narrowed. Ava caught a whiff of White Diamonds as the old lady tilted her head.

"I don't think *you* understand. This door is for the dancers only." The bouncer stuck his thumb over his meaty shoulder. "If you're not here for amateur night, then you can't get in."

Granny inhaled slightly, before she relaxed her stance. "Well, why didn't you say so?"

The bouncer cringed. "Don't tell me you're here to strip."

Granny propped her hands on her hips, her face set in a schoolteacher scowl. "Are you trying to tell me I'm too old? Is that what you're saying? Because there are laws against discriminating against senior citizens. Did you know that?"

"Umm, it's not that..." He dug the toe of his shoe into the dirt, his weight shifting, apparently at a loss for words.

"Are you trying to discriminate against me because of my age?" Granny wagged a boney finger dangerously close to his chest. "Is that what this is about?"

"I didn't mean..." He ran his large palm back and forth across the nape of his neck, glancing at Ava for help.

Ava bit the inside of her cheek, trying not to grin. The guy outweighed Granny by two hundred pounds. It didn't matter. Granny was more intimidating.

"Well, just so you know, it's not me that's planning on stripping. It's her." Granny jerked her thumb toward Ava.

Ava's stomach lurched.

The bouncer sighed, obvious relief spreading across his face.

"But..." Ava inhaled sharply at Granny's poke in her side.

"Now if you don't mind, I've got to get her changed." Granny shoved Ava in front of her as the bouncer stepped aside, opening the metal door.

"So what's your name?" The bouncer gave Ava a wide smile, showing way too many crooked teeth.

"Av..." Granny gave her an elbow to the side. Ava rubbed her bruised ribs and glared at the old lady.

"He means your stage name." Granny shook her head and turned back to the bouncer. "Not sure. Got a red thong and some pasties." The old lady patted her bag as she gave the bouncer a thoughtful look. "What kind of names have the amateurs been using tonight? We don't want to take someone else's stage name. We want to be unique."

Ava wrinkled up her nose, her stomach churning faster than ever.

"Well, I've seen a few use astrological signs, like Aquarius and Taurus. Another girl came in using a name from a cartoon movie."

"What do you think? What name suits her?" Granny touched the bouncer on the arm as they stood there together looking at Ava from head to toe.

The bouncer's grin widened. "With all that beautiful black hair, and a red thong, I'd say she looks like Little Red Riding Hood."

Granny snapped her fingers.

"That's perfect. All we need is a hood." Granny clapped her hands together.

"I bet one of the regular girls would let her borrow something." The bouncer didn't take his eyes off Ava. She glared. Unfazed, he gave her a wink.

Grabbing Granny under her elbow, Ava gave her a tight smile. "Come on, Granny, we need to hurry if we're going to get me ready in time."

The old lady nodded and gave the bouncer a grateful smile as Ava hurried her though the door. When she heard the steel door slam shut she stopped in her tracks.

"What?" Granny frowned.

"I am not stripping." Ava spat out the words.

Granny shrugged. "I didn't intend for you to. We just needed to get inside." Granny gave her a thoughtful look. "But we do need to get you in costume."

"For what?"

Granny waved her hand dismissively. "In case the bouncer comes inside. If he asks why you aren't dancing just tell them you're still waiting your turn."

Ava rolled her neck from side to side and inhaled deeply. "Okay, that makes sense." Ava glanced down the hall to the nearest door. She nodded.

"I'm guessing from the noise level this is the where the strippers get ready." Ava lifted her ear from the door and looked to Granny.

Granny nodded and turned the knob.

The dressing room was crowded with dancers who were either walking around in their bra and panties or topless. All the girls were heavily made up, with smoky eye shadow and bright red lipstick.

Some of the girls were tall and thin, like trained dancers, while others were petite and curvy. But all seemed to have one commonality. They were all comfortable with their naked bodies.

Ava expected everyone to stop and turn when the door opened, but they didn't. Instead they kept on inhaling cigarettes with one hand while applying eye shadow with the other. Apparently, stripping required a girl to be skilled at multi-tasking.

"Come on in, ladies." An older lady gripping a clipboard pushed Ava forward.

She was surprised that the deep voice belonged to an attractive older lady. Slim and trim, she wore a business suit and her blond hair was molded into a loose bun at the nape of her neck. A cigarette dangled out of the corner of her mouth.

The woman looked Ava up and down and frowned. "Don't tell me you're getting cold feet."

"What? No, I..."

"We left her red cape at home." Granny stepped in front of Ava and gave the lady a confident smile. "We were wondering if you had one back here we could borrow."

"She plans on wearing something other than a cape?" The woman lifted her aggressively plucked eyebrow. "You know the rules. The cookie jar has to be covered."

"Cookie jar?" Ava frowned.

The woman in charge lifted her bored eyes to Ava. "Your vagina, pussy, beaver. Whichever term you prefer."

Ava closed her eyes and silently wished for a quick death.

"No need to worry. We'll have her cookie jar all wrapped up." Granny patted her bag. "I've got her thong and some pasties in here. She's little Red Riding Hood, you know. Just need a red cape."

"Fascinating." The woman lifted the cigarette out of her puckered mouth with two long fingers. She exhaled her smoke. Ava coughed and waved the smoke out of her face.

The woman pointed toward the corner of the room. "Look in the closet. One girl was a vampire last Halloween and I think she had a red cape." Ava started in that direction when the woman's gruff voice made her hesitate. "Just be sure you put it back."

"I will." Ava narrowed her eyes. What the hell was she? The cape police?

Granny slid up beside her as Ava absently searched through the costumes. "I take it she's gone?"

"Yeah. She gave me this waiver for you to sign." Granny shoved the paper under Ava's nose.

"Waiver? Why would I need a waiver?"

Granny shrugged. "In case you get hurt, you won't sue the club."

Ava turned and faced the old lady. "Get hurt doing what?"

"That." Granny pointed a finger at a passing dancer wearing platform heels.

Ava wrinkled up her nose. "How many dancers have gotten hurt wearing those heels?"

A passing stripper stopped in front of Ava. "Why this month alone, we've had two girls break their foot when they slipped on something on the stage. Hell, even my insurance won't pay for me to have these bunions removed." While balancing on one leg, the stripper lifted a long limb and shoved her deformed foot in Ava's face.

Ava's eyes widened and she leaned back.

The stripper straightened and shrugged. "If you don't sign it, you don't get to dance." With that she strutted away on her platforms.

"I'm not stripping."

Granny ignored her and continued to dig through the rows and rows of costumes. She stopped and pulled out something red. "What about this?"

Ava held out the red cloth and shook her head. "That's a cape but it doesn't have a hood." She pointed to the blue shiny material next to where Granny had picked up the cape. "Probably goes with the Super girl costume."

Granny shoved the cape back on the rack and continued to sort. She paused and pulled out something else. "Here."

Ava held the long red cape in front of her. "I don't think Little Red Riding Hood's cape was that long."

Granny snorted. "Well it's the best we can do. Besides there's enough material to cover your whole body while you're searching for Jayden." Granny's voice was but a whisper.

Being covered sounded good to Ava. Sighing, she held her hand out to Granny. "Fine. Give me the rest of the costume."

The old lady smiled as she hurried her over to a private corner with a dressing screen. Ava stepped behind it and began to change.

"Are you finished yet?"

"Are you sure you can't find something else for me to wear instead of these pasties?" Ava glanced down at the red circles covering her nipples. She sniffed. They really did smell like strawberries.

"Don't they cover your nipples?" Granny's head peeked around the screen.

Ava cringed. "Yes, they cover my nipples."

Granny shot her a frown. "Then what's the problem?"

Ava gritted her teeth. "They don't cover anything else. I'm completely naked." Ava held her hands out and looked down. "Not to mention the fact that I'm afraid to take a step in this edible thong. It feels like it's going to rip in two every time I move."

Granny smiled. "That I can assure you won't happen. In fact there's a money-back guarantee that those panties won't rip, not until someone actually takes a bite out of them."

"That's comforting." Ava closed her eyes and rubbed her pounding temple.

"Here, take one of these." Granny held out a small mint.

Ava narrowed her eyes at the lady. "What is it? Arsenic?"

"Just something to help you relax. Don't worry. I take one all the time when I have to host a sex party." Granny smiled

"It's not a roofie is it?" Ava lifted her brow.

"No. I wouldn't even know where to get that." Granny paused and lifted her finger to her lip. "Although, my friend, Ester, has a grandson who is a drug dealer. I bet he could hook me up with some hoofie."

"It's called roofie, not hoofie." Ava cringed, the throbbing in her head getting louder. She shoved the pill back into Granny's palm. "I'm not taking it."

Granny shrugged and slipped the tablet back in her purse.

"All right, here's the plan. Keep the girls busy with your edible whatever and I'll go look for Jayden." Ava grabbed the cape and wrapped it around her like a cocoon.

"Good luck." Granny gave her an encouraging squeeze on the arm before walking to the middle of the room. Putting two fingers between her lips, she whistled. The screeching noise halted the movement in the room as all the dancers turned to look at the old lady.

"Listen up, girls. I've got everybody's order from the sex party!" The excited girls immediately descended on the old lady like buzzards on road kill. A few of the girls didn't gather in the center of the room, obviously college girls here for amateur night. Instead, they took the opportunity to seize seats at the coveted makeup tables and brushed eye shadow over their lids and swiped lipstick across their lips.

Opening the door, Ava peeked out. Thankfully, the hall was empty. Slipping out the door, she made her way down the hall. The carpet was pink and the walls were deep red with gold crown molding at the ceiling.

Ava looked back over her shoulder to make sure no one was following her. Picking up her pace, she stopped when she reached the door at the end of the hall.

She reached for the doorknob, expecting it to be locked. To her relief, it turned. Slowly pushing the door open, Ava groped for the light switch on the wall in the darkened room. When her fingers brushed the plastic tip, she held her breath and flicked the switch.

Her heart lunged. Tied to a chair in the corner of the room was Jayden, his head hanging limply on his chest. His blond hair was matted with blood from where they had beaten him. His arms, bruised and cut, were tied behind his back while his legs were tied to the chair.

Ava took a step closer, Jayden jerked his head up and it was then she saw his face. His right eye was swollen shut and his left barely open. He glared at her with a hatred so intense it actually made her stomach hurt.

Swallowing hard, Ava held up her hand and removed her hood. "Jayden it's me, Ava. I'm here with Granny to get you out."

His eyes went from hatred to confusion to relief as she stepped closer. "Ava, you need to leave now. They're looking for you."

Kneeling at his feet, Ava reached into the large plastic purse and pulled out a knife. "I know. I'm not alone.

Damon's out front in the club and Granny's with the strippers."

His head jerked over to her. "Damon let you and Granny come?" He gritted his teeth and shook his head. "I'm going to kick his ass."

Ava gave him a slight smile. "He didn't bring us." She ducked her head and quickly worked the knife against the thick ropes.

"He doesn't know you two are here." Jayden's voice sounded oddly hollow.

"He's not going to know until we get back home, got it?" Ava released his legs and went to work on cutting his hands free.

When the last thread snapped, she stood.

"Damn." His good eye roamed over her near naked body.

"Shut up." Ava frowned and wrapped her hooded cape around herself.

Jayden managed a crooked grin. "What are you supposed to be?"

"Little Red Riding Hood. Believe me, the irony is not lost on me." Ava shook her head. "Look, we've got to get you out of here." Cracking the door, Ava peeked out. "We'll go out the back door."

Jayden snorted. "The bouncer guarding the back door isn't going to let me out. He's the fucker who did this to me."

"Well, you can't go out the front." Ava looked back at him. Jayden leaned against the wall, pain etched in every line of his face. Ava looked down at the floor, her hand running the red cape between two fingers, feeling trapped. How was she going to get Jayden out?

Ava's head jerked up, her mouth settling into a big smile.

Jayden frowned. "What?"

"I got an idea."

CHAPTER THIRTEEN

Damon eased himself onto the corner stool at the bar, careful not to hit his sword against the metal bar running under the counter and make a clinking sound. The bar wasn't as crowded as the tables were, but he still had to wait for Braxton to finish filling drink orders before the bartender ambled toward him.

"What can I get you?" Braxton nodded slightly, while running his tan cloth across the counter, his eyes scanning and assessing anyone nearby.

"Just a beer." Damon felt for the plastic bag at his waist and palmed it, waiting for the opportunity to pass it to the bartender.

Braxton pulled a mug off the shelf and placed it under the beer tap and filled it. He slid it to Damon, who took a drink.

"Consider it on the house." Braxton kept his bar towel moving in circles, wiping up invisible condensation and spilt beer. "I hear you need a special drink."

"Something like that." Damon flattened his hand on the counter, hiding the bag he'd palmed. He slid his hand closer to the napkin next to his mug. A cold female hand across his neck made him freeze.

"I'm done." The stripper purred near his ear.

"So, I see." He turned his face toward her and she slipped her free hand toward his crotch.

"Are you ready?" She poked out her lips in a sexy pout.

"I need to drink my beer first." Damon forced an interested grin to his lips. He nodded toward Braxton. "Can I buy you a drink?"

"I'm working. I'm not supposed to be drinking." She shot a nervous look at Braxton as if she expected him to chastise her.

"What if I buy you a Red Bull?" Damon asked.

She turned back to him and her full lips curled up. "Sure. Make sure it's loaded." She winked.

Damon caught Braxton's' attention and ordered a Red Bull and vodka. Braxton nodded and left his bar towel to mix up the concoction.

The stripper wrapped her arms around Damon's upper arm like a boa constrictor.

"Why don't you go make sure our room will be empty in about five minutes?" Damon put his empty hand around the stripper's waist. Finally, she complied. When he turned his attention back to the bar, he noticed Braxton's bar towel on the counter.

Lifting his beer, he took a long swig. As he placed it back on the counter, he dragged the towel closer and slid the plastic bag underneath. As soon as he moved his hand away, Braxton's hand came down on the towel pulling it toward him and under the counter in one easy motion.

"Here's your drink." Braxton shoved the Red Bull and vodka toward him. "Make sure Cindy gives the bouncer his drink." Braxton slid another drink over to Damon for the bouncer.

Damon frowned. "Who's Cindy?"

"Cindy is the name of your stripper." Braxton didn't bother fighting a grin.

"She's not my stripper." Damon growled.

Ava managed to grab another red cape from the stripper's dressing room and make it back to the office without being seen.

"Here put this on." Ava tossed the red material toward Jayden before she took up her post of peeking out through the cracked door into the hallway.

She glanced back over her shoulder to see Jayden standing there with the red cape covering his massive shoulders. Though it would cover his face and his upper body, there was no way to conceal his muscular legs.

"Shit. I don't think this is going to work. You look like a drag queen."

"I just need to get by the bouncer. I don't have to look as hot as you."

Ava tugged on her bottom lip with her teeth. "You're right." Her gaze met his. "Are you ready?"

Jayden nodded slightly. Ava knew if they waited any longer he wouldn't have the strength to make it out the door.

Ava retrieved Granny's plastic white purse and peered inside. Her lips parted slightly then curved into a wide smile. "Actually, all we have to do is make it out the back door."

Swinging around, Ava peered out the crack of the door. Pulling the door open wide, she gave Jayden the all clear sign. When she stepped out into the empty hallway, Jayden was right behind her. He shot his hand out in front of her, stopping her from continuing.

"I need to go first." Despite his condition, Jayden was still being protective.

Not wanting to step on his manhood, Ava looped her hand through his arm. "We go together." His eyes squinted as his lips pressed into a defiant thin line. Quickly she added, "We'll blend in better. Girls usually walk side by side."

Indecision reflected in his eyes as he considered her logic. His face relaxed slightly as he gave her a brief nod, then covered his face with the hood.

She held onto Jayden, not so much out of fear, but to give him the extra support. With each step he limped, and when she glanced up into his face she could see his jaw clenched, swallowing back the pain.

They almost made it to the exit when the dressing room door swung open.

They froze.

Ava's heart plummeted and she was certain it would never start again.

Granny stepped into the hallway.

Ava sucked in a breath and rubbed her hand over her heart, making sure it was still working. "Shit, Granny, you scared me."

"Ava, I..." The old lady's words trailed off as her eyes traveled over the covered figure that was Jayden. "Oh, my God."

"I'm okay, Granny," Jayden mumbled but didn't bother lifting his hood. Granny brought her hand up to his hidden face, but he grabbed her hand. "It's not anything that won't heal."

"We need to get him out of here now." Ava looked over her shoulder making sure they were still alone in the hallway. "We'll go out the back door."

"What about the bouncer?" Granny posed the question to Ava, but kept her eyes on Jayden.

"We will keep Jayden covered. If the bouncer stops us then we'll use that piece in your bag." Ava handed Granny her purse.

Jayden's head jerked up, the red hood slipping to one side, exposing his face. "You got a gun? Jesus, Granny, how the hell did you get a gun?"

Granny gasped at Jayden's beaten face.

Ava cringed and pulled the hood over Jayden's face. "She doesn't have a gun. She has a Taser."

"Who the hell gave you a Taser?"

Dotting at the moisture at the corners of her eyes, Granny gave him a stern look. "One of the girls at my last sex party was short about fifty dollars on her order. She bartered with me."

"For a Taser?"

Granny shrugged. "She said she needed a vibrator more than a Taser. Poor girl hadn't had a date in over a year." Granny's brows came together. "I didn't have a heart to tell her that the only way someone was going to attack her was if she was wearing a paper bag over her head. But even then, it was doubtful. She was not very big on personal hygiene."

"She didn't use deodorant?" Ava wrinkled her nose.

"She didn't shave."

"Her legs?"

"Nothing. Not her legs, not her armpits, not even her hoo-hah."

"Jesus, will you two stop talking about vibrators and hoo-hahs? This is worse torture than what they did," Jayden hissed through gritted teeth.

"Here, give me my purse." Granny stuck her hand in and came out with a pink Taser.

"Give it to me." Jayden stuck out his hand. "I'll go first. That way I can Taser his ass before he can let the others know what's going on."

As Granny walked out the exit door with Jayden concealed in a red hood, a large hand clamped down on Ava's shoulder. Her heart jumped into her throat as she met Granny's wide eyes with her own. She knew what she had to do.

Ava slammed the door shut behind them, shutting out her freedom but securing theirs.

"What are you doing back here?"

Ava slowly turned, gripping her cape in her fists. She wrinkled her nose and her eyes watered at the horrendous smell of rotten eggs coming from the beaver costume.

"I asked..." The enormous stinky beaver stopped and turned as loud voices came up behind them.

"What the hell is this?" Two large men filled the hallway as they stared between Ava and the Beaver.

Ava gasped, her stomach clenching so hard she was sure her lunch was about to make a second appearance. Standing not six feet in front of her were her kidnappers.

Grasping her hood, Ava burrowed deeper, hoping the dimly lit hallway would prevent them from recognizing her.

Forcing her feet to stay planted, Ava spoke. "I'm here for amateur night." From out of the corner of her eye she saw the Beaver jerk his head in her direction. "I got confused how to get to the stage."

"Stage is that way." The younger of the two jerked his thumb across his thick shoulder.

"Thanks." Wrapping her cape tighter around her, she walked past them. A hand reached out and yanked her to a stop. Holy shit. She had come so far only to be caught.

"Say, sweet thing, what're you supposed to be?" His rancid breath crawled across her like spiders and she couldn't stop shivering.

"Little Red Riding Hood." Ava was shocked to hear the calmness in her own voice.

"Nice." He released her and swatted her bottom. She dug her fingers into the palms of her hands, refusing to give in to the urge to turn around and punch him in the balls. Putting one step in front of the other, Ava forced herself to walk down the hall toward the stage.

Barrett watched Ava walk away, making sure she was out of the way before the shit hit the fan. He knew she'd come to help save Jayden, but doing so had put her in danger. Now he was going to have two people to save.

"What the hell are you supposed to be?" one of the men snarled.

Barrett turned his attention back to the two large red wolves standing in front of him. He'd smelled Ava's fear rolling off her and Barrett knew she'd recognized them as her kidnappers.

"He's a beaver."

"He's a stinky beaver." The older of the two waved his hand in front of his face.

"You two don't smell much better." That was actually the truth. Red wolves had a distinct smell, a cross between cat urine and musk.

The younger wolf lunged. Barrett swung, his furry fist meeting the jaw of the pissed off red wolf. The wolf stumbled back, slamming his back into the wall. His dazed eyes met Barrett's for a split second and then they closed while his feet slipped out from under him. He slid down the wall like a wet noodle.

"That wasn't very nice." The older red wolf bristled and slowly advanced.

Barrett removed the beaver head. "You should have kept your boyfriend on a tighter leash." The beaver's head landed with a thump on the floor.

The red wolf snarled, reaching behind his back and pulling out a gun. Barrett was quicker. He threw his full weight at the wolf. They landed in a pile on the floor. While the red wolf was busy trying to suck in air, Barrett grabbed the gun and tossed it over his shoulder.

"Fucker." Barrett threw his fist in the guy's face, knocking him out cold.

The creak of the steel door had Barrett scrambling for the gun. Jumping to his feet, he aimed the weapon at the door just as three large Weres ran through.

Zane, Lucien and Jaxon stopped short when they saw he leveled a gun at them.

"What's up? Boss?" Jaxon lifted his chin in a greeting, while Lucien and Zane's gazes swept the hallway looking for trouble. Granny shoved her way through the wall of men and muscle.

"Shit." Barrett lowered the gun. "Granny. What are you doing here?"

Granny pursed her lips. "Getting my boy out."

Zane scowled and then looked back at Barrett. "We got here just as Jayden and this one here"—he jabbed his thumb towards Granny—"attempted to Taser the guard outside the door. It didn't do anything but piss him off. We took him out."

"The perimeter is secure. We set up Guardians around the building, but we did see a lot of rogue wolves enter the front door. Not sure how many." Jaxon shrugged.

"How many Guardians did we get inside?" Barrett asked.

"Half a dozen, not including us." Lucien smirked. "I think it's a fair fight."

"Yeah, for them." Zane shoved his thumb in Granny's direction. "I told this one to stay with Jayden, but she doesn't listen too well."

No shit. Barrett shook his head. "Granny you need to get out of here before they know Jayden is missing."

"I can't leave without Ava." Granny stuck her chin up. "Where is she anyway? She was wearing a Little Red Riding Hood costume."

Barrett went still. Ava in a stripper costume and Damon in the crowd. Those two things did not mix. There was no way he could get to her before Damon saw her.

Reaching into his jeans pocket, he pulled out his cell phone and dialed Braxton.

The second it connected, he said, "Restrain Damon, and do it now."

"What the fuck?" Damon jerked against the fuzzy pink handcuff Braxton slapped on his wrist. The other end was tightly cuffed on the metal railing of the bar.

"Sorry, man, Barrett's orders." Braxton held his hands up and took a generous step back just as Damon made a grab for him.

"Barrett?" Damon gritted his teeth, dread free-flowing into his gut. "Barrett wanted me handcuffed? Why?"

Braxton held up his palms and he shrugged. "Don't know, man. He just said to restrain you."

"You chose to restrain me with fuzzy handcuffs." Damon tugged against the metal trapping him. Who would have thought handcuffs that resembled cotton candy would be so strong.

"It's the only thing I had on hand."

"I don't even want to know why you have pink fuzzy handcuffs." Damon narrowed his eyes at the bartender. "I would have at least thought you more of a blue kind of guy."

"Smartass. They're not mine. Someone turned them in."

"Yeah, right." Damon looked under the counter. The railing was one long piece that ran the entire length of the bar instead of multiple pieces fitted together. Sitting up, Damon shot Braxton a glare.

Braxton shoved a shot glass of whiskey toward him and then darted out of his reach. "Here, might as well drink this since you're kind of stuck there."

"What's going on?" Damon glanced around the crowded room, anxiety crawling around in his stomach. He sucked in air as the room started to shrink. A drunken guy wearing a doctor costume stumbled and slammed into his shoulder. Damon snapped and growled. The doctor quickly straightened, mumbled an apology and scurried away.

"I'm not sure." Braxton's smirk slid off his face when his gaze landed on the main stage. Damon turned his head following the path of Braxton's eyes. His gaze landed on the

leggy stripper wearing a red cape, the hood obscuring her face. His body leaped to life, his dick hardening with such a speed, he was shocked.

Gritting his teeth, Damon forced himself to look away. He was shocked at his body's reaction and guilt flooded his chest. No woman had ever had that kind of control over his body. No one, except his Ava.

Damon's nostrils flared as the dancer walked toward the pole in the middle of the stage. Her long legs peeked out from the blood red cape with each step. Her matching hood enveloped her face, with only her long dark hair draping out from under the concealing material.

Nickleback blared over the sound system, her slow movements matching every sensual beat. Slowly, she relaxed her white-knuckle grip on the blood red material. The DJ introduced her as Little Red Riding Hood.

The cloak rippled away from her thigh making his dick harden.

"Are you ready for your lap dance now, sugar?" Cindy the stripper stepped in between his legs. He leaned back, her overwhelming sickening scent making him nauseated. Damon couldn't take his eyes off the stripper on stage. Though he couldn't see her eyes, she seemed to be staring straight at him.

Little Red Riding Hood reached up and slid her hood off her head.

Air whooshed out of his lungs and his mouth dropped. His already hard dick twitched as liquid hot lust flowed like lava through every cell of his body.

"Hey, Little Red Riding Hood, I got something you can nibble on." Damon jerked his head toward the group of college guys crowding the edge of the stage, waving dollar bills and hollering sexual innuendos at Ava. His Ava.

Fuck no.

Damon jumped to his feet, ready to tear those guys limb from scrawny limb. Pain shot through his wrist as his body held fast to the handcuff. Looking down at his restraint, he growled. "Fuck!"

"Hey, sugar, we can do that, too, if you like." Candy trailed her palm down his chest past his waist to his crotch and grabbed a handful of him. "Oh my, looks like you're all ready for me."

Damon grimaced and snatched the girl's hand away.

He heard it, a growl so low only another wolf would perceive it. He knew who it belonged to. Only this time it wasn't male. It was female.

It was Ava.

Standing in front of the stripper pole, Ava held Damon's gaze across the crowded room. How could he let a skanky stripper paw all over him?

The look of shock that crossed his face when she removed her hood was priceless. At first she thought his scent of arousal was because of her. Then Ava saw the stripper was practically humping his leg.

Keeping her eyes on his, Ava pulled the tie at her neck, letting the cape slip from her shoulders like rain and puddle at her feet. Hollers and catcalls rang out over the song she'd been dancing to. She'd been scared when she had first stepped on stage, but after watching Damon and that damn stripper, anger replaced any fear she'd felt about taking her clothes off.

She slowly slid her hands down across her breasts and between her thighs as she danced to the seductive music. Turning, she faced the pole and bent over, making sure she showed every inch of her ass. She knew the thong wasn't doing anything to hide anything.

Ava heard Damon's growl over the noise of the crowd. She smiled in satisfaction. Good. Let's see how he liked it.

Standing up, Ava faced the crowd. Reaching high on the pole she jumped and wrapped her legs around it. Leaning back until she was upside down, she caressed her breasts and slowly slid down the pole in a controlled slide.

When she reached the bottom, she rolled over until she was on all fours, crawling to the edge of the stage toward a group of young college boys. She didn't look at Damon. She didn't have to. She heard his violent growl above the music, making the hair on her neck stand up.

"Hello, boys." Sitting back on her knees, Ava smiled at the guys as she pulled her thong aside with her thumb for them to slip money inside. "I don't bite. Hard."

The guy swallowed, his eyes glued to her breasts. Ava fought the impulse to punch him in the throat.

He slid his fingers along with a couple of dollar bills in the waist of her thong. "Baby, you're the best-looking thing I've seen on the stage tonight."

"Thanks." Ava bit her cheek, trying to refrain from telling him to fuck off.

"How about you let me and my buddies buy you a drink?"

"No, thanks. No drinking on the job, you know."

"Maybe this will sweeten the deal." He held up a hundred-dollar bill, slipping it in the top of her edible panties.

Ava reared back to knock him on his ass when the unmistakable roar of a wolf, splintering wood, and the grinding wail of bending metal hit her ears.

She pulled her leg back just in time as a beer bottle shattered on the stage and fights broke out throughout the club. Two burly men scrambled to grab her, instead knocking her backward toward the center of the stage. Then all hell broke loose.

Security guards rushed to all areas of the club trying to separate and contain the different fights, only to have three more break out. Women screamed and strippers dropped to the ground, picking up money that scattered to the floor.

Ava stood and then ducked, missing a chair flying through the air. Crouching, she glanced around to the group of college guys. Damon was in the middle of them, fists flying, while something pink and silver dangled from one of his wrists as he pummeled them.

Guilt and regret washed over her. The second they put their hands on her, Damon had gone after them. Her stomach tugged with remorse. She had baited Damon into fighting. Now, he might get hurt.

Damon knocked out two of the guys and was working on the other three. Ava frowned when she saw another guy coming up behind him with a knife glinting in his hand.

Taking off her platform heel, Ava scooted closer and hurled the shoe at the asshole's head. It hit him square in the face before bouncing off. A confused look crossed his face before he dropped to his knees and collapsed.

Glancing over at Damon, she froze. He laid the group of guys out like a fan around him and was staring hard at her, anger radiating out of his eyes.

"Ava, what the hell do you think you're doing?" His voice carried over the fighting in the club.

Jealously and anger flashed in her veins like electricity. "Me? What about you, Spartacus, and that fucking stripper?"

He jumped, gracefully landing on the stage like a lethal animal. Bending, he swiped her cloak off the stage and wrapped it around her until nothing but her head and feet were sticking out.

"What the hell were you thinking coming here tonight?" His eyes were like blue fire, hot and angry.

"I came to help get Jayden out." Ava smirked, cocking her head to the side. "And I did."

His glare slipped. "You did what?"

"Granny and I already got Jayden out. Through the back door."

"Is he okay?"

She nodded. "He's beat up pretty good, but he's going to be okay."

"So you stayed behind because you felt the need to shake your little ass on stage and get groped?" Damon's glare was back.

"If you stop being an asshole for five minutes, I can explain what happened." She clenched her jaw so tight her cheek ached.

"Asshole is my nature, sweetheart." He tossed her across his shoulder.

From her upside-down position she saw three large men run up to Damon. She knew from their size they had to be werewolves.

"What the fuck are you guys doing here, Zane?"

"Barrett called us in. We've got Guardians surrounding the perimeter and some inside as well. Jayden is out. We'll clear a path for you so you can get the female out," the one called Zane answered.

"Put me down, I can walk." Ava pounded on his muscled back as he ignored her and ran for the exit, dodging fists and beer bottles as the crowd continued to fight over the blare of the Black Eyed Peas song "My Humps."

Shouldering open the front door, Damon headed out into the night. Ava waited for him to slow down and return her to her feet.

He didn't. Instead, he ran toward a Hummer.

Heaving her off his shoulder, Damon propped her against the vehicle.

"Get in the backseat, lock the door, and lie down. I'm going back in for Barrett."

Ava frowned. "Barrett's inside? I never saw him."

"You wouldn't recognize him in his costume."

Climbing onto the leather seats, Ava shivered, the October night soaked into her bones. She wrapped her cloak tighter around her. "What costume did he have on?"

"A beaver."

Ava froze. "That was him?"

He jerked his head toward her. "You saw him? Where?"

"In the back, where I saw two of my kidnappers."

Damon reached under the front seat, pulling out a very large handgun, and tucked it in the waistband of his Spartacus costume. "Stay here, I'll be back."

Ava didn't have time to stop him. Damon ran across the parking lot, heading around the back of the building, back into danger.

Her gut twisted, her muscles momentarily frozen at what might happen. Swallowing the knot in the back of her throat, Ava forced her fingers to hit the lock button and then curled into a ball on the back seat.

Damon turned the corner of the building. A stream of screaming strippers poured out of the back door, stepping over something very large lying on the ground. As he pushed his way to the exit door, he paused. A bouncer lay sprawled on the ground, completely motionless.

Damon kicked the bouncer with the toe of his boot, expecting him to jump up. The bouncer didn't move. Leaning closer, he noticed a large red welt on the side of his neck. Just about the size of a stun gun.

Damon stepped over him. Entering the building, he glanced down the hallway. A headless beaver was kicking some serious ass.

Barrett dodged a hit and returned it with one of his own. He sent the guy flying into the wall. Two more bouncers ran into the hallway, knives in hand.

Damon jumped into the fray. He kicked the knife out of one guy's hand and turned, rushing the other guy. Grabbing the guy's hand, he twisted. The guy screamed and dropped the knife. Damon released his hold at the nauseating sound of snapping bone. The guy crumbled to the ground, cradled his arm and cried like a pussy.

Barrett stood in the middle of a pile of security guards sprawled out on the floor.

"Did you get Ava out?" Barrett glanced over his shoulder as he headed to what appeared to be a door to the office.

"I did. I take it that's the reason you had Braxton handcuff me to the bar," Damon snarled just as Barrett threw open the door. Tied to a chair and gagged was none other than David Jenkins.

"I didn't need you causing a scene and drawing attention to yourself until I could get Jenkins secured." Barrett put his oversized beaver foot between Jenkins's legs and pushed, sending the chair flying backward into a wall. The shelf above Jenkins's head trembled. A glass vase tumbled off, thunking him on the head.

Jenkins groaned. His eyes turned up in his head as his lids slid closed.

Barrett pulled out a flash drive and plugged it into the computer, his fingers tapping across the keys.

"Ava caused a scene, herself, prancing around practically naked."

"She wasn't naked. She had those pasties on, and a thong." Barrett pulled the flash drive out of the computer and went to tuck it into his pocket. He frowned as he realized the beaver suit had no pockets.

Damon grabbed Jenkins by his shirt collar, dragging him down the hall toward the exit, Barrett at his side. "You sure as hell better not be looking at Ava."

Jenkins moaned. Rousing, he began thrashing around like a cat in a wool sack.

Keeping his eyes on Barrett, Damon stopped and punched Jenkins in the face. Jenkins went still again.

"How could I not look? She was standing in front of me before she went on stage." Barrett opened the exit door, grabbed Jenkins by the legs while Damon grabbed under his arms. They headed for the Hummer.

Damon gritted his teeth so hard, his jaw cracked. Dropping their heavy package on the ground, Damon unlocked and opened the back of the vehicle.

"Ava, it's us." Damon and Barrett tossed Jenkins into the back like a rug.

Ava's head popped over the seat. "Who's that?"

"Jenkins. He jumped in the fight when I was going after those two red wolves." Barrett slid into the driver's seat. Damon climbed into the passenger's side.

"Red wolves?" Damon eyed Barrett and clenched his fists.

"My kidnappers." Ava sat back, buckling her seatbelt.

"They ran away, leaving Jenkins behind." Barrett snorted. "I tied him up so I could go after them, but security showed up."

"We don't have Ava's kidnappers."

"We have the ringleader who orchestrated the kidnapping. I'm sure the others are in hiding." Barrett nodded over his shoulder. "More importantly, with Jayden's help we found Haley."

"Is she okay?" Ava asked.

"She's fine." Barrett pulled out of the parking lot.

"Jenkins will face Tribunal for what he's done." Damon growled the words hot in his throat.

"What's Tribunal? Where are we headed? Back to Granny's?" Damon watched in the rear-view mirror as Ava leaned forward in her seat.

"You two are stopping for the night at a hotel, while I get this asshole back to Little Rock. You can come home in the morning," Barrett said.

"What about Jayden and Granny?" Ava frowned.

"I've sent some Guardians to take care of Jayden. After they check him out they are going to transport him and Granny to Arkansas for the Tribunal."

"I'm not used to being a wolf, remember?" She arched her eyebrow at Barrett. "What's Tribunal?"

"It's like a trial. David Jenkins will be presented before the wolf Pack and will have to answer for his crimes." Barrett glanced at Ava.

"And he will pay for them with his blood." Damon hissed, hoping he would be the one to mete out justice.

Barrett dropped them off at a motel on the outskirts of Shreveport. Though it was old with dark paneling and shag carpet, it was clean. It reminded Ava of the first hotel they'd stayed in together, the night he rescued her.

Clutching her red cape in front of her, Ava looked at Damon. "You haven't spoken three words since we left the club. You can't still be mad."

Damon turned, his eyes furious and narrowed. "Braxton is coming to pick me up so I can go get my bike."

Ava's heart slammed in her chest as she straightened. "Are you coming back?"

He said nothing, his fury palpable, filling the room until she shivered.

"Damon?" Her voice sounded small in her own ears. When she reached out to touch him, he stepped back, away from her touch.

Ava let her hand fall to her side, her heart breaking into a thousand brittle shards. She had only been trying to help. But in doing so she had broken her promise to him. He didn't trust her anymore.

Soundlessly, his footsteps tread across the puke green carpet. Damon shut the door behind him. Just like that he was gone.

Ava melted onto the floor, unable to move, afraid her bones might shatter like her heart. Blinking, she tried to dam up the sharp tears that threatened to spill. It was too late. She couldn't hold it in any longer.

Intense pain shot through her chest, her aching heart ripped into strips, bringing her to her knees. Tears streamed down her face as the searing pain of heartbreak intensified. Cradling her stomach, Ava pushed herself up off the nauseatingly green carpet. Pain gripped her again and she screamed. Nausea rolled over her like a wave as sweat beaded her body. Something was terribly wrong. She felt as if she were dying.

God, she'd never been this sick before in her entire life.

Gritting her teeth, she forced herself to stand. She would not get sick right here on the floor. She had to make it to the bathroom. Each step was an effort of concentrated will.

On her fourth step, her legs buckled, sending her crashing to the floor.

CHAPTER FOURTEEN

Damon parked his bike in front of the motel room, killed the engine and slid off the Harley. Usually a ride on his bike calmed him whenever he was in a bad mood, but not tonight. Nothing would help tonight. Anger boiled beneath his skin.

He wasn't going to let Ava off the hook and it didn't matter that it was 3:00 a.m. Damon stepped inside and locked the door. They were going to have a conversation that involved her being stupid enough to put herself in danger.

The inside of the dated motel room was dark. He squinted at the bed, but didn't see Ava. The orange bedspread was untouched.

"Ava?" His head snapped toward the closed bathroom door. She was in there—he could smell her scent.

He took a step and froze, his muscles tensing. Light spilled out from underneath the tiny crack of the bathroom door.

Damon pounded on the door. "Ava, we need to talk."

Shuffling noises came from behind the closed door.

"Ava, open this goddamn door right now!" Patience was never a virtue he aspired to have and he wasn't going to start striving for it now.

"What the fuck were you thinking strutting around naked on that stage with all those males in there? Or, were you even thinking?" Every time he closed his eyes, Damon saw that man putting his hands all over Ava.

"Do you have any idea what those assholes were thinking when you came out on that stage? Do you?"

No answer.

"I'll tell you, sweetheart. They were all thinking how many ways they could fuck you!" Damon pounded on the door again. "Do you know what I was thinking? Do you even care?"

Damon snorted. "I was thinking how many men I was going to have to kill for even looking at you, let alone touching you." His chest heaved as he fought to suck in air.

Glaring at the door, Damon hit it again.

Fuck it. Turning, he strode toward the motel door. He needed some air, some space.

The bathroom door opened. He turned back and she struck him in his chest, knocking him to the ground, with her paws pinning him there. He sucked in a deep breath.

Magnificent and beautiful with fur black as midnight, the wolf stared back at him with emerald green eyes.

Ava.

She'd finally shifted.

She whimpered, but her silken tail thumped against his thigh as she scented his chest, and then she licked his face. She cocked her head to the side before sitting back on her hind legs, still sitting on top of his stomach. She whimpered again, almost howling and then her eyes rolled back in her head. Her bones creaked, changing and stretching and accommodating, until she was back in her human form.

Still straddling him, Ava pinned his chest down with hands instead of paws.

"Are you okay?" Damon caressed her cheek. "God, Ava. I should have been here." The pain she endured must have been horrific. He swallowed hard. "Were you in pain?"

"Yes."

He was fucking pathetic. He had let his anger overwhelm him and the result was he hadn't been there for Ava when she needed him the most. "I'm so sorry, sweetheart." Damon swallowed the lump in his throat as images of Ava writhing in pain settled in his brain.

"How are you feeling?" Damon searched her eyes for any hints of lingering pain, wanting to make things better for her.

She said nothing as she leaned into his caress, rubbing her cheek against his palm, and her eyelids shuttered.

"Ava, is there anything you need?"

She stilled, her eyes opening. A slow, seductive smile spread across her face.

"Yes. I need to fuck."

The memory of her first shift from human to wolf would be forever etched in Ava's brain.

As soon as she realized what was happening to her, that she was actually shifting into a wolf, she had been terrified.

Writhing on the floor had been one of the most frightening experiences of her life. Pain shot through every vein in her body like unrelenting jolts of electricity.

Crawling to the bathroom, she grabbed the counter and pulled herself up to see her reflection in the mirror. Her hair was stuck to her sweaty face, her feverish eyes were red-rimmed and glossy.

White-hot pain struck her gut like a knife, and she cried out as she crumbled to the floor, and writhed. Every muscle in her body screamed as her bones lengthened and bent, tendons straining beyond their normal form. Her screams blended into growls until the angry pain that ravished her body had finally stilled.

Opening her eyes, she glanced down at her body, half afraid of how repulsive she might appear. What she saw was fur, thick and soft and shiny like expensive mink. Holding up her right hand, uh paw, Ava examined her new body. She didn't think she looked repulsive at all. Instead, she looked lean and strong and predatory.

The second that Damon had walked into the motel room, his distinct scent wafted over her like a five-course meal to a homeless beggar.

She rolled, jumping to her feet in a swift, easy motion. She grinned, liking the power racing through her body. Lifting her head, she sniffed the air. Damon's scent mingled with the anger he couldn't throttle.

Bang, bang, bang!

Narrowing her wolf eyes at the door, she heard him yelling, demanding she come out.

He obviously wanted to argue.

She wanted something else.

Ava heard a *thump, thump, thump,* behind her. She cocked her head. Her tail patted rhythmically against the linoleum.

Damon took a step away from the bathroom. Was he going to leave? She needed to stop him but wasn't quite sure how she was going to open the door with paws.

She stood on her hind legs, clamped her teeth down, hard, on the doorknob and turned her head. The door opened an inch. Nosing the door open all the way, she ran through it, just in time to see Damon reaching for the front door.

The look on Damon's face was priceless.

Not sure how she managed to shift back into human form, she straddled him and rubbed against the denim of his jeans and cotton T-shirt.

Grinding her crotch against his, she stroked her wetness against his jeans and judging from the scent of his arousal, he wanted her just as much as she wanted him.

Leaning down, she nipped at his ear as she licked his neck.

"I said I need to fuck." Nuzzling his neck, she pressed her bare breasts into his chest, her nipples hardening against his muscle. Reaching her hand between their bodies she stroked his cock before nimbly unzipping his jeans and pulling him out.

He groaned, wrapping his hands around her waist and pulling her closer. She smiled. Good. Now they were on the same page.

He pulled her mouth down to his, kissing her with blistering heat. She was afraid she was going to come before he was inside her.

Pulling away, Ava grabbed his jeans, stripping them away from his body while he ripped his T-shirt off.

Climbing up his body, she straddled him. He twisted his body, flipping her over on her back. "Not on the floor. You deserve better than to be taken on shag carpet."

"I don't care about the carpet, I just want you inside me." She strained toward him, but he held her away. He lifted her in his arms and carried her to the bed. Gently, he laid her down, apparently not in a hurry. She pulled him down, needing his mouth on hers, his skin against hers. He gazed at her with such intensity it burned her soul.

He covered her body with his, touching and stroking with his fingers until her body cried out for release. His mouth found her breast and he tugged her nipple into his hot mouth. She gasped, holding his head to her breast as he sucked. Pleasure arched through her body, making her grow even wetter.

"I want you in me, now," she panted, digging her nails into his back.

He nudged her thighs apart and entered her in one swift motion, burying himself deep. He groaned as he bit down on her neck, sending shivers racing through her quivering limbs.

"God, that feels so good," she moaned. He filled her, stretching her until she thought she would explode in pleasure.

"You're so fucking tight." He pulled back looking down at her with his intense gaze, muscles straining not to move.

"No. Don't stop." She hooked her ankles around his legs and ground down on his dick.

He growled as he withdrew and then thrust deep inside her body, his breathing becoming more ragged, his breath hot on her cheek. Ava arched off the bed, clutching him as his thrusts grew faster.

He claimed her mouth as his tongue tangled with hers, marking and claiming his territory. Their skin heated and slid against each other as sweat pooled between their bodies from their frantic lovemaking.

She quivered as pleasure streaked inside her body.

"Come for me," he commanded, his gaze fixed on her.

Throwing her head back, her orgasm swamped her, making her cry out as blinding white lights filled the edges of her vision.

His fingers dug into her hips, as he thrust faster, groaning loudly as his own orgasm spilled into hers.

He collapsed on her, a load of sweaty hot muscle. Wrapping her heavy arms around his back, Ava stroked his skin, loving the salty taste of him on her tongue, his scent on her body, his breath on her neck.

He shifted and rolled until she was lying on top of him. His calloused fingertips stroked her back, soothing her, as her eyelids grew heavy.

Neither spoke. They didn't need to. They'd spoken volumes more in the last hour than they had the last few days. Within minutes, his cock stirred to life against her thigh. She smiled, straddled his waist and slid down on his length, sighing as she began to rock against him.

"Ava," he whispered her name like a prayer as he gripped her hips and set the pace.

This moment, this one moment, would be all she had with Damon. He'd told her just having sex alone would not be enough to mate. She wanted this night seared into her memory so it would last her a lifetime.

She closed her eyes against the burning tears and buried her face against his neck.

This time when she came in a heated rush, she cried out his name as tears streaked down her face.

Racing down the highway toward Little Rock, Damon's chest tightened. The closer he got to their compound, the more he couldn't breathe.

When he woke that morning, he had jumped in the shower, careful not to wake Ava. They had shared an amazing night together, a sweat filled night of touches, caresses and endless lovemaking. He'd stayed awakee most of the night trying to fight the impending daylight. But morning had come all too quickly and with it the truth.

All that morning, Ava had tried to touch him, kiss him, but he'd brushed her off and pushed her away with excuses of phone calls he had to make. She tried to kiss him as she climbed on behind him. But Damon had ducked his head, acting like he hadn't noticed.

He'd noticed. He tried to distance himself since he woke up, knowing it was for the best. Ava was to be Barrett's mate. Barrett had the bloodlines, the breeding, the prestige.

Not him.

He was an orphan, no bloodlines, or status.

He'd seen the hurt in her beautiful green eyes. Damon swallowed down the pain that crept into the back of his throat every time she'd looked at him. It destroyed a little bit of his soul, that he'd caused her so much pain.

His misery increased as they crossed into Little Rock, nearing their destination.

He'd crossed the line. He'd had sex, no—made love— with Ava, knowing she was intended to be Barrett's mate.

The penalty for that crime was death. Damon knew without a doubt that Barrett would rip his throat out for his transgression against his Pack Master.

He slowed his speed as he drove into town. He glanced at the Council building that had been bombed, assessing the damage. A huge black hole, where the bomb had exploded, marred the otherwise pristine front of the building.

Damon continued until he came to the Guardians bunker-style living quarters. He turned into the parking lot.

Killing the engine, Damon waited for Ava to dismount first.

"Are you never going to talk to me again?" The tone in her voice betrayed the hurt she felt from his silence.

He gritted his teeth, forcing himself not to say a word. If he did, he was going to end up begging her to run off, find an Alpha that would to mate them together, and have a life.

Instead, he got off the bike and entered the building.

"Fuck." Ava slid off the bike and curled her fingers into fists as she followed Damon into the building, ready to scream at him for not fighting for them.

"Ava, thank God, you're all right." The General stepped out of a room and scooped her up in a tight hug. She smiled and met his worried gaze.

"I'm fine. Thanks to Damon." She looked at Damon under her lashes, who stood quietly.

"Then I owe you my eternal gratitude for keeping her safe." The General shook Damon's hand.

"You owe me nothing. Ava's safety was always my priority."

The General narrowed his eyes and looked between them. Ava could feel the tension in the room.

"I've talked to Barrett." The General pinched the bridge of his nose and looked back at Ava. "He told me what you found out in Louisiana, about who you really are."

"I think it's more than that, General." Damon took a step forward.

The General narrowed his eyes and straightened. "I don't think this concerns you, Guardian."

"His name is Damon and he risked his life for me. So in my book this concerns him as well." Ava's anger boiled in her veins, now aimed at a different target. "Why didn't you tell me who I was?"

The General gave her a weary smile. "I was trying to protect you."Damon stepped up beside her. "She had every right to know."

The General's head snapped up. He gritted his teeth and let out a snarl.

"He's right," Ava said.

The General let out a long sigh. "Ava, your father was my best friend. After your mother died, he was devastated. He lost his mate and he was worried that he might lose you, too, if someone found out your royal bloodlines. Back then, the Packs weren't as organized or as large as they are now. We couldn't risk losing you."

The General ran his hand over his tired eyes. Ava noticed he'd added a few bags under his eyes since she'd last seen him.

"Your father never told you that you were a wolf. That's why you were raised away from the Pack, to help protect your identity. When your father realized that you were getting close to puberty, he obtained a drug that would prevent you from shifting."

Ava shook her head. "I never took any kind of medicine. Not even as a child."

"But it can be hidden in food. Isn't that right, General?" Damon snarled.

The blood rushed from her face and she looked at the man she'd considered her father for so many years. "Is that right?"

"Yes." The General closed his eyes and shook his head. "Your father put it in your food. After he died I continued doing it as well."

She shook her head. "But what about after I moved out? There's no way you could have put it in my food then."

"That coffee you like so much, the one that I always have sent to your house?" He had the decency to look away

"My coffee. You put it in my coffee." She snorted and looked around. "I thought you belonged to a coffee-of-the-month club and that's why you always sent me so much."

"That's probably why you had headaches in the morning. It wasn't caffeine headaches, it was the withdrawals from the drug." Damon crossed his arms and narrowed his eyes on the General.

The General took a step toward her. "Ava, I didn't do this to hurt you."

She held out her hand and took a deep breath. "Yes, but you still hurt me all the same."

The General stood silent and, for the first time in her life, Ava realized he didn't have a clue how to fix the problem.

"Barrett is expecting us, Ava." Damon's husky voice sliced through the silence.

She nodded and then looked back at the man she called father. "I understand why you did it. I don't agree, but I understand."

The General looked lost. Her heart tugged and she walked into his arms and hugged him. When she pulled back, she whispered, "I still have a lot of questions."

He nodded and smiled. "I have all the time in the world to talk. Just let me know when."

"Are you okay?" Damon frowned and shoved his hands in his pockets.

"I will be."

The front door opened and Jayden limped in on crutches. "Damon, my man." Jayden limped toward him and stuck out his hand. Despite the bruises, Jayden had a big smile plastered on his face. "Glad to see you two got out of that club last night without incident."

Damon nodded and looked at Jayden's leg.

"Can't say the same about you. How's the healing?"

Jayden shrugged. "Bastards broke it with a baseball bat. Should be completely healed in a couple more days."

Ava looked between him and Jayden. "A bone will heal that fast?"

"When you're a werewolf, yes." Damon nodded. "The bones and tissue heal ten times quicker than that of a human."

"Well, if you guys are ready, we can head out to the back. The Tribunal has been waiting for the two of you to arrive."

"I get to come too?" She rubbed her palms on her jeans.

Damon started forward, then turned to face Ava. "Of course. The crime Jenkins committed was against you and Haley."

"Haley's here?" Ava gave Jayden a wide-eyed look.

"She is. She's safe. She will stand with you when the Tribunal begins."

Ava let out a relieved sigh. Damon couldn't help but smile. While he had doubted that Haley was still alive, Ava never did. Ava never gave up hope.

"Come on, they're waiting for us." Jayden took a step, hesitated, then looked back at Ava.

"What's wrong?" Damon looked from Jayden to Ava.

"I don't know." Jayden cocked his head to the side, looking at Ava. "You look different."

"What do you mean?" She reached up and ran her hands through her hair. "Is my hair sticking up?"

Jayden froze, his mouth dropping open, fascinated by the motion of her hand.

Damon's hackles raised as Jayden's scent filled the air. He whacked him across the chest with the back of his hand. "What the hell has gotten into you?"

Closing his eyes, Jayden inhaled deeply as he leaned toward Ava. "My God, you smell good."

Damon shoved Jayden back a few feet as possessiveness ripped through his gut. "You need to step the fuck back."

Jayden, balancing on his good leg, kept staring at Ava, his eyes glossing over.

"What the hell's wrong with Jayden?" Her breath tickled Damon's neck as she looked across his shoulder. Her scent, even more wonderfully potent today, was like she'd rolled around in pine needles in a forest.

Fuck. His stomach bottomed out, hitting the floor in a thud. He should have known what had happened, but he'd been too blinded by his lust for her.

Keeping his eyes narrowed on Jayden who was trying to get a better look at Ava, Damon spoke over his shoulder. "Ava, last night after we..."

"I swear Damon, if you say 'after we fucked,' I'm going to rip your balls off myself."

Damon turned. "I was going to say 'after we made love.'"

A slow grin spread across her face. "You were?"

Jayden took a step closer. Damon growled.

"What's wrong with Jayden?"

"He ...desires you." Damon curled his hands into fists. Jayden was closer than a brother to him, but when it came to Ava, Damon wouldn't hesitate to knock him out. "The Queen, when ready to mate, will always draw wolves to her.

"Is that what happened last night between us? Were you just looking to get laid?" Her smile faded.

Damon gritted his teeth. "It was more than just sex, Ava. We both know that."

"You wouldn't say two words to me. I thought you regretted last night."

Damon felt like someone had sucker punched the air out of his lungs. He looked at her. "Are you serious?"

She nodded. Jayden inched closer. Damon punched him in the face. Jayden fell to the ground, out cold. Damon looked back at her.

"Ava, last night was the best experience I've had in my life. I've never thought I would be worthy of a female like you. Last night you gave yourself to me without inhibitions, without ulterior motives." Damon brought her hand to his mouth and kissed her knuckles. Damon looked into her eyes. He knew what he must do. He'd known it all along.

"I love you, Damon." She wrapped her arms around his waist, burying her face into his chest. "I don't care what that stupid law says about me being mated to Barrett. I don't want Barrett. I want you."

Joy, unexpected and complete, swelled in his chest until he thought he was going to explode. Grabbing her around her waist, Damon pulled her against him and claimed her mouth. Her sweet taste made his head dizzy as her scent enveloped him and seeped into the recesses of his heart.

Holding her face between his hands, he looked into those emerald eyes he'd fallen in love with. "I want to mate you."

"Well, that's going to be a problem." Ryker's voice echoed menacingly in the room.

Damon tensed, every hair on his body rising. Ryker was Barrett's second in command. It was no secret that Ryker couldn't stand Damon's guts. Hell, the feeling was mutual.

"From what I've been hearing, you seem to have your hands on Barrett's soon-to-be-mate. You know there are rules about that." Ryker smirked, his lips curling up over his white teeth as if he envisioned disemboweling Damon himself.

"Look, asshole, this is none of your business." Ava whirled around, lasering her gaze on Ryker, who actually looked a little surprised at her blatant lack of respect.

Damon fought a grin.

"I'm not Barrett's anything and I'm sure as hell not his mate." She took a step closer and jabbed her finger in Ryker's face, his expression going from surprise to deadly serious. "I will mate one Alpha and that's Damon."

Ryker growled and Damon pushed Ava behind him. Protective instinct swirled through every inch of his body as the wolf inside roared to life, ready to tear the male to pieces.

Ryker advanced on Damon.

"What the hell's going on here?" Barrett's voice boomed through the building as he strode in, owning the room.

"I will not let you have her, Barrett. Let's be clear about that." Damon angled himself so he was facing both Ryker and Barrett.

"Yeah, well, I'm still Pack Master here, so I'm in charge." Barrett thundered. "I have a Tribunal to preside over and you two are holding me up." Barrett shot a withering glare to both men.

"Barrett..." Damon addressed his leader, but Ava stepped in front of him.

"I refuse to mate anyone but Damon." Ava tilted her chin up looking him in the eye. "Just thought I'd let you know since you're the head cheese around here."

"Head cheese?" Barrett arched his brow as he gave Ava a disbelieving look.

Damon didn't know whether to laugh or yell at Ava's lack of respect for Barrett. Instead, he reached for her and cradled her into his side.

Barrett narrowed his eyes, first on Damon and then on Ava. "It seems your female has a lot to learn about respect to her leader."

"Look, I..." Damon clamped a hand across Ava's mouth.

Ryker stepped forward. "Wait, did you call her Damon's female?"

Damon's heart skipped a couple of beats. He'd thought he'd misunderstood, but if Ryker heard it too, then...

"I'm still Pack Master and I decree who mates who," Barrett bellowed, his voice low and deadly.

"You said Ava is a pureblood and she is to only to be mated to another whose blood is pure." Ryker looked at Damon and sneered. "Damon is an orphan."

Barrett turned his attention to Damon. "You may have grown up an orphan, but after doing some research, I found out who your parents were."

Damon's mouth went dry. There was a small part of him that was too afraid to unlock that door of truth. But he knew there was no turning back now. Not if he was going to claim Ava for his own.

"And?" Damon held his breath waiting for Barrett to answer.

"Damon, your parents were Jean Claude Trahan and Marie Le Blanc."

Damon frowned. "They were French?"

Barrett chuckled. "Not just French, they were descendants of the Duke and Duchess of Villeneuve."

"What?"

"Damon, you're royalty." Ava tightened her arms around his waist.

"I don't understand." The air left his lungs as he stared back at Barrett as he tried to comprehend what his Pack Master had just said.

"It means your bloodline is just as pure as mine and Ava's." Barrett grinned.

"How did I end up an orphan?"

"Your uncle, who was your only surviving relative, died suddenly. There seemed to be no other relative, so the nuns took you in at the orphanage."

A million thoughts flooded his mind. "I'm of royal bloodline."

"Yes, you are."

Only one thought swept into his mind. He met Barrett's gaze. "As of royal lineage, I exercise my right to claim Ava as my mate from this moment on, never to be parted from her except through death."

"You sure that's what Ava wants?" Barrett slid an amused look at Ava. "Women can be quite fickle."

"I chose Damon to be my mate. I don't want anyone else." Ava buried further into his chest and he couldn't stop the smile spreading across his face and across his heart.

"So, it is said, so be it." Barrett put his hand on Damon and Ava's heads. A warm sensation shot through his body. He glanced at Ava and realized she'd felt it too.

She gazed up at him with love and awe. "Is that it? Are we now mated?"

Damon grinned. "That's it. You are now my mate."

"As far as Ava being a queen, we'll have to see what the Council says. It may take some time to figure out if this will change the Pack and how it rules. This hasn't happened in a long time. Until then, I suggest you take advantage of the time and go on a honeymoon. Once you're in charge, your life is no longer your own." Barrett glanced at Jayden lying on the floor before turning toward the door. "Someone drag Jayden to the Tribunal so we can get this over with. The Hogs are playing LSU tonight."

CHAPTER FIFTEEN

The Tribunal was not at all what Ava had expected. The werewolf Guardians, about fifty in total, formed a circle around the accused, David Jenkins. At first, Jenkins refused to talk, but the second he saw Damon coming for him he started spilling his guts.

Jenkins told them how he was paid money to seek out the purest females and kidnap them. Luckily for them he'd only manage to find Ava and Haley. Their intent had been clear all along, to repopulate their dwindling numbers so they could once again go to war with the gray wolves that now controlled all the territories in North America. Jenkins claimed he had no knowledge of where the serum came from that forced females into heat.

Ava caught a glimpse of Haley as she was ushered in. She was as beautiful as her picture, blond hair and blue eyes that were red from crying. She trembled as she faced Jenkins, visibly upset to be in the same room with her kidnapper. Ava's heart ached for the girl.

"David Jenkins, you've been found guilty for the egregious offense of kidnapping two females. As you are well aware, the penalty for this crime is death."

"Fuck you, gray," Jenkins snarled.

Barrett growled and picked Jenkins up by the throat and hurled him against the wall. Jenkins landed on the floor in a heap.

"As Pack Master for the state of Arkansas, I shall allow your death to be carried out by one of my own Pack members. As much as I would like to end your life myself, I will allow him to carry out the execution. Damon Trahan is mated to Ava Renfroe, one of the females you kidnapped, and he has the honor of killing your sorry ass." Barrett faced the crowd. "Everyone is commanded to leave while the execution is carried out."

Damon waited until the steel door slammed shut before facing the red wolf. His body hummed with blood lust, his veins surging with the need to shred Jenkins's body into tiny pieces.

Jenkins snarled, his lip curling over his yellow teeth. "I would have raised an army of red wolves with that bitch and now you ruined everything."

Damon growled. "Ava is my Queen and my mate. You are going to pay with your blood for what you did." He removed his shirt and toed off his boots.

Jenkins's eye twitched and he took a step back.

"You can shift or stay in your human form. Either way, I will kill you." Damon shoved off his jeans and stood naked before the red wolf. He wasn't waiting any longer to take his revenge.

The wolf took over, shifting from his human form into the beast inside. His bones lengthened, muscles stretched, as hair lengthened over his body. He opened his eyes and stared at his prey.

Jenkins shifted into wolf and leapt. But Damon was faster and much bigger and pinned him on the ground with his massive paw. Damon stared down in the wolf's eyes filled with horror at knowing his life was about to be ended. Tilting his head back, Damon growled in rage and then clamped down on the wolf's throat.

Damon dressed and, as best as possible, tried to wipe off the blood before he left the room. Ava wouldn't understand what he had to do and he didn't want to frighten her.

Ava stood waiting for him in the next room.

Crossing the floor, he headed straight to her. He picked her up and she wrapped her legs around his waist, pulling him into a kiss, ignoring the hoots of the other males.

He pulled back and looked down into Ava's glowing face. "I guess we need to start looking for a place to live." He cupped her cheek. "I'm sorry about your house."

Ava shook her head. "Don't be. I don't care where I live as long as you're with me."

"I promise to always love you and protect you with my life." Damon pressed his forehead to hers.

"I promise to love you and honor you as your mate." Ava tightened her arms around his neck.

"This means you're mine, Ava." He'd never loved someone so much as he loved his Ava.

"I've always been yours, Damon."

He kissed her long and deep. When he broke the kiss, she met his gaze.

"It also means I get to be on top." She arched her brow and rubbed up against him.

"Is that so?" His lips curved into a slow grin.

"Yes." She nuzzled his neck.

"How about we find a room and settle it that way?"

"I think that sounds like a perfect idea." She kissed her way back to his mouth. "You do realize that you belong to me now."

"I wouldn't have it any other way." He grabbed her butt and pulled her close.

"Good. Cause Damon Trahan, you are stuck with me for life."

"I couldn't be happier, sweetheart." His heart swelled as he began to think of a future with his Ava. He would take her any way he could, angry or happy, irritable or moody. Hell, he'd even let her be on top if that's what she really wanted.

"You're my life, Ava. I won't ever wander this earth without a purpose." He nipped her neck. "Now, why don't we take Barrett's advice and start on that honeymoon?

The End

OTHER BOOKS BY JODI VAUGHN

Paranormal Romance
RISE OF THE ARKANSAS WEREWOLVES series
BY THE LIGHT OF THE MOON (Book 1)
BENEATH A BLOOD LUST MOON (Book 2)
DESIRES OF A FULL MOON (Book 3)
DARKSIDE OF THE MOON (Book 4)
SHADOWS OF A WOLF MOON –coming summer 2016

Contemporary Romance
CLOVERTON Series
LOST WITHOUT YOU (Book 1)
LOST ALL CONTROL (Book 2)

SOMEWHERE, TEXAS series
SADDLE UP (Book 1)
TROUBLE IN TEXAS (Book 2)
BAD MEDICINE (Book 3)

AUTHOR BIO

Photograph by Adi V Photographee

Jodi Vaughn is a Southern Paranormal Romance author. When she's not busy playing with her characters and typing away at her laptop, she can be found enjoying a cup of tea (or a very large glass of wine) in her home in Northeast Arkansas. She resides in Jonesboro with her handsome husband and brilliant son, as well as a temperamental swan and a yellow lab that is fond of retrieving turtles when duck season is over.

Made in the USA
Columbia, SC
26 July 2017